Praise for *Boyfriend from Hell*

"Unlike many down-on-their-luck heroes who never seem to suffer, Quaid's characters are genuinely desperate, lending a real sense of danger and urgency. Without a vampire, werewolf, or fallen angel to be seen, this strong debut is a pleasantly fresh take [on the genre]."

—*Publishers Weekly*

"Quaid jumps into the urban fantasy genre with a bang. . . . She quickly establishes a unique cast of characters, full of flaws and mystery. There is plenty of humor, wild action, and vigilante justice in this truly excellent beginning of the Saturn's Daughter series."

—*RT Book Reviews*

"Fast-paced and action-packed entertainment . . . A fun read . . . wonderfully crafted."

—*Seeing Night Book Reviews*

"Engaging and energetic . . . *Sexy*, *fun*, and *dangerous* are perfect words to describe this book."

—*Books, Bones & Buffy*

"Action-packed from beginning to end, sparkled with a great dose of humor."

—*Tynga's Reviews*

"A quirky romp of a ride . . . A cute twist on the paranormal genre."

—*Night Owl Sci-Fi*

Also by Jamie Quaid

Boyfriend from Hell

Available from Pocket Books

JAMIE QUAID

DAMN HIM TO HELL

THE SATURN'S DAUGHTER SERIES

Pocket Books

New York   London   Toronto   Sydney   New Delhi

Pocket Books
A Division of Simon & Schuster, Inc.
1230 Avenue of the Americas
New York, NY 10020

This book is a work of fiction. Any references to historical events, real people, or real places are used fictitiously. Other names, characters, places, and events are products of the author's imagination, and any resemblance to actual events or places or persons, living or dead, is entirely coincidental.

First Pocket Books paperback edition July 2013

POCKET and colophon are registered trademarks of Simon & Schuster, Inc.

For information about special discounts for bulk purchases, please contact Simon & Schuster Special Sales at 1-866-506-1949 or business@simonandschuster.com.

The Simon & Schuster Speakers Bureau can bring authors to your live event. For more information or to book an event contact the Simon & Schuster Speakers Bureau at 1-866-248-3049 or visit our website at www.simonspeakers.com.

Manufactured in the United States of America

10 9 8 7 6 5 4 3 2 1

ISBN 978-1-4516-5637-4
ISBN 978-1-4516-5638-1 (ebook)

DAMN
HIM
TO
HELL

1

On a noisy Friday night inside Chesty's pole-dancing bar and restaurant, no one heard the gargoyles scream until the front door crashed in.

The pounding rock music in the bar screeched to a halt—not an unusual occurrence or a reason for alarm. The DJ often had to spin albums with a hand crank, since anything electronic developed a personality of its own in the Zone. But this time, the shrill *aiieeeee* of the town gargoyles shattered the abrupt silence.

Like most of the other patrons, I'd been boogying hard and was annoyed with the abrupt cutoff.

Glimpsing two old people falling through the distant door, whacking at each other, I shrugged off the fight but puzzled over the earsplitting shrieks. The rest of Chesty's clientele returned to eating and drinking. The girls on the poles put their clothes back on and wandered off until the DJ could get the music rolling again.

Drunk on appletinis and sweaty from dancing off my exultation, I wiped my brow with the back of my arm. The persistence of the unholy screams raised my hackles, despite the buzz I'd been working on. The bar area didn't have windows, so I slipped inside the office I used to share with Ernesto, the club manager, to look out the small one there.

In the blue glow of the Zone, I could barely make out the outline of a stone gargoyle sitting atop the gutter of the building next door. It seemed to be stretching its neck and screeching bloody murder. While they were supposed to be mere architectural details, gargoyles in the Zone occasionally strolled the alleyways. They'd even been known to mutter insults. But they never just sat there and screamed.

Not knowing what to make of this nonstandard alarm system, I returned to the main room and sought Andre to see whether he'd gone for the battling old guys, the DJ, or an AK-47 to shoot the noisy gutter. Andre Legrande owns Chesty's and most of the businesses in the Zone. He's also an amoral enigma, but I was confident he'd know what it meant when gargoyles cried.

I caught sight of him across the room, pushing through the weekend crowd toward the struggling pair who'd broken in the door. Out of a sense of curiosity that will be the death of me one of these days, I slipped along the sidelines to do the same. Once upon a time I had been invisible to most of this crowd—a gap-toothed, four-eyed, limping nerd so innocuous that I disappeared into the woodwork. Nowadays, thanks to the rewards my patron saint, Saturn, bestowed upon me for damning people to hell, I was more noticeable, and had a reputation. People tended to shift out of my way of late.

A puff of green and pink cloud drifted through the open doorway. Andre picked up his pace. So did I, my unease climbing.

What kind of craziness produced pink-and-green clouds? The Zone's massive pollution had created serious anomalies over the years, like the neon-blue buildings and the ambling gargoyles, but so far it hadn't changed the weather.

I winced as one of the old drunks smashed a chair over his opponent's head. Instead of collapsing in a bloody heap, his victim simply shook a shaggy mane in bewilderment—which was the moment I recognized her. A her, not a him. *Nancy Rose!* Why would mild-mannered, motherly Nancy Rose the hippie florist be in a barroom brawl with a bum?

Hurrying, I shoved aside a drunk who got in my way.

Unlike other Zone inhabitants who changed because of the chemical pollution, I have a cosmic birth defect for which toxic waste can't be blamed. It seems I was born in the seventh house under a wrong asteroid or something, which warped my chromosomes and made me one of Saturn's daughters. Mostly, it gives me an innate ability to screw up my life seeking justice. Repeatedly.

I couldn't let Nancy Rose's assault go uncontested. I was about to drunkenly conjure a whammy to turn the old bully into a toadstool when—to my astonishment—the chair wielder keeled over, blocking the entry with his bulk.

Seemingly unharmed, short, stout Nancy Rose stood dazed and swaying over her assailant's sprawled body. Only when he didn't get up to finish the fight did she slowly topple herself.

Weird. Staggering drunks might be mother's milk around here, but not fighting florists.

The pink and green cloud continued to seep through the doorway.

Andre reached the entrance before me. He stepped over both bodies and glanced in the direction of the chemical factory to the north. I made it to his side just in time to hear him mutter "Frigging shit" before cursing in three languages that I understood and a few more that I didn't. Formerly Special Ops, Andre Legrande has a colorful background, and I could tell he was about to harsh what remained of my mellow.

My gut churned as I knelt beside Nancy Rose to check her pulse.

Verifying she was alive and breathing normally, I stood up and stepped over the bodies into the street.

On the harbor along this industrial south side of Baltimore, the Zone glowed blue neon on a normal night. A series of chemical floods over the past ten years had polluted the land along the water where tanks had once stored the output of our neighborhood chemical companies—the kind of places that create nerve gases for wars as well as personal hygiene products.

After the last flood, the EPA had cordoned off the blighted harbor and abandoned the Zone's commercial district to the shadow of the rusted-out chimneys of the derelict plant. Acme Chemical had rebuilt up the hill to the north of us. Tonight, a noxious pink and green cloud drifted down that hill.

Holy crap. Acme sent gas and not a flood this time? Did they *want* to eradicate us?

"That pink looks really bad against the blue," I pronounced with drunken brilliance.

"Shut up, Clancy," Andre said angrily.

My name is actually Mary Justine Clancy, but no one gets to use my first name. Most people just call me Tina, except Andre the All-Knowing.

"I'll handle Nancy Rose and clear the club," he snapped. "You need to go home and wake up Pearl and my father and herd them into the basement until we know what's happening. I'll be up right behind you."

I was too buzzed to panic but not too drunk to register fear at Andre's fury.

I stared in trepidation at the chemical plant, trying not to believe we were being gassed in the middle of the night. Lights were popping on all over the plant, but I didn't think they had a night shift.

"And here I thought tonight would be our night. I was really ready to celebrate that you're no longer my boss," I said with drunken regret.

After years of struggling and a fortune's worth of law school debt, I'd just received my official notice welcoming me to the Maryland bar. I was a *real lawyer* now, no longer a dispenser of street justice or Andre's flunky. And I was about to be gassed by a pink cloud before I could find out what was beneath Andre's silk shirts.

Familiar amusement flickered in his dark eyes as he checked out my revealing halter top and micro-shorts.

"I don't do lawyers," he replied, mocking my earlier rejection, when I'd told him I didn't do bosses. Andre holds a grudge. "I'm sure the senator does."

I punched his arm for that snide remark, but the cloud rising ominously larger and more luminous had me heading up the street at a fast clip.

If Andre was going to handle Nancy Rose, I needed to save my neighbors and my cat. Milo was aberrant enough—the whole Zone was aberrant enough—without being nuked by a Disney cloud.

Checking over my shoulder to see how much of a head start I had, I jogged uphill toward our neighboring town houses. Trying not to panic, I determinedly clung to my moment of joy and triumph. After all these years of hardship, I deserved a celebration for achieving my goal of being able to *officially* defend the law instead of relying on my unpredictable Saturnian vigilante instincts.

Well, for the moment, I was merely a law clerk, but I was finally on the straight-and-narrow, doing-it-by-the-book path. Law libraries, not planets, ruled my world these days.

I would not let a bilious green cloud extinguish the sweet future I had planned.

Except, instead of calling 911, I was obeying Andre's orders. Not out of habit, mind you, but because what happened in the Zone stayed in the Zone. Police hated melting their tires on our tar, and if officialdom came down here too often, they'd eventually realize the whole slum needed to be bulldozed instead of just the harbor.

Or if the wrong people saw shrieking gargoyles, we could be turned into a freak circus. Some of our community members would take umbrage at that, and mayhem would be the least that ensued. There was safety only in privacy. Gas clouds were problematic for their ability to both hurt us and reveal us.

I glanced back again, in some vague hope that the cloud would dissipate. Instead, it had all but obliterated any sight of the far end of town. I assumed the lighted windows meant someone at Acme had called for help, but one never knew.

I tried my el-cheapo cell to warn my friend Cora and reached a Greek restaurant—in Athens, if the language was any indicator. The Zone was perpetually hungry, and cell phones were unreliable at best down here.

As I tucked my phone away, one of the homeless bums from the encampment along the water darted out from between two buildings. He looked a little moon-mad with his gray hair straggling to his shoulders and his shadowed eyes darting from side to side. I intelligently halted—until he brandished a knife and shouted incomprehensibly in my direction.

Mostly, the weird ones never gave me any trouble. This one ran straight at me, slashing the air in large strokes as if he carried a sword. What was it with old guys tonight?

Fear robbed me of caution. I kicked high and connected with his wrist.

The knife flew into the street. The bum stopped, blinked in astonishment, then slowly crumpled to the broken pavement, just as Nancy Rose had.

Damn, I hadn't hit him that hard! The bum's belly alone was twice my size. Hauling him off the street was out of the question.

I almost panicked, but Bill, the giant who operated the bar and grill down the street, lumbered out and noticed my predicament. "I'll handle it," he called. "Get out of here and warn the others."

I liked Bill for a lot of reasons.

Checking the progress of the gas cloud, I sprinted faster. A street light pole twisted as if watching me run. I'd had some time to grow accustomed to aberrancy, but I still despised being spied on. Swiveling lights were a nasty reminder of the bad old days when I had snoops on my tail every minute.

My apartment was in a Victorian row house a few blocks beyond the Zone on the south end of the harbor, half a mile or more away from Acme's perch to the north. I could hope the gas didn't reach this far. The gray flicker of TVs lit some of the windows, but none shone in the darkness of my building. Inside, I pounded on my landlady's apartment door to wake her up, yelling at her to get to the basement.

Then I ran up the stairs for my tufted-eared miniature bobcat. He'd grown too large to be called a Manx kitty.

Milo raced to greet me, dragging the messenger bag I used as a carryall. He had a bad habit of running toward trouble, so I didn't see this as a good sign. Before I could scoop him up, he dashed into the second-floor hall and raced up the stairs to the top floor. Shit. Running up into a sky full of gas didn't seem to be the wisest course of action.

Just as Milo reached the landing, heavy feet lumbered down. Milo turned, jumped past the bottom two steps, sped by me, and threw himself at the door of the apartment across the hall from mine.

I had lived here only a few months. Caught up in study, exams, two jobs, and the tracking of a murderer, I hadn't had time to make the acquaintance of any of the other tenants.

That was about to change.

"Basement," a voice rusty from disuse called from above. A pair of shabby brown corduroys appeared on the stairs above me. *Paddy!*

I recognized the crazy inventor who occasionally stopped at Chesty's. The waitresses fed him gratis, and I'd assumed he was homeless. His graying chestnut hair fell lankly to his shoulders, and his lined and bearded face was nearly as wrinkled and faded as his corduroys.

I'd been told that once upon a time, he'd been a renowned research scientist at Acme Chemical, which is owned by the Vanderventers, his wealthy, powerful family. After the disastrous flood, he'd fallen apart. From the looks of him now, he had deteriorated even more since I'd seen him last. He might not have taken the death of his nephew—my boyfriend Max—in a fiery car crash too well. Especially since Paddy's son, Dane Vanderventer, had died shortly after, because of little old me.

Well, sort of died. I had sent Dane's wicked soul to hell for cutting Max's brake lines, so in a strange twist of fate, Max's soul now inhabited Senator Dane Vanderventer's body.

This caused a number of problems, but the point is I was a wee bit hesitant to tell Paddy about the Dane/Max *arrangement*. It didn't seem like an explanation I could give to a man I barely knew and who wasn't precisely in his right mind.

Right now didn't seem an appropriate time to strike up *that* conversation.

"Basement," Paddy repeated, taking the next flight of stairs. "I'll get Pearl."

Pearl Bodine was our elderly landlady. I grabbed Milo before he could take out the door with his scratching, pounded on the old oak panel as hard as I could, and shouted, "Gas attack!"

The heavy panel swung open to reveal a blurry-eyed Lieutenant Schwartz—in his knit boxers and nothing else.

My tongue stuck to the roof of my mouth, and I gaped at ripped abdominals and bulging pectorals. This was what the good detective hid behind rumpled suits and uniforms? By all that was holy . . .

Milo leapt from my arms and bolted down the stairs after Paddy.

"Gas?" Schwartz asked, sniffing the air.

"Acme. I think there's been an explosion. Paddy says to get to the basement."

"Just a matter of time," he said fatalistically. "Be right there."

I rushed after Milo.

Paddy was already assisting a chattering Mrs. Bodine down the cellar stairs. I wasn't entirely certain following a crazy scientist into the basement was the wisest means of avoiding a gas attack. If the cloud hadn't spread, we had time to get the hell out of Dodge. My Miata could hold us, barely. Besides, Pearl had cobwebs on her chandeliers. I didn't want to imagine what her basement was like.

I waited to see what the good detective intended to do.

Milo yowled and flung himself at the front door, disturbing my fuzzy internal debate. The appletinis hadn't completely dissipated.

"You can't attack gas, you idiot." I scooped him up again, but he jumped off my chest to the top of an ornate armoire, putting him in reach of the open transom of the aging town house.

"Milo!" I screamed as my cat disappeared out the opening. Damned cat, if the leap to the porch didn't kill him, the gas would. He'd pretty much used up half his nine lives already.

Torn between the desire to protect myself and the urge to find my cat, I lingered long enough to hear

Schwartz clattering down the stairs. Clattering? What was he wearing, a suit of armor?

Not waiting to find out, I raced after Milo.

If I died rescuing a cat, maybe I wouldn't go to hell for all my vigilante justice after all. Although right about now, I was thinking the Zone was pretty close to hell on earth. All we needed was the stench of sulfur. I took a second to sniff the air, but other than the usual fishy odor from the harbor, I only detected a faint whiff of burned ozone. A few freaked-out gargoyles could still be heard.

Milo leaped from the porch rail to the railing of the next town house, skipping stairs and the yellow jacket nest in the bushes. Feeling plucky, I followed suit, but landed with a thud far less graceful than my kitty's feline pounce.

"Milo, my white-knight cat." With renewed urgency, I shoved him in my messenger bag before he could run again, then pounded the door knocker. Andre owned this town house and shared it with his father, Julius. He'd also taken in Tim, the invisible kid. If they were all still asleep, they needed to be warned.

When no one answered, I let myself in and shouted, "Julius! Tim! To the basement, now!"

I knew they had one. I'd been in Andre's underground tunnel that led to an empty warehouse across the road. Should I ever have time to spare, I'd look up the history of these old houses, but I was more concerned about any illegal operations Andre might be running.

"We're coming down!" Julius's familiar voice

shouted back. "Open the basement door for us." Elegant, imperturbable Julius sounded edgy.

Hoping this house was identical to Pearl's, I ran down the hall toward the kitchen, located a flat painted door almost hidden by an Oriental wall hanging, and tugged. It opened silently on well-oiled hinges. I flipped a light switch and, thinking a grown man and a teenager could make their own way downstairs without my aid, I hurried to get out of their way. I knew Andre's cellar was a heck of a lot cleaner than Pearl's would be.

The gargoyles' cries were lost behind these thick brick-and-plaster walls. Andre didn't settle for filthy damp coal cellars, no sirree. His cellar had plaster, and wall sconces, and some kind of rugged stair-tread protector over mahogany-stained and polished wood stairs. Hell, his cellar looked better than any place I'd ever had my bedroom.

The bottom step led to some kind of speckled-tile floor like they used to have in banks and city halls. Doors led off to either side of the corridor, but I had no idea which one to take. The only one I knew was at the end and led to the warehouse.

What the devil was taking Julius and Tim so long? The way they were stumbling and staggering and bumping into walls, it sounded as if they were carrying a pirate trunk down with them.

You'd have to understand Andre to get why my mind leapt to pirate trunks and not sixty-four-inch flat-screen TVs, which most normal men would try to take with them to the grave. Andre reminded me of Jean Lafitte, the gentleman pirate in old New Orleans—complete with slick black hair, swarthy complexion, flashy white teeth, and a distinctly European mind-set.

Even though he called himself Legrande, I knew he'd grown up right here in blue-collar Baltimore. He'd gone to the same school as the wealthy Vanderventers, except I figured he'd done it on a scholarship.

I nearly jumped as the object of my thoughts yelled down the stairs at me. "Dammit, Clancy, doors! Open doors!"

Andre must have taken care of Nancy Rose and cleared the customers out of Chesty's in record time.

Not bothering to waste breath asking why he couldn't open his own damned doors, I started flinging open every one in sight. He knew better than to yell at me like I was some kind of low-IQ sheep.

No hoards of pirate gold or exotic harems down here—very disappointing. I'd expected more from our alpha male.

One room had tubes and paraphernalia like a chemistry lab. Another was filled with computer equipment. A third contained a pretty damned extravagant theater that would have made any Hollywood director proud. I was pretty sure the flat-screen TV in here was bigger than sixty-four inches. Clearly either we were far enough away from the Zone for Andre to have his play toys or the underground bunker acted as a buffer against the Zone's eccentricities.

I threw open the only remaining barrier and found a *hospital* room. Damn, Andre just kept getting spookier and spookier. I could almost believe vampires, but Frankenstein was out of my territory.

"Tina, give us a hand here. Tim's fading out."

"Am not," Tim argued—faintly.

I spun around to see Andre and Julius holding up the corners of one of those shiny, colorful comforters they sell in fancy department stores. Sure enough, Tim had disappeared, and his corner was sagging.

On the comforter lay Sleeping Beauty.

2

"Color, Tim," I scolded, grabbing the sagging duvet at Beauty's feet. "Concentrate."

Tim had been only five when the first chemical flood had spilled through the home of his drug-addicted mother. Small, bullied, and neglected, he'd grown into a terrified gay adolescent who loved plants—and turned invisible when frightened. Made sense in a completely Zonish way, but he's one of the reasons we don't like strangers around.

He colored in enough for me to see his hands and feet so I didn't step on him. I nodded at Julius, whose face was lined with weariness and worry.

Still dressed with flawless elegance, Andre held up the opposite side of the blanket all by himself. This mysterious Sleeping Beauty was sufficient argument to keep my distance from my former boss. Who the hell was she and where had they been hiding her? A few months back, I'd lived in this building for days and hadn't seen or heard another woman. And how could anyone sleep through this commotion?

That was, assuming we weren't carting a dead body around. The Zone was paranormal enough—I didn't need to *read* fantasies about zombies and vampires. I was probably living with them. I'd left normal far behind with Max's death.

Andre backed through the doorway of the hospital room and maneuvered the duvet over the naked cot with a skill born of experience. Anywhere else, and I'd worry about the cleanliness of a bare mattress in a damp cellar, but I was pretty sure Andre would have ionic air cleaners and space shuttle technology to prevent anything resembling so much as a mote of dust.

Andre wasn't poor, just weird, in a controlling kind of way. He always knew what was needed and where. Maybe it was his Special Ops training.

I'd learned enough not to demand explanations if there was any chance I wouldn't like the answer, so I didn't ask any. Yet.

Now that I had time to look, I could see that Beauty was breathing. The wrinkles in the corners of her eyes framed a face too old for her to be Andre's wife and a little too young for her to be Julius's. Like her fabled namesake, she appeared lovely and healthy, but also as in the fairy tale, she didn't wake up, despite the jostling acrobatics of the clumsy men and Andre's irritated growls.

I'd have said something witty about kissing her awake, except Julius's mouth sagged with sadness as he tenderly arranged her nightgown and used the long end of the duvet to cover her bare feet. I liked Julius, even if he was Andre's father. Besides being kind, he had aristocratically chiseled features, distinguished silver streaks in his hair, and an elegant mien Andre might someday aspire to.

Come to think of it, so did Beauty.

"Linens in the cabinet," Andre stated tersely, punching up numbers on his cell phone. Cell phones worked down here?

I don't know who he had meant to order about, but Tim was the one who obeyed, not me. After being deemed a Saturn's daughter, I'd checked out Saturn, and sure enough, Capricorn is ruled by the planet Saturn. If you want to believe astrology, my late-December birthday means I'm goal-oriented, pessimistic, and cautious. And I don't do orders.

Still suspended between drunken disbelief and fear, I whipped out my phone, too, intending to warn my friends not to come to work in the Zone for the next few days.

I verified that Milo was still with me. From my bag, he batted my hand with his head. Reassured, I ignored a rattle on the stairs.

As I punched buttons, a space suit clattered into sight. My eyebrows probably met my hairline, but I had a sleepy Cora on the other end of the line and couldn't manage to question and yell at the same time.

Still on his phone, Andre joined me in the hall, seemingly unfazed by Space Man. So I yelled at Cora to stay away, kept Milo in my bag to keep him from being stomped on, and pretended I was on a *Star Trek* set.

Since Cora lived outside the Zone and could count on a functioning phone, we'd worked out a telephone tree by the time Andre finished yelling at his flunkies to batten down the hatches. He had a right to be short-tempered if Acme was gassing his employees.

The level of his rage expanded the dimensions of my fear, but I was still having a hard time accepting that Disney clouds from a regulated company could kill me. Wouldn't the plant be sounding warning alarms and the police and medics be swarming down here if there was a chemical disaster?

Stupid, I know, but Denial is my middle name. I hadn't grown up in the Zone, as Andre had. I was still looking at this as a normal problem to be approached with reasonable solutions, even though I knew that tactic wasn't common in the Zone.

Andre and Space Suit hurried to the tunnel door at the end of the hall, and I tagged along, trying to keep Milo in my messenger bag. He wasn't kitten size anymore. I needed a larger bag.

"Where the hell do you think you're going, Clancy?" Andre snarled, stopping at the door and glaring at me.

"To fetch a nurse for Sleeping Beauty?" I suggested.

Andre in Special Ops mode was intimidating. He glared as if he would snap off my head, which meant I'd succeeded in crawling under his skin. Score one for the girl.

"You can't go out without a hazmat suit," Space Man said, sounding like a mechanical Schwartz. He kept hazmat suits in his apartment?

"So where do I find one?" I asked politely, figuring Andre was heading for a storage room already well supplied for any conceivable emergency.

"The gas is spreading. Until we know what we're up against, we'll need trained nurses and emergency personnel using our limited number of suits, not lawyers," Andre said snottily. Women generally didn't reject his advances, so he was taking mine personally. "Stay here and man the phones."

I didn't like it, but he had a point. "Lawyers are trained to communicate," I reminded him. "Use me as communication central. Do I need passwords to get into your computers?" I nodded at his technology room.

Andre looked as if he'd rather eat flesh than agree with me, but just as I was forced to admit I was useless outside, he had to admit I'd be effective inside.

He sent Schwartz through the tunnel while he backtracked to the communication room. Powering up servers, a small generator—I raised my eyebrows again—and an entire array of networking devices, he typed in passwords and opened windows on the world.

Score two for the girl.

I didn't even have the money to buy a small PC, and he had a duplicate Pentagon. The why of this over-the-top preparation remained unclear.

The generator appeared to vent outside, I cautiously noted. One thing you learned when spending a childhood in strange places was how to check for potential hazards. Carbon monoxide from generators could be deadly.

"Ventilation down here?" I asked.

"Filtered. This is an old bomb shelter. We can house forty if we have to. Food storage in the warehouse, but if the gas reaches as far as the hill, you'll need hazmat suits to get it. There's another suit in the closet, but it's only for chemical spills, not gas. I don't recommend using it unless necessary."

If he and Schwartz don't return went unsaid. The seriousness of the situation was finally harshing my buzz. I'd been treating the smoke cloud as just another of the Zone's eccentricities, like the blue buildings. I was playing along with the default script, not really thinking.

But if the gas cloud was truly deadly, all hell was about to break loose. The last vestiges of alcohol fled my brain—I was totally in the Zone now, physically and mentally.

My ex-boyfriend had spent weeks in the outer rings of hell, yelling at me through a mirror, so I knew hell existed. Or limbo. Or some fiendish dimension beyond this one. I'd seen enough of the afterlife to know I didn't want to experience it again.

Fear got me focused. Setting Milo and my bag on the floor, I sat my butt in the desk chair and listened intently as Andre gave curt instructions about websites, networks, and e-mail. Apparently all his businesses were connected. Terrified messages were already pouring in—although a good third of them came garbled or as advertisements for pork rinds in Georgia . . . which are toxic in their own way.

The Zone had a sense of humor. I didn't. Not if lives were at stake.

Milo crawled out of my pouch and prowled the room. Apparently tired of playing nursemaid, Tim wandered in and shifted nervously from foot to foot. I gave him my cell phone and told him to start calling everyone on it. There weren't that many names. I'd been too busy to have much of a life.

"We're survivors, Clancy," Andre said as I opened the first of the obscenity-laced rants on the screen. "Just keep your cool . . . and your boyfriend out." With that reassuring pep talk, he hurried away, leaving me to the silent cellar.

Max. Or rather, Dane/Max. He meant for me to keep Senator Dane Vanderventer out of the Zone. Normally, United States senators would not visit a backwater industrial area with few voting constituents. But now that Max's do-gooder soul was inhabiting his powerful cousin's body, keeping him out of another environmental disaster was akin to averting it in the first place. Wasn't happening. I'd have to hope for a terrorist attack to distract him. Max would have the Zone torn down if he knew how truly weird it was.

"Don't call the number labeled Max," I warned Tim. "And come to think of it, don't call Jane Claremont, either. She doesn't live down here."

"Too late." Tim handed the call to me while I scrolled through incoming messages on the monitor. One e-mail contained video from someone's smart phone. The gas was spreading downwind, in our direction.

"Tina, what's happening?" Jane asked sleepily.

I could hear her kid crying in the background. Tim had probably woken them up. Jane is an accidental friend and a journalist—a poor, idealistic one with a two-year-old son.

"Is it a story I can sell?" she demanded, knowing I wouldn't have called her at this hour for anything less than a good reason.

"First off, don't come anywhere near the Zone," I warned. "At dawn, you're going to see a spectacular cloud over the chemical plant that is spreading onto the streets. We don't know much more than that. Call Acme and see if they stonewall. Start calling police and fire stations and find out what they're reporting, and get back to me if they have any real news." I glanced at the computer clock. Three a.m. No one would know anything yet.

"I might be able to hit the network with this. Bless you!" she exclaimed before hanging up, eager to sell a story.

The possibility of real disaster hadn't sunk in for her yet, either. We're all so inured to catastrophe from watching TV, complete with commercial interludes, that we don't have an appropriate respect for the reality of ground zero.

Damn, I didn't have Sarah's number. The daughter of a serial killer and apparently another of Saturn's dangerous band, she could be volatile under stress. She'd be out there whacking old men if we didn't get her somewhere safe. My buzz was safely harshed. I wasn't certain I had the character to save an entire community.

Without my phone to keep him entertained, Tim had been peering over my shoulder at the #zone Twitter feed scrolling across the monitor. "Hey! That says it's coming from my boss's phone but she doesn't even know how to text. Who's got her phone?"

Oh, crap, Tim didn't know about Nancy Rose. I scrambled to divert him rather than break the news now. "Why don't you scout around, see what supplies Andre has down here?"

I suspected the warehouse above held the bulk of Andre's supplies, but I needed Tim to stay busy.

I scanned the next few text messages. Bill, the bartender, called to say he was transporting a van of locals upwind. Most people were smart enough not to move into the Zone. But I knew he meant elderly people who had never left their familiar neighborhood, transients who camped in the dead buffer along the water, and the poor with nowhere else to go. Plus people like Paddy who defied explanation. Although apparently he was living up here and not in the homeless camp, as I'd thought.

I monitored wind currents on one computer and local news on another. So far, Jane's exclusive hadn't hit the airwaves. Other than a few brawls and the pretty cloud, there wasn't much to report. Unless there were dead bodies lying in the street, we didn't rate headlines. They'd do breaking news for the morning TV shows, when they could get good video.

But Andre obviously hadn't wasted time stirring up the populace. More smart-phone videos started making it through. They showed a cloud that had grown spectacularly ominous—thick and greasy and . . . colorful. Sluggish in the pre-dawn humidity, the chemical fog rolled widespread and low along the harbor. Beneath it, small figures dashed about, either escaping or trying to mug each other. It was hard to tell.

Around four a.m., Frank, the detective who owned Discreet Detection, called in. "We've got two geezers behind Chesty's trying to kill each other here."

What was it with geezers beating up on each other tonight?

"Where's Andre?" he asked.

"Chasing vandals out of Bill's bar," I told him. "They're breaking windows already. Want me to send Schwartz your way?" I didn't know how many hazmat suits they had on the ground, but Frank was apparently in one of them.

"Nah, I'll just dump one in a Dumpster," he said. "They'll wear themselves out trying to get at each other. Nice to know a catastrophe brings out the crazies but not the cops."

He appeared to be right. Rather than falling dead

in the streets, people in the Zone were becoming increasingly violent—and there was nary an official policeman in sight, despite our calls. Maybe they were unpacking their hazmats.

Andre had to establish a bunker in front of Bill's Biker Bar and Grill to keep people out of the liquor. I hoped he wasn't guarding it with his AK-47; alcohol wasn't worth human life.

Schwartz called to say he was barricading the kitchen at Chesty's. A cook had caught thieves running out with everything they could lay hands on. They were hauling their loot back to the homeless camp, fighting over it and then dropping like flies.

"Where are your buddies at the precinct?" I asked.

"Acme's told them the air has neutralized the gas," he said flatly. "And I'm not inviting mundanes to learn the hard way that Acme lies." He hung up before I could ask more. I'd never heard Schwartz sound so cynical. He'd be beating up bums next.

On his next call, Andre was shouting. "Clancy, send Tim next door for Paddy and Pearl! You've got incoming."

Incoming? Andre didn't talk about his military career much, but I'd seen him crash through locked doors with automatic weapons in hand. Even though I didn't know what to expect, I jumped when he hit commando mode. And if Andre thought it was safe for Tim to run next door, fine. I couldn't imagine what crazy Paddy or doddering Pearl could do to help.

By the time I finally heard sirens, it had been more than three hours since we'd first seen the cloud. It was now practically covering the entire Zone, officialdom was just checking in, and Milo was fast asleep at my feet.

Propping the cell phone against my ear as Bill reported relieving Andre at the bar, I checked the corridor at the sound of pounding on a door. Emerging from the hospital room, Julius waved me away to indicate he had matters in hand.

I liked Julius, but he was a neurotic hermit and not necessarily dependable. I told Bill that the authorities were heading his way, then took a quick survey of the premises, as it had occurred to me that by *incoming* Andre likely meant new patients, not bombs or cops.

Three more cots had been set up in the room with Beauty—who hadn't flicked an eyelid. She lay there in eerie stillness even as voices shouted from the tunnel and wheels and running feet racketed outside in the hall.

"They were pounding the stuffing out of each other, then *whap!*—just like that, they keeled over," a sharp, curt voice said from the hallway. *Frank.* Frank was a detective because he had a talent for finding what was lost. Strange, but again, it was best not to question. Not with Frank. Not with Cora, my best friend down here, who conjured snakes. And definitely not with Sarah, who was even weirder, not to mention scarier, than me—and I'd sent my boyfriend to hell.

Life in the Zone was never boring.

I left the infirmary to watch Frank rolling a gurney carrying a frail old man. Julius tested his pulse and checked under his eyelids. I got out of their way.

The patient on the gurney wore the rough clothes

of the homeless encampment. He didn't move a muscle or make a sound as he was unceremoniously rolled from one mattress to another. Just like Sleeping Beauty, and Nancy Rose earlier, he was stone-cold out of it, and my skin crept with uneasiness.

At this rate, we could have an encampment of zombies by noon.

3

I shoved an overgrown hank of hair out of my face and started making calls, attempting to discover what had happened to Nancy Rose. My shampoo-ad hair had been a reward from Saturn for sending Max to hell. Thus it was a source of both guilt and pleasure. Still dealing with my over-developed conscience, I hadn't learned to accept my hair yet.

I hadn't *meant* to send Max to hell. I still didn't have a rulebook about this Saturn's daughter business. All I had was impossible-to-contact Themis, my dotty grandmother. And she wasn't exactly what I'd call clear about facts, which made me assume there weren't any. For all I knew, she could be one of the homeless living in the encampment, not that I'd recognize her if they rolled her in on a gurney.

Sarah, the only other Saturn's daughter I was aware of, looked more and more like a chimpanzee every time *she* took someone out. Without my knowing exact criteria one way or the other, her example had cured me of experimenting with my special abilities. Fearing that I was selling my soul to the devil for pretty hair had been a game changer that had me vowing to behave and never to use my erratic Saturn power again.

Except . . . I'm not what you'd call a passive person. I'd spent a lifetime being bullied for looking like a wimpy geek—and I'd learned to fight back. So yeah, I was lying to myself if I thought I could stop using my planet-god-given ability to wreak havoc.

"Where is Nancy Rose?" I asked when I finally reached Ernesto.

"Still here. We've got a probl—" The phone went dead.

I pounded the damned receiver against the desk.

Can you see my dilemma as I watched my neighborhood crash and burn? I conceivably had the super-ability to fry all of Acme Chemical's management in eternal flames for gassing my friends. But no matter how crazy-making furious I might be, I couldn't convince myself anyone would deliberately explode chemical tanks. Who would I damn? And if I damned the wrong person, would I, in turn, be damning myself?

Milo climbed on my lap, and I stroked him in an effort to calm down.

"More incoming!" Andre shouted a little later, this time in person while I was helping Julius peel grubby clothes off comatose old people and scrub their withered limbs.

I made a lousy nurse, but my landlady was worse. Pearl held her nose and picked up the rags with tongs to carry them to a covered trash can. Paddy hadn't arrived with Pearl. Tim had said our mad scientist had come out of Pearl's basement, sniffed the air, and wandered off without a hazmat. I half expected the incoming to be him.

But instead this new arrival was someone else I recognized—Nancy Rose. I still hadn't told Tim about her, hoping she'd have recovered by now. Stupid of me.

Praying the chemical company hadn't been experimenting with infectious diseases, I helped roll her onto a cot. She was younger and in better shape than the homeless guys, if totally zonked. But Tim started crying when he saw her.

"She's just asleep," I said, trying to be comforting. I'd had enough crying for a lifetime, and under these conditions, it could be contagious. Tim had had a rough life, and I didn't want to see him hurt. "See if Andre has more cots anywhere."

"Why can't we take her to a hospital?" Tim sniffed and wiped his eyes.

Andre folded up the gurney. "Because Acme is covering up the disaster by sweeping everyone into trucks and hauling them to the plant." He'd removed the hood of his hazmat. His expression was grim and his hair was wet with sweat.

"What—taking them to the plant?" I gaped in horror at the monstrosity of first nuking, then kidnapping the helpless.

Andre tapped my jaw shut. "You said it yourself: we're guinea pigs. Tim, move the theater seats to the walls, and Julius knows where there are more cots. I have all my men scrambling to pick up bodies as they drop, before Acme can steal them."

Murderous red rage must have shown in my eyes. Andre didn't know precisely what I was capable of, but he'd seen my powers flood his bar and allow me to talk to Max in hell. He knew I wasn't normal. He caught a hank of my overlong hair in his glove and tugged, then leaned over and planted a hot kiss on my cheek that seared my skin.

"Don't, Clancy," he purred in my ear while my blood pressure went up in flames. "Whatever you're thinking, just don't. We need you to keep Senator Boyfriend on a leash."

My neglected breasts perked to attention and my libido sparked. Who wouldn't melt if the sexiest man on the planet expressed concern like that? But no matter how hot Andre might be, I was too smart to fall for his considerable charms. The bastard was simply hoping to distract me, and talking about Dane was a bigger distraction than the kiss.

I resented that all the world thought a slimy U.S. senator was my boyfriend, just because Max in Dane's body claimed I had saved his life and kept calling me.

I'd saved Max's soul maybe, but the senator's was burning in hell, where it belonged. My place in the scheme of things was murky, but I was quite clear that I wasn't anyone's girlfriend. I hadn't had sex in months.

Still, Andre had succeeded in bringing me down from my wrathful cloud enough to realize he was right about leashing Dane/Max. The senator's conscience would have us shut down, and we'd all starve and go homeless.

I would have to be the one to rein in his righteous huff, but we had more immediate problems. "Can't we send cops after the body snatchers?"

"The cops think Acme is being generous in offering in-house facilities to a bunch of homeless people with no insurance. You want to tell them otherwise? Keep it cool in here, Clancy. I've gotta get back to the street."

He had a point. The outside world thought we were slimy deadbeat trolls living in a slum. To them, Acme was a shining example of capitalism at its best. In People vs. Corporations, people lost every time.

Leaving Julius and Pearl to clean up the patients and make them comfortable, Tim and I began moving theater seats. Cora found us a while later.

"I told you to stay home," I said ungratefully as she began hauling benches.

"And I love you, too," she retorted.

Cora is gorgeous. Tall, voluptuous, with creamy mocha skin stretched over dramatic cheekbones and hair cropped to accentuate the angles, she should have been a model or an actress. Instead, she manned the secretary's desk at Discreet Detection and produced snakes from thin air. We all have our hang-ups. The Zone's were just more *intriguing* than most.

"Yeah, that and three bucks will get me a cup of coffee, for which I would kill right now," I said. I hadn't seen a kitchen down here, but I was betting there was one. It just required thinking like Andre to find it.

I didn't have the time or inclination to kink my mind that badly. I returned to communication central, wishing I knew how to fix things.

Messages had piled up in my absence. I glanced at the clock—past six. I was dead on my feet and about to starve.

Checking online, I saw that the morning news had finally picked up helicopter views of the gas cloud at dawn—a spooky roiling green and pink wide enough to spread over the dead zone by the water and a little way up the hill to the residential area above Edgewater Street, creeping closer to us on the far south side from the plant.

Feeling sick thinking of the little kids living in those tenements on the hill, I turned off the TV and tuned in to the reports feeding directly to me through the computer.

Which was when Frank's all-caps subject header caught my eye—SARAH.

Shit. I'd hoped she'd stayed home. With trepidation, I clicked the link in Frank's message.

It opened a video of guys in fancier hazmat than

Andre owned loading Sarah onto a stretcher. It was unmistakably Sarah—frizzy bronze hair, torpedo breasts, and hairy chimp hands and feet. She must have passed out mid-change. Normally, when Sarah was startled, she morphed instantly into a chimp.

Fear sank deep into my bones. Acme scientists would take every cell of her body apart to figure out how she did that—one of the many, many reasons we stayed under the radar. If she woke up, she had the potential to damn everyone in sight, even the good guys. Provided there *were* any good guys. Maybe I should just let Sarah take care of the justice problem for me. . . .

Which brought forth another conundrum—did I go to hell for letting Sarah execute Acme officialdom when I knew she wasn't qualified to judge fairly? I was beginning to think I needed to live in a hut in the Himalayas to avoid these mind-boggling moral dilemmas.

The disaster was taking on new and deeper proportions, and my head was starting to throb. Milo put his paws on the keyboard and purred at me. Stupid cat. I put him back on the floor and buzzed Andre the video link. Answering a cell phone while wearing gloves is tricky, even if the Zone let him get the message, so I didn't expect an instant response. But someone had to go after Sarah. I was enough of a coward not to want to be the one.

Light-headed with hunger and fear, I pushed away thoughts of lawyers joining the souls of angry senators in hell. Cora came bearing steaming mugs of coffee and nuked Krispy Kremes from someone's freezer. In return, I showed her Frank's video. Her curses were more creative than mine.

"Put your hair back, Medusa," I chided when her favorite garden snake materialized and wrapped around her toned, bare arm.

Cora nuzzled the snake, then sent him back to whatever dimension he occupied. Two years ago, when I'd first moved to Baltimore, I would have freaked out. After living with roaming Dumpsters and shape-shifting chimps, very little fazes me anymore.

"Where's Paddy?" she demanded.

"Wandering the streets as usual as far as I know. Why?"

"He's the only one of us who can get inside Acme. He has to go after Sarah or they'll have the body snatchers sweeping all of us into their zoo."

"We belong in a zoo," I pointed out, but I got her drift, and it wasn't a pretty one.

History lesson: The brothers Vanderventer created Acme and built it into a wealthy powerhouse. Then they died and left the mess to their frustrated wives. Max's grandmother had vacated her responsibilities, leaving Paddy's evil mother, Gloria Vanderventer, gripping Acme with an iron fist. I held Gloria at least partially responsible for Dane's diabolical involvement in Max's death. Even so, body snatching was a new low for the woman.

"Does Paddy still have an office at Acme?" I asked. He wasn't reliable, but he was all we had. I just had to hope he wasn't evil like his mother and son. Optimism doesn't become me, so that was desperation speaking.

"Paddy has free rein to wander over there," Cora said, watching over my shoulder as I opened more messages. "Who knew Bill had an iPhone?"

Hulking bartender Bill had videoed a gray-haired lady with a cane pounding the crap out of an ambulance attendant trying to pick her up off the street. She looked a hundred years old and not more than ninety pounds, but she beat the two-hundred-pound attendant away. Then fainted. She appeared lifeless, but my bet was that she was comatose like the others.

Cora whistled. "That's some wacky gas."

The video spun crazily, as if Bill had dropped the phone. Abruptly, we were watching a toppling blue mountain. I wanted to shake the screen to get a better perspective. A gloved hand grabbed a blue elbow. We caught a glimpse of a big shoulder being rolled onto a stretcher. And then all we saw was a plain white van driving away and pink particles drifting to the ground from a cloud of green.

Bill had been wearing blue.

Too appalled even to curse, I stared silently at the pink and green scene. Bill was a gentle bear of a man. He fed fish to Milo and looked out for me. He was my rock. Even though he wasn't violent, he'd once raced to my rescue and chased baddies out a window for my sake.

They couldn't have taken Bill! Bill couldn't be down. Why hadn't he been wearing hazmat?

Cora leaned over and punched off the message, then opened the next while cursing under her breath. Milo fled the room, and I couldn't stop him. I needed to know what they'd done with Bill.

We hastily clicked more messages, searching for more videos. We needed cameras on the street, damn it. Who had Bill?

Of course, given the scrambled messages and photos of the Eiffel Tower the Zone was currently sending, even if we had street cameras, they would probably photograph Pluto and Mars. It was as if once the video of Bill had been allowed through, the Zone decided I'd had enough reality and needed a world tour.

"I'm going out there. You can do this." I got up and headed for the closet Andre had pointed out. If the only danger out there was pink gas and feisty old ladies, I could handle it.

Cora didn't argue. She slid into my seat and took over the controls. She worked computers daily, loved technology, and owned more equipment than I owned shoes. She was better at sitting still than me.

The hazmat suit stank. I was barely five-five—if I stretched—and the suit was obviously intended for someone half a foot taller. It sagged around me like a bridal gown on a six-year-old. The boots flopped awkwardly despite all the adjustments.

My biggest threat would be falling on my face and not being able to get up.

Or Andre, if he caught me.

He'd said this suit was only good for chemicals, not

gas. I could ditch it, but I figured the breathing apparatus was better than breathing gas.

My Saturnian need for justice was welling, undeterred by practicality. I had to see for myself that my pal Bill was safe before I blamed the world and wiped it out.

With my temper, I couldn't rule out the possibility of Armageddon.

4

South Baltimore is industrial. On any given day we can expect to smell garlic from the spice-packing plant, dead fish from boats in the harbor, or a rotten-cabbage stench from one of the chemical plants. Today, the air reeked of ozone, that fried electrical smell you get when a wire is going bad.

Being able to smell the air probably meant I'd better figure out how to work the suit, but it didn't come with instructions. I'm good at reading rulebooks and manuals, not so hot at intuiting technology on my own.

Staggering around in a hazmat suit—even one of the lighter ones—isn't as easy as it looks. But I couldn't tolerate watching injustice without taking someone down. My first goal was to find Paddy and see if he could be directed into Acme to find Sarah and Bill. I'd drag the eccentric scientist by the hair of his chinny-chin-chin if I had to.

Milo trotted after me. I sighed, glanced back to verify I'd firmly closed the warehouse door, then picked him up and put him in a pocket of the suit. He'd saved my life more than once. Who was I to argue?

Shuffling downhill, I gathered momentum and a little stability. Deciding I'd rather not meet Andre coming up, I took the alleyways and practiced judicious concealment, sort of like in the good old days when I used to keep my head down and my mouth shut.

That's how I'd learned our Dumpsters traveled. I'd thought they were spying on me until one night I caught them dancing.

A big rusted green bin rumbled into my path now. In a hurry, I tried to squeeze past it. When the stinky Dumpster tried to crush me against a brick wall, I kicked it in a rusted patch, tearing a hole in it. Then I clambered up the side and over. I spit into the garbage as I crossed, to show it who was boss.

The erratic videos I'd been receiving hadn't adequately depicted the fantastical image of the main business strip. The gas covering the Zone and harbor was more like drifting smoke than a heavy wet cloud. Sunlight filtered through, highlighting the sparkly pink particles. It made a great Disney effect. All we needed was a pink castle.

Instead of frivolity, though, we had eerily empty

streets in the shadow of the looming remains of burned-out storage tanks and incinerator chimneys.

Since Chesty's was the largest business in the Zone and had both liquor and food to attract crowds, I'd figured it was a good starting place for my hunt. Paddy sometimes hung out there. But I wasn't ready to go in without scouting the territory. After the videos I'd received, I'd expected brawls on every corner. Where was everyone? Nervously, I peered from the alley beside Chesty's to the main drag of Edgewater. Two people in the fancy style of hazmat suit were loading Officer Leibowitz into an unmarked van. Not an ambulance, a van. Now, I had no love for Leibowitz, our street cop. He was a rolling ton of lard who'd terrorized me, blackmailed a gay teenager, and used the law badly—but he was *our* crooked cop, and no human deserves to be treated like a guinea pig.

I was wondering if I could visualize blowing up the van's tires, and engaging in my usual internal debate on morality, when Ernesto came rampaging out of the shadows with his wheelbarrow. Ernesto is pretty much a Danny DeVito doppelganger with a bad attitude. The hazmats he was attacking were twice his height and muscle. And there were two of them. Had he lost what passed for his mind?

Ernesto rammed the heavy wheelbarrow into the back of the first hazmat's knees. With a cry, his victim lost his grip on the stretcher and crumpled backward into the barrow. His abrupt release caused the end of the stretcher to fall to the road, and in a very smooth chain reaction, Leibowitz flipped—unconscious, face-forward—into the barrow on top of the hazmat.

No way was Ernesto holding up that mass of flesh. The overloaded wheelbarrow tilted forward. Ernesto struggled to keep it upright, but he couldn't balance the weight of two men. With a clunk as the metal hit blacktop, Leibowitz was unceremoniously dumped back to the street. Without the cop's deadweight on top of him, Ernesto's hazmat victim scrambled out of his ignominious position.

Both body snatchers started swinging fists.

I didn't like Chesty's sleazeball manager any more than I liked Leibowitz, but the unfairness of two young, strong men beating up on one little old guy hit me squarely in the justice button.

It would be wiser for all if I could learn to think these things through in quiet contemplation, but that's not really possible when fists are involved.

Without much practice at my new talent, I was flying without radar. The image of body snatchers cracking knuckles against solid ice appeared in my head, and, hidden in the alley, I went with it. No idea where that visual came from. I just got mad, visualized, and *boom*! It happened.

Unfortunately, the enactment of a visualization was not always literal, but this time I came close. The whack of knuckles hitting a hard surface and the howls of shock that followed said I'd done *something*.

With my back to a brick wall, I peered around the corner again. The body snatchers nursed cracked bones—or smashed hazmat gloves—cursed, and glared in disbelief at the iceberg between them and Ernesto. The pink ice was already melting into Edgewater's chemically enhanced blacktop. So maybe I'd frozen gas.

Ernesto tugged at Leibowitz's nearly three hundred pounds, attempting to load him into his rusted wheelbarrow. Disguised in my suit, I considered it safe enough to saunter out to help him.

The diminutive manager sent me a suspicious glare but refrained from questioning pink rock candy mountains as long as I was helping him load the cop. Weirdnesses happened in the Zone. We left the attendants bandaging busted knuckles and shoved our unorthodox gurney toward Chesty's.

Before I entered the bar, I stared down the oddly empty street. It felt like a science-fiction film: earth after a nuclear war had wiped out all life forms. Or maybe that was just the effect of the moonwalking suit I was wearing.

Beneath the wispy weird cloud, I could see that the police had barricaded off the end of Edgewater that led up to Acme Chemical. Were they keeping Acme in or us out?

Since there were a dozen official vehicles at the plant and zero on our side, my bet was that they had sealed off Acme in the foolish belief that the cloud wasn't hurting anyone down here. If a tank had blown, they probably had multiple injuries inside the facility. Out here, we were invisible. Or unimportant guinea pigs.

I followed Ernesto into Chesty's . . . and walked in on an impromptu town hall meeting.

Or maybe it was a triage camp. Ernesto trundled his burden to a pallet on the floor and unceremoniously dumped him out. Comatose old people sprawled on blankets littered the floor between tables. And men in hazmat congregated around the bar, arguing, giving the place the appearance of a tavern on the moon.

Oddly, there were several people in hospital scrubs circulating from pallet to pallet, testing pulses and bandaging injuries. They didn't seem any older than me. Medical students? The cheap housing in the industrial district attracted penniless students from the various universities and even Johns Hopkins, but the Zone seemed an unlikely hangout. Why weren't they wearing hazmat suits?

I saw no sign of Paddy, but Ernesto had returned to the bar, where he was passing out drinks. Hazmat helmets were off or open. My stomach rumbled, reminding me that none of us had eaten this morning. Alcohol on donuts and empty stomachs was unappealing and not a particularly smart idea.

Accepting that Ernesto had been helping and not harming for a change, I tramped through the kitchen as if I owned it. I'd worked at Chesty's as both flunky and waitress, had friends back here who fed me for free, so I knew my way around.

Pulling off my gloves, I set the coffee machines running, gathered every edible in sight, and, wondering if gas had contaminated the food, carried it to the bar.

"If you're not worried about the air in here, then I'm assuming the food is safe," I announced mechanically, still stupidly wearing my hood in hopes of reducing the gas effect. "Coffee will be ready in a minute."

"Thanks, Tina." The tallest suit pulled off a glove and swiped a whole mini-loaf of bread from the tray. Polite, with big hands—that would be Schwartz.

Andre was leaning with his back against the bar, watching the students and their patients, only half-listening to the hubbub around him. He'd removed his hood and gloves, so he could only narrow his eyes at my arrival and not complain too loudly about lawyers being a waste of suit.

"Are they dead?" I asked as Andre swiped a handful of brownies.

"Comatose." Frank pulled off his hood gear and took one of the mini-loaves and a bucket of butter.

"Why aren't you taking them up to the house then? Isn't it dangerous down here?"

"Hard to say," Andre growled. "Paddy was out there earlier. He says the gas is only affecting those who are already sick. But it knocked out Sarah, so keep your suit on."

Andre didn't fully grasp what Sarah and I were. Neither did we, actually. But he'd seen the identical tattoos of justice scales on our backs, and he wasn't stupid. In fact, sometimes, he was freakily prescient.

"Unless you have him, I think Acme got Bill, too," I warned.

There was true remorse under Andre's curses this time. If Paddy was right, did that mean Bill had been sick already? He'd seemed plenty healthy, although he'd once been a heavy smoker. Like most men, Bill probably thought himself invincible and had never bothered with doctors.

So I kept my suit on, even though I was starving. But I snatched the last brownie and crammed it under the hood to munch, and fed a sardine to Milo in my pocket.

"Where's Paddy now?" I asked, intent on my goal of rescuing Sarah.

Ernesto produced a tray of coffee. The aroma was heavenly, but I couldn't figure out how to drink coffee and keep my hood on. Frustrated, I took it off despite the warning. I could die of starvation or get some caffeine and go berserk with gas. I chose the latter as more interesting.

At my defiant action, Andre asked, "If I was mayor and passed a law forbidding you to go outside without a suit, would you obey it?"

"What do you think?" I greedily sucked down coffee.

"I think lawyers ought to obey the law," Andre replied grumpily.

"And mayors only make laws the voters want, so you don't get to be dictator. This voter wants coffee. Now, again, where's Paddy?" Andre's charm didn't work so well on me, and he knew it. Neither did his attempts to distract, although the kiss still burning my cheek had potential.

"Paddy's probably locked up with Sarah and Bill in the decontamination chamber," Schwartz answered, averting further squabbling. Leo didn't talk much, but when he did, it was effective.

"Decontamination chamber?" I'm quick. I got it. I just wanted it spelled out clearly before I flew into a vengeful fury. I was starting to recognize the signs of mindless red rage that meant I was headed for full-out ballistic. Now I had to figure out how to control it.

Hearing the anger in my voice, Andre broke a bread loaf and stuffed a piece in my mouth. "Don't go berserk on an empty stomach."

Even a day old, the bread was good. Rosemary with a hint of garlic. I couldn't yell with my mouth full, but I could glare daggers at the back of Andre's thick head.

Schwartz added cream and sugar to his coffee. "Acme," he said.

I rolled my eyes at his terse explanation. "They're decontaminating the plant but not us?" I asked, chewing as fast as I could but still talking through a mouthful.

"Yup. They've got the EPA and all the pros running all over the building, vacuuming up blue goo or whatever. The official reports say the air quality is good, that once the gas hits open air the harmful particles are disbanded, and so the danger is only inside the plant." Andre sipped his coffee black.

I followed his gaze to our elderly patients. "Right. The best kind of air quality, one that kills the old and homeless and cops. They're just an albatross around society's neck anyway." My opinion of cops wasn't high, Schwartz notwithstanding, but in this case, I was being sarcastic.

"Ouch," Frank said. Frank had once been a bum

who lived under bridges, according to Andre. The Zone had been good to him, sort of cleaned him up. Short, dark, and wiry, he tended to lurk in shadows, kind of like me. So I didn't know him well.

"Tina's a cynic," Andre said, but he didn't argue with my assessment.

That's the thing about me and Andre. We might verbally gouge each other's eyes out, but underneath, we were often on the same page. Our methods of solving problems widely differed, however. He was sneaky. I was rash, although I prefer to think of it as being blunt and straightforward.

"I want Sarah back," Ernesto said, surprisingly. "She's creepy, but she works for peanuts."

I repeated *ouch* under my breath and bit back a comment about working for bananas. Sarah couldn't help her chimp affliction.

At least now I had some clue as to his motive for being helpful. "Did those guys help you load up the wheelbarrow?" I nodded at the scrubs.

"Yeah. They're med students who live up the hill and sometimes cruise the camp to patch people up," Frank explained. "They're the ones who warned us the vans weren't going to the hospital, and they've been helping us hijack the victims from Acme. But we didn't see Bill go down."

Impressed, I watched the med students with more respect. They might be using the denizens of the homeless encampment as lab rats for their studies for all I knew, but they risked life and limb out there. I wouldn't have done it. The EPA had labeled the fenced-off area around the harbor a dead zone for a reason.

They were wandering around without suits. I wanted out of mine.

"So the assumption is that if you don't keel over after exposure, it's safe to breathe the gas?" I asked.

"If you don't beat the crap out of anyone, *then* keel over," Andre corrected, giving me an evil look. "Feel the need to off anyone, Clancy?"

"I feel like that all the time," I countered. "Maybe if I stop feeling murderous, I'll figure I've been gassed and check myself in at Club Acme. Maybe I'll do that anyway. I want Sarah and Bill out of there."

"Not easy," said a weary voice from behind us.

Paddy staggered in, covered in pink particles, like he'd been confettied.

Paddy hadn't collapsed. Given his odd behavior and weird mutterings, I'd figured he was *mentally*, if not physically, ill. Except right now, he sounded more rational than I'd ever heard him. He'd actually replied to a direct statement instead of talking about plastic and wandering off.

I watched skeptically as he shuffled over to the food, helped himself to an apple, and settled on a bar stool as if he were a hundred years old. I did a few mental calculations. His son Dane had been in his mid-thirties when I sent his soul to hell. Chances were good Dane's father was over sixty. Good lord, that calculation had Gloria Vanderventer closing in on ninety. I mentally voted to bring her to the Zone to see how she reacted to green gas.

"Why won't it be easy?" I demanded when no one else spoke. "I'll say Sarah is my sister, she has a dangerously infectious disease, and they'll all turn into monkeys if they don't let me have her."

Andre snorted. Paddy almost smiled. I'd never ever seen the man smile. He'd muttered imprecations, deconstructed appetizers, and ignored me. Just getting him to talk had been a chore. Smiling might be fatal.

"Acme's on full lockdown," he explained, sounding perfectly normal. "They have security at every entrance. The EPA thinks they're in charge, but they haven't been allowed into the underground labs, don't even know they exist. They're just removing the mixing tanks."

I stared in amazement. Whole, coherent, unpalatable sentences. I glanced at Andre, who shrugged.

"Problem is," Paddy continued, "the machine they want is underground and could blow again if they don't stop the experiment. Bergdorff, the guy in charge, is obsessed and not particularly rational."

Silence rippled outward as we absorbed that news. I debated the validity of one madman judging another, but I could practically feel the ground shiver beneath my feet.

"Do we need to go in and take Acme down?" Andre asked ominously.

Paddy shrugged and threw back a slug of juice. "They'll halt for a while. But if the plant closes, this area really dies." His voice still sounded rusty.

That had been the problem all along. People needed jobs. The Zone needed customers. Acme provided both. This part of Baltimore was not particularly thriving, so any business closure was a blow. I'd once threatened Max after he became a senator and vowed to shut down his family's business.

My cell phone rang "The Star-Spangled Banner." Speak of the devil . . . I very decidedly had not programmed in that tune, but my messenger bag was practically rattling with urgency. Taking off my gloves, I dug out my new pay-as-you-go phone.

"Justy!" Max shouted as soon as I opened it. "What the devil is happening down there?"

"Good morning, Senator Vanderventer," I purred, knowing every ear in the room had suddenly turned to me. Even Milo listened. I scratched behind his ears. "What can I do for you on this fine and glorious morning?"

"Get the hell out of there," was his retort, not unexpected. "Did Acme have another spill?"

"Spill? Of course not. What would make you think that? And if there were, I'm sure your grandmother would be right on top of it. Why don't you give her a call?"

Max hated Gloria, Dane's grandmother. Living in someone else's body was a complicated business.

He swore like the biker he was and not like the senator he was supposed to be. "I'm coming down there," he threatened.

"I won't be here," I cooed. "Really. Talk to your grandmother. Better yet, bring her down here," I added meanly. "And if you truly want to help, have one of my friends hired at the plant."

That produced silence. Max had been trying to get the goods on Acme's dirty R&D for years—until they killed him. Playing the part of a senator, he avoided the place to prevent any appearance of favoritism. If he wanted to get reelected, he'd have to stay out of the family's dirty business, one way or another. So all my ribbing was a little in jest.

But totally unexpectedly he said, "I can get someone my security clearance. Check at the guard gate in half an hour. Use it wisely." He hung up.

Every man in the place stared at me, waiting.

"So . . . I have one get-out-of-jail-free card. Do we draw straws to see who gets into Acme?" I asked into the silence.

5

I'd spent years keeping my head down and my mouth shut after the college protest (read: riot) that had ended with me being arrested, shoved down some stairs, hospitalized for months with a mangled leg, and expelled from school. After Max's fiery explosion, I'd been running on scared. In consequence, I'd developed some grandiose notion that once I passed the bar exam, I'd miraculously morph into a respectable citizen standing on firm moral ground, with rulebooks all around me.

Obviously not. I knew what I had to do. Even though I generously offered the opportunity for someone to develop a better plan for getting into Acme, I really wanted to be the one to save Bill and Sarah. But if

I tried, the likelihood of my damning someone to hell was pretty high. It wasn't as if Acme would let a woman with chimp hands escape without putting up a fight.

Besides, I had a whole lot of enemies in the Vander-venter camp—like maybe all of management and anyone related to them. They probably had wanted posters bearing my face tacked to the walls. They couldn't prove I'd done anything to Dane or sent their goons to Africa—one of my more brilliant visualiza-tions—but after months of spying on me, they had reason to suspect it.

"None of that drawing straws nonsense," Andre announced. "We only have this one chance, and we have to do it right. Paddy, can you get back in without clearance?"

Our scientist shrugged, slumped his shoulders, let his straggly hair fall over his face, and crumbled bread into his beard. "Yeah," he muttered.

Wow, and I'd thought *I* was good at keeping my head down! Paddy had me beat by a mile. Or maybe he had just miraculously recovered and simply mocked his prior behavior. In the Zone, it was best to keep an open mind. Or an empty one, ignorance being bliss and all.

"Schwartz, if you put on your uniform and showed up at the gates, do you think you could get access as a policeman?" Andre continued his Lord of All He Sur-veyed act.

Schwartz squirmed uncomfortably at the notion of suiting up and faking authority he really didn't have, but he nodded.

"Clancy and I are persona non grata up there, so we're out," Andre continued. "Paddy, do you think we can reach both Sarah and Bill and carry them out, or will we be limited to finding out where they are so we can go in later?"

We were up to the royal *we* now, were we? I bit my tongue and tried listening instead of reacting.

"Locate first," Paddy decided. "They've been adding underground bunkers even I don't know about."

Andre rubbed his eyes tiredly at this information. He muttered a few epithets under his breath. I knew the feeling. I wanted to go in, guns blazing, like Clint Eastwood and John Wayne rolled into one. As previously noted, subterfuge is not my strong point. I wanted the good guys to wear white hats. Even Paddy appeared pretty shady right now.

"Frank it is," Andre ordered.

Which made sense. Frank was our Finder. But just *finding* didn't save my friends from Acme's depredations. I couldn't justify leaving them in there. I wanted Bill out because he'd hate being a guinea pig, but I was the only one who knew what Sarah was capable of. She could damn us all to hell if she woke up suddenly and didn't see a familiar face. I didn't particularly want to spend eternity dancing in flames, but I couldn't risk seeing my friends do the same, either. Rescuing Max's soul from hell had been a one-time fluke.

"Nope. I'm going," I decided, against all common sense. I didn't even have the strength to lift Sarah should we find her. "Schwartz, meet me at Pearl's in half an hour. Can you get an official car?" I stood up and stalked toward the door before anyone could react. "Paddy, once you get inside, keep a lookout for us, please?"

"Clancy, don't be an ass!" Andre warned, blocking my path.

"I can clock you in one," I told him. "I don't want to, but I will. You don't know what Sarah is, but I do. Trust me on this—you don't want to leave her in there and find out."

He'd seen our tattoos. He'd seen Max in my mirror after Max died, and he'd been there when I'd whacked Dane with my flaming compact. There was a lot he didn't know, like about Max being Dane now, but he knew I wasn't normal. Still, he glared.

"How can you find Sarah if Paddy can't?"

"I have no friggin' idea," I admitted. "But she's less likely to fry me than Frank. So get over it and let me by."

Got him smack in the old curiosity with the word *fry*.

Andre had once explained his weird prescience as the ability to add two and two and find three. I could see the wheels in his head spinning now, but I didn't intend to linger while he added up Sarah's husband dying, her mother being neutralized behind jail cell bars, and similar incidents. I jerked on my hood and gloves as a futile security precaution and opened the door.

Lieutenant Schwartz didn't generally approve of my pressure tactics, but he was an old-fashioned gentleman who looked out for me when others didn't.

He accompanied me back up the hill to our respective apartments. Technically, we both worked on the same side of the law. Maybe he harbored some foolish hope that in return for keeping me safe, Senator Dane would coerce the police into giving him another promotion.

I didn't disillusion the poor guy. We all had dreams.

I twitched uneasily at that thought. My dream of someday being a judge would be in serious jeopardy if Acme caught me trespassing. I reassured myself that Max's clearance made my activities perfectly legal—unless I took up body snatching or got mad and nuked a chemist.

As we reached Pearl's place, Schwartz removed a glove and glanced at his watch. "Be down here in twenty minutes. Pretend you're a research scientist or something, will you?"

"You're a good liar, Schwartz." Leaving him with that ambiguous compliment, I trotted up to my apartment with all the agility of an overweight turtle. I should have shucked the suit downstairs.

I shut Milo in the kitchen with his food and litter box. He gave me the evil eye, but I could worry about only so many things at once. Bill and Sarah had to come first.

Scientist. Crap. What did a scientist wear? Nervously, I dragged my heavy, hair into a clip on top of my head. I'd bought suits at a consignment store for my law clerk gig, but I didn't think scientists wore pinstripes. Blazers, maybe. Khakis. Button-down shirts. I had those from law school days. I added the dark-plastic-framed reading glasses I used to wear before Saturn Daddy fixed my eyes. I donned a pair of sensible pumps. All I needed was a tablet computer, which I couldn't afford. A backbone of steel would have been convenient as well.

After finding Max in my mirror, I was still wary around reflective surfaces, but I did a quick double check, added some pale lipstick, and toned down my natural Persian bronze with too-light face powder I'd bought out of a bargain basket. I wouldn't fool my friends, but maybe I could trick a security guard or two who didn't really know what I looked like.

I debated returning the hazmat to Andre's bomb shelter but figured I didn't have time for arguing with Cora. So I left it to be delivered later and made tomato-mozzarella-basil sandwiches for me and Schwartz.

He accepted his gratefully when I ran out to his unmarked vehicle right on time. Cop cars are never really unmarked. Security would recognize the official plates and extra antennas.

"Will Paddy stay sane enough to help us?" I asked before tearing into my bread, hoping to stifle my fear by feeding my hunger.

Schwartz frowned. "I've been wondering about that, too. Did he suddenly get sane or has he been sane all along?"

"Huh, so it's not just me he's been fooling? Doesn't exactly make him trustworthy." Max hadn't been worried about the family eccentric—did he believe Paddy was crazy, too?

"He's all we've got," the good lieutenant said with a shrug. "Just don't do anything that will cost me my job."

"Yeah, yeah, I know, you've got orphans in Haiti to support." I hated being reminded that Schwartz didn't think me capable of behaving responsibly. He was probably right. I don't know what gets into me sometimes. I can't save the world. I *know* that. I was having a hard time saving myself. But here I was anyway.

We drove straight through the lingering remnants of the gas cloud, down Edgewater, past the swiveling streetlights and sleeping gargoyles. Schwartz pulled the car up to the police barricade blocking the plant driveway at the end of the street, waved his badge, and cruised on through to Acme's security gate while I tried to appear innocuous.

The guard handed us clip-on passes and waved us past after checking his log to verify the senator had called in about a guest pass. I cringed at knowing that respect came from having friends in high places.

Losing a boyfriend had been a hard way to gain a senator. Even after it turned out that Max had been using me as a spy, he had still rated as one of the good guys, and the sex had been incredible. I was sooo not getting it on with Max in his cousin's body, though. That was just too freaky.

As a consequence of my vowing to lay off both Max and Andre, even the respectable lieutenant was starting to look good. And I hated cops.

Acme's reception area was unassuming, at best. Old linoleum-tile floors, a spindly banana-type plant near the front window, a wooden desk guarding the hall-ways leading off left and right—straight out of the fif-ties or an old people's home.

Obviously, the Vanderventers didn't spend their money on décor. Schwartz again flashed his badge, and the nondescript receptionist gave us directions to command central, or whatever cops called it.

"Best if I don't show my face to anyone who knows me," Schwartz murmured, steering me down a dark corridor of closed office doors and veering from the directions given.

"Watch it, or your Dudley Do-Rightness will wash off," I warned. My smart mouth hid a variety of fears.

Schwartz was a hunk and a half, but his shining armor was seriously out of place in the world I lived in. Maybe I could grow into his world—after I swal-lowed my terror and rescued Sarah and Bill. I checked directional signs and decided labs would be a good starting point.

"Someone has to uphold the laws," he muttered, shoving his muscled arm in front of me and check-ing around a corner before letting me proceed. The entry-level floor seemed to be mostly gray walls leading to manufacturing facilities. "Place is weirdly empty, isn't it?"

"Saturday," I reminded him. "Who in here would be working weekends besides security?"

"Paddy should know. It would help if he'd carry a phone. The crazy old coot gives me the creeps."

For closemouthed Schwartz, that was an I-wantabe-friends moment. And it worked. I studied him with interest. After all, he had great abs and I'd been without sex way too long. He was looking back. But this wasn't the time for overtures of that sort. I hid my gap-toothed smile, and we both glanced away at the same time.

Following signs, we took the stairs down. We'd been directed to an office on the top floor, so we were safely heading in the opposite direction of authority. I just hoped we weren't aiming for a nest of vipers. I'd had some pretty hazardous encounters with Vanderventer security in the past.

The ozone stink seemed stronger in the stairwell, but I didn't notice any green gas. I kept checking myself to be certain I didn't somehow start disappearing like Tim or shifting like Sarah. The ozone and rattling metal steps gave me cold shivers.

At the bottom of the stairs, we found another corridor, this one of concrete blocks painted two shades of beige. Signs indicated Lab A was on the right, Lab B on the left. Voices carried down the corridor from the left.

Confronted by the peril of what we were doing, knowing Bill was strong enough to take care of himself, I had a WTF-am-I-doing-here moment until I recalled Sarah's condition. To avoid nuclear damnation, we had to find her.

Which meant going where the people were. Grimacing, I turned left. Schwartz grabbed my elbow. We had a brief, silent wrestling match that I was going to lose unless I used dirty fighting. Not wanting to actually hurt one of the good guys was a deterrent to violence.

Paddy resolved our nonverbal argument. He peered out of an unmarked door, held a finger to his lips, and gestured us in.

I swear, the room we entered was straight out of *Bride of Frankenstein*. I expected Boris Karloff to pop out of a closet. Wooden lab tables! Beakers, test tubes, burners, clamps . . . I hadn't done well in high school chemistry, but I could recognize the ancient apparatuses.

A battered desk covered in papers and notebooks was nearly hidden in one corner by a metal cabinet. Dust covered everything. Nary a computer in sight. And no Sarah, not that I'd expected our hunt to be that easy.

"Where to now?" I asked, trying to keep the doubt from my voice. If this was Paddy's lab, it didn't appear as if he'd worked in it for years.

Paddy had donned a long, dirty white lab coat since we'd seen him at Andre's. His beard was as scraggly as his hair, but his eyes were clear and perceptive as he rummaged through a drawer and produced blueprints.

"I confiscated the building plans. Here's us," he rumbled, pressing his finger to a little square in the sprawling complex. "They've put the EPA up here." On a top management floor, away from the action.

"The technicians they've called in are meeting down here." He pointed to a slightly larger rectangle roughly in the direction from which we'd heard voices. "The stairs to the hidden sublevels are here."

I gulped. He was pointing at a door accessible only from the room where all the technicians were meeting. "What's in the sublevels?" I asked, just because I couldn't think of anything else to say.

"The Magic labs," Paddy replied.

Okay, so maybe he wasn't totally sane after all.

6

Schwartz didn't bother hiding his skepticism. "Magic lab? Is that some kind of acronym?"

"Code word," Paddy acknowledged. "About twelve years ago, Acme acquired a new element from a top secret source. If anyone asks what we're working on, we just say magic."

"Swell, a new element to blow up the world, like uranium, right?" I asked. "And they've got Sarah down there with your crazy exploding experiments? What about the other zombies?"

"Zombies?" Schwartz and Paddy both asked, glancing up from their study of the blueprints.

"Like Sleeping Beauty back at Andre's—dead, but not dead," I explained impatiently. "What's up with that?"

Paddy wiped his big hand over his face, but I thought I caught a glimpse of sadness before he turned back to the table. "That's not our concern. We have to remove Sarah first."

Okay, I got that. Sarah was one of those "special" people that the Zone residents hid from the outside world. They'd been hiding Sleeping Beauty, too. And I aimed to find out why, eventually.

"Will Bill be there, too?" I demanded.

"I think they'd gather all their victims in one place," Paddy acknowledged. "There's not a lot of places to hide them."

"Can we call the authorities once we find them?" I asked bluntly.

Paddy shook his head. "Acme will stonewall. That's why they have the victims hidden. I think Gloria bribes the police chief or someone to play down incidents here. Schwartz, if Tina called you on an official basis and told you there were homeless bums in Acme's secret basement, what would you do?"

"I'd go for a search warrant." Schwartz glanced at me and shrugged apologetically. "And even if my boss gave me permission to try, which would be a hurdle, the judge would deny it unless I had proof that Acme was harming innocent people. No one believes Acme's dangerous but us."

Which was where me and my "magic" powers came in. Justice for those the law ignored. Got it. Didn't like it.

"Does Acme have security cameras?" I asked,

changing the subject. "Can they see what we're doing right now?"

"Not in here. They have cameras in the corridors, but there won't be anyone monitoring them today. They can check the footage later, though," Paddy warned. "They'll know we've been here."

"Stink bomb then," I said. "After the gas leak, your people will be as jumpy as Gary Cooper's neighbors at high noon. One whiff of a stink bomb, and they'll be out of there so fast, they'll burn rubber."

Schwartz made a snorting nose that sounded suspiciously like a laugh. Paddy glanced at me approvingly.

"Perceptive. Simple. It might even work."

"Fair is fair," I said with a shrug. "They gas us, we gas them."

The truth was, I was the one who was jumpy. Being in the basement of this mausoleum with no telling how many mad scientists and their machinery—not to mention security goons with guns—had my skin crawling. I wanted out as fast as we could get there.

Or maybe it was knowing I didn't like Sarah well enough to go to hell for her that made me edgy. Yeah, I didn't want her frying innocent people, but how innocent were these people, after all? Did the government know Acme's scientists were experimenting with a new element? Was the green cloud a new nerve gas?

One thing I know from my environmental scientist mother—corporations earn more money off weapons than health care. If Acme had a magical new element, they were intent on building bombs with it, not saving the world from disease.

So maybe I should be taking out the lab and not just my friends.

Man, I hate indecision! This is what courtrooms and legal processes are about. They might take awhile, but decisions were made. There was a proper guideline.

Had he been here, Andre would have worried about my unusual silence while the boys mixed their stink bomb, but Schwartz and Paddy were clueless. I studied the blueprints and kind of wished I could talk to Max. I even took out my mirror and pretended to remove an eyelash while wishing I could see just a flicker of his reflection. But he was gone, from hell and from my life—mostly.

Besides, he'd just scream, *Justy, get out of there!* Not very useful. I missed him.

At least Schwartz and Paddy didn't order me to stay behind when they made their bomb run. To disguise ourselves from the cameras, we all donned gas masks so we'd give the appearance of having been outside, without the burden of wearing the heavy suits. And then we marched down the long corridor.

The door to Lab B was shut but not locked. The voices rising from behind it did not sound happy. No whistling while one worked at Acme.

Wearing my pretend-scientist attire and a face mask, I leaned against the beige concrete and watched as Paddy entered the lab as if he belonged there, which, I suppose, he did. He left the door open for our benefit.

The angry voices rose higher at his entrance.

Paddy put on a good mime performance, gesturing to his mask and waving his hands, urging everyone to run. Nice that he was actually trying to warn the assholes—not that they cared. They cursed, grabbed his arm, and tried to force him out.

Schwartz and I glanced at each other and, in concert, rolled our little bombs across the tiles.

Everyone was too focused on poor Paddy to notice. He slumped. He shook his shaggy head. And when the rotten-egg stench exploded, he staggered out with the rest of them.

By that time, Schwartz and I had concealed ourselves in a cleaning closet. It's hard to get intimate while wearing a gas mask, but I had my back practically pressed into his front, and my libido was not minding one bit. Maybe because I was trying hard not to laugh my head off at all those brilliant scientists blown away by a juvenile joke.

"What the devil is Bergdorff doing now?" one of the lab coats shouted as he coughed and raced ahead of the stench.

"We sent Bergdorff and Ferguson and their crew home!" another of the coats shouted back as they ran down the corridor. "Must be the freaking EPA morons."

"Why would the EPA have hydrogen sulfide?" another asked, slowing down and sniffing the air.

"If that's just sulfide and not Bergdorff stirring his brew, what are we running for?" someone smarter than the average suit asked—from the far end of the corridor. "Just find the damned leak."

Uh-oh. I dived out of the closet and across the hall to Lab B before they all decided to turn around and brave the stink. Schwartz stayed hot on my heels.

Once inside the forbidden lab, we hastily worked our way through far more modern paraphernalia than that in Paddy's pitiful closet. I watched for potentially explosive machinery, but the place was all computers, stainless steel, and glass. The back wall had no discernible door, just a suspiciously uncluttered lab table stretched across the width of it. We hunted for switches or hinges, me diving under the table and Schwartz leaning above it.

The argument in the corridor didn't seem to be coming closer. Paddy probably had to stick with his comrades, so we couldn't count on backup from him.

I'm a lawyer, not an engineer. I couldn't figure out how the lousy door worked. Or if Paddy's blueprints were all wrong or if he was just crazy. Frantically, I tried visualizing a door opening while muttering, "Open sesame," and pounding the wall. Nothing happened, not even a pink iceberg. Not surprising. Door opening didn't involve issues of justice, apparently.

"Stand back," Schwartz whispered. "I've got it."

I scuttled out from under the table and out of the way as Schwartz slid back a well-oiled door, with lab table attached. Devious. And obviously designed for secrecy. I'm in favor of an everything-in-the-open policy myself. Secrecy just isn't healthy. It means someone is doing something they shouldn't be.

Before Schwartz could order me to stay behind or lab coats could show up to ask what we were doing, I dashed through the opening, hitting the wall in search of a light switch. Found it in one. An ecologically sound fluorescent bulb whimpered on, giving off just enough light for me to see the stairwell.

At the bottom of the stairs, I cursed when faced with green concrete blocks and the same Lab A and Lab B layout as upstairs. Unimaginative bastards. Was it my imagination, or did I feel the rumble of machinery?

Not wanting to imagine being blown to hell while we were so close to it, I hastily took the A side. Schwartz turned left to the B side.

I opened every unmarked door in my path. No machinery. I wondered if I could visualize disintegrating bombs but figured inanimate objects were probably not on Saturn's duty roster.

The room below Paddy's was a supply closet down here. I debated dropping my dangling gas mask and donning a lab coat and surgical mask but figured I wouldn't fool anyone without a more official badge than my visitor's one.

As I approached the main lab, I heard more voices. Damn, we'd known it wouldn't be easy. I was supposed to just locate Bill and Sarah and scram before anyone knew we were here. There was no way I could throw them over my shoulders and carry them out. Especially not with people guarding them.

My mind churned as I explored farther down the corridor, past the main lab. Nobody came out to ask me what I was doing. I figured I could always tell them I'd gotten turned around and lost. What could they do, call a senator's guest a liar?

Well, yeah, if they recognized me. Last I'd heard, they'd labeled me Max's bitch. Oh well.

I hit pay dirt on the last door, the one on the same side as Lab A. Head Honcho's office, I diagnosed, even in the dark. Big shiny desk, lots of plaques and certificates—and a big old two-way mirror overlooking the well-lit lab.

Well, looka there, would you? I mentally imitated John Wayne, even though the Duke would never have come close to a setup like this one.

No explosive chemical tanks, but through the mirror I could see lab tables of unidentifiable equipment and an array of computer monitors. In between the tables, they'd hastily erected a row of cots—six that I could see. Instead of nurses or physicians walking among the patients, people in lab coats monitored machinery attached to each comatose body. They whispered among themselves as they recorded heartbeats and blood pressure. All the patients lay still as death, even when one of the coats prodded and pricked them, testing for reflexes.

Then I noticed a particularly luscious tech lady patting Bill's springy ginger hair. He might not mind waking up to that.

I couldn't immediately find Sarah, until I noted a curtain erected in a far corner. Outside the curtain was what might have been a portable blood-testing table, with more lab coats huddling around it. *Gotcha!* Maybe I couldn't save the world from Acme, but I intended to save it from Sarah. The world wasn't prepared to see whatever was in her DNA.

I rummaged through Honcho's desk, hunting for anything that screamed "official." I collected a tablet computer, a remote-control device, and a name badge with a purple frame. I slid my visitor's badge into the fancy frame. Then I returned to the supply closet in the hall for a lab coat and a surgical mask. I clipped the remote device to the coat pocket to complete my appearance of authority.

And then, as a last-minute thought, I grabbed a handful of rubber gloves and paper slippers and shoved them in one of the coat's pockets. Sarah couldn't thank me, but they might make our escape easier.

As I emerged from the closet, Schwartz strode down the corridor in my direction, narrowing his eyes at my getup. In his spiffy blue uniform and shiny badge, dangling his gas mask, he was my final piece of armor.

I gestured at a folded gurney in the supply closet. "We're getting Sarah out now."

It hurt like hell choosing psycho Sarah over my good friend Bill, but we could only move one patient, and Sarah was the loose cannon. Sometimes I'm rational, even if I resent it.

Before Leo could give me any male guff, I struggled with the gurney hinges, giving the good detective something more useful to do than question or complain. He finished unlatching it while I played with the tablet.

I couldn't afford fancy tech, not even a smart phone, but I grasped the basics. I played with the keyboard until I hit the right button, and Head Honcho's preprogrammed password fed itself in. Voilà. I was sooo keeping this.

Not if Schwartz could help it. He was still eyeing me suspiciously. Hiding my fear and my larcenous distraction, I straightened my lab coat, made certain my fancy badge was visible, placed the tablet in the crook of my arm, and marched into the lab across the green hall, a uniformed policeman pushing a gurney trailing behind me.

The coats inside the lab glanced up in surprise. I rudely ignored them and gestured at the curtained area. "Hurry," I ordered brusquely. "We don't have time to waste."

Bless Schwartz's pea-pickin' heart, he followed orders as if he were made for them. Ex-military, I surmised. One of these days, I'd have to get to know him better instead of just lusting after his bod. I handed him the rubber gloves and gestured for him to steal Sarah while I stepped between him and the huddle of coats.

"What are you doing?" one of the female lab coats demanded. "Who are you?"

She had a long syringe in her hand. I remembered those needles with a shudder. What did she have in this one?

"Just following orders," I said in my most officious voice. "Senator Vanderventer said this was a matter of national security."

Max would probably kill me, but the coats stepped back, out of my way, to consult with each other.

Someone pulled a cell phone out of his pocket. Not good.

"I'll need your names," I commanded, forcing cell phone guy to stop what he was doing and look at me. "The senator is grateful for your promptness in an emergency situation. He will see that you receive appropriate recognition for your help with this very dangerous matter."

I might have been shaking in my shoes, but I didn't get to be a lawyer by being stupid. Their ears perked right up. The syringe disappeared back into the pocket. I scribbled names in the tablet with a stylus, nodded curtly, and gave them another officious speech.

After taking one wistful look at poor Bill, I deposited the tablet in my lab coat pocket and marched off after Schwartz. All I could see of Sarah was a sheet covering most of her body, thank goodness. We didn't need to attract any more attention than necessary. If Schwartz had pulled the gloves and slippers over her chimp appendages, she would be less conspicuous.

I couldn't damn innocent scientists so I could save Bill. Wouldn't it be convenient if I could wield constructive instead of destructive justice? Experimentally, I whispered as we hurried down the hall, "Bless Sarah and Bill and let them wake up."

Nothing happened.

"Pretty please, Saturn? Just let them wake up?"

Nada.

Maybe I needed red rage to reach Saturn, but at the moment, I was too terrified to be angry. I never wanted to enter these bowels of hell again. Scientists with needles and hidden cellars were a Frankensteinian death trap if I ever saw one.

Leo had the gurney halfway down the hall and was hitting buttons to summon a hidden elevator he must have discovered in his search, when we heard a shout.

"Wait a minute!" We heard footsteps pounding from the other end of the corridor—just as the elevator door opened.

This was the reason I hadn't dared rescue Bill, too. He was too heavy for running like hell.

I glanced at Schwartz. He nodded and, clenching his jaw, shoved the gurney into the elevator. Remembering his request that I not get him fired, I hit the up button and prayed to escape from the antiseptic depths of hell. Not that I expected prayers to be answered.

7

"Gas mask." I pointed at Schwartz's, reminding him to cover his face. "Security clearance." I held up my purple badge.

I could tell he got my message because he scowled as he adjusted his mask, and I whipped out my phone. Did cell reception even reach through this bloody building? Better yet, would the Zone let me call out?

I hit Andre's number. I got voice mail for a cheese shop in Wisconsin. Worried that I was about to blow this, I tried to think of some way to carry Sarah out of there without better transportation than Leo's cop car.

She seemed pretty pale, and my gut knotted. What had they done to her? She was the only person remotely like me that I knew, and I felt more than a little protective. Schwartz had managed to pull the gloves over her paws, because one dangled outside the sheet. I had just carefully tucked it under when my phone played "Here Comes the Judge."

Unhappy with the inappropriate interruption, I seriously considered getting the hell out of the Zone if this electronic comedy routine continued. Wondering how Acme operated computers if I couldn't even use a phone, and realizing that I could not *not* answer the Judge's call if I wanted to still remain a lawyer, I punched the button just as the elevator doors opened on the main floor. No welcoming committee. Yet.

My employer's secretary spoke in clipped tones in my ear. "Clancy, Judge Snodgrass needs you to research a case this afternoon. Can you be here by two?"

I glanced at my watch as we rushed the gurney down the main hall of offices. It was after one already, and it was just research. On a weekend. "We're having a bit of a public emergency down here, Jill," I told her. I knew she wouldn't like it. She didn't like me. She liked men and didn't think women ought to be attorneys—or near her favorite judge. But I needed this job. "Can this wait until tomorrow?"

"I'm not coming in on a Sunday," she said acidly. "And you don't have clearance for office keys. If you want this job, you'll be here by two."

She cut me off. I generously refrained from damning her to hell, but for a minute there, she hung on the precipice.

One more stressor added to my day. *You can do it, Clancy.*

A couple of security goons in uniform were coming at us, looking mean. Since they hadn't hurt anybody, I couldn't wish them to Hades or anywhere else any more than I could Jill. Apparently, my attempts at anger management were working. A pity, that.

I kept talking loudly into my phone as if it hadn't gone dead. "Yes, Senator. Of course, Senator. Is the ambulance outside yet? Your cousin is in good hands, I assure you. We'll let you know as soon as we arrive."

I stalked past the guards as if they weren't there. Schwartz stoically propelled the gurney. If anyone could read my pulse, they'd know I was running on terrified and pushing a heart attack, but I'd had a lifetime's practice faking it.

"Wait a minute!" one of the guards shouted as we passed.

I held my purple badge over my shoulder, waggled it, and kept on walking, talking to my imaginary friend.

Behind us, I heard them consulting some authority on their phones. Schwartz muttered incomprehensible curses and pushed faster. Getting arrested wouldn't do either of us any favors.

We burst into the reception area at a full run. The receptionist glanced up in surprise. I shouted, "Emergency!" and hurried ahead to open the doors.

The clowns in uniforms spilled into the lobby just as we hightailed it out. Without a word, Schwartz hoisted our patient over his shoulder, abandoned the gurney, and raced for his car.

Whatever worked.

The worst of the pink and green cloud had dissipated, leaving a thin film of pink confetti particles everywhere it had touched. Schwartz's cop car had been parked elsewhere before the explosion, so it was relatively unscathed in comparison to the parking lot and streets. I opened the back door, Leo practically flung Sarah across the backseat, and we both dived for the front just as the guards tottered after us. They were on the brink of corpulent, not joggers by any stretch of the imagination, and they were struggling with gas masks as they ran.

No way was I letting them have Sarah. Thank Saturn, our Zone cop apparently felt the same.

Schwartz gunned his engine, backed up, swung the car around, and hit sixty before he reached the gate. The guard didn't dare close it, especially after Leo turned on the siren. I do love a siren.

The police barricade allowed one of their own to pass but blocked the path of the Keystone Cops rattling after us in their security truck.

"Win one for the Duke!" I crowed, pumping my fist in the air. We rocked!

Leo sent me a strange look. Obviously, he didn't watch old westerns. Taking my triumph where I could find it, I checked on our patient. Despite all the commotion, Sarah lay still as death. That worried me, but I was no doctor. I'd done all I could do. Except rescue Bill. That burned. Triumph was fleeting.

I glanced out the back window, but the gates had closed. There wouldn't be any going back in. Telling myself I wasn't responsible for anyone but myself, and that I had to focus on keeping my job, I clenched my teeth and plotted how to reach the judge's office by two.

Leo took a right off Edgewater away from the harbor, as if we really were heading for a hospital. Once out of the Zone, he switched off the siren, swung down a garbage-strewn alley only a policeman would dare drive, and maneuvered us back to the hill and Andre's warehouse.

I glanced at my watch. One thirty. The judge's office was almost half an hour away, depending on traffic. Sarah needed help I couldn't give her. I had to let others save the day.

"I love and adore you, Leo," I said appreciatively, "but I have to run or get canned. If I bake you a cake, can you take it from here?"

"I can take it from here without the cake," he said grumpily, parking behind the warehouse. "And if anyone took my license number and I get called to the carpet, you better bring out the big guns."

Meaning Dane/Max. I didn't want to ask favors of a man I could barely talk to, but I nodded. "You got it, big boy." I leaned over, smooched his bristly cheek, and scooted out before he could react. He hadn't had time to shave or shower this morning, and he smelled like hot male—not a bad scent, all things considered. I tried not to think what I smelled like after a night of partying and a morning of running on terrified. I needed superhero deodorant.

Dashing for my Harley across the street, I ran through a mental checklist: Milo safe upstairs, messenger bag over my shoulder, blazer and khakis okay for a weekend, ditch lab coat . . . keep computer tablet!

I'd apparently shoved the pretty toy in my pocket while running. Ooooh, cool. Who needed the devil to reward me? I'd rewarded myself for keeping my head on straight.

I flung the lab coat into the shed my Harley leaned against, stuffed the tablet in my messenger bag, and roared off to the office.

Riding from the blacktopped industrial wasteland of the Zone, north on the interstate, and into the leafy suburbs of Towson was like leaving the Sahara for an oasis. They had trees here. Even in September there were buckets of flowers around lampposts and on doorsteps. Businesses thrived. Traffic clogged every major artery. I took a few stone-fence-lined back roads, then zipped my bike down the yellow stripes of the main thoroughfare until I reached the county court building.

I dashed up the stairs and, out of courtesy to my associates, stopped in a washroom. My reflection over the sinks glittered with pink. Damn.

It was already two. I didn't have time to do much. I doused my armpits, buttoned up, and hit the office at two after two.

Judge Snootypants and his secretary, Miss Goody Two-shoes, glanced up at my entrance. Both donned identical frowns.

"Industrial accident," I said casually. "You'll hear about it on the news. What's the case and where would you like me to start?"

"Reginald is already in the library. Bring us some coffee and file the briefs in my office, will you?"

Okay, here's where anger management is a good thing. I didn't visualize the old fart leaping off tall buildings—that's pretty good, right?

I'd been filing briefs and carrying coffee for weeks. The only time I'd been allowed in the library was to return books. I was damned good, and they were underutilizing my services, not to mention pissing me off big-time by getting me down here under false pretenses.

I practically saluted and marched off to the break room. I'd spent twenty-six years working toward this goal, and I refused to blow it. I was going to be the best damned lawyer in Maryland, at the very least. I just had to prove myself.

Proving that I could pour coffee was not a good starting place. I noted the books on the library table when I delivered the cups, glanced at the names on the file folders, and suggested another case file they might want to check out. Reginald all but snarled at me. Reginald was a Yalie who'd worked for the judge for the past year. He wore a tie even on Saturday and had his hair styled once a week. Jill adored him. I had despised him on sight.

His Honor nodded at my suggestion and told me to pull the book.

I opened it to the case mentioned, set it in front of Snodgrass, and sauntered out in my secondhand blazer, shedding pink glitter across the carpet. I would prove myself one casebook at a time if I had to.

I spent the rest of the afternoon filing and wondering what was happening at home. Lives were at stake and I was making coffee!

I was hot under the collar and itching all over before the judge decided we'd done enough for the day. I was paid by the week, not the hour, so I didn't expect any reward for my efforts. Telling myself this was just the first rung on the ladder, and that I was making connections to pave my way up, I took the stairs faster than the elevator and hit my bike.

Max's bike, actually, but he wasn't here to ride it. Since he'd crashed my car, it had seemed like a fair trade. If I thought too hard about that time, I'd cry, so I just let the wind cool my cheeks and disperse the glitter. I refused to cry anymore.

Rain clouds were moving in by the time I parked the bike behind the house and trotted around to Pearl's front door. The gloom hid the glittering Disneyland effect. Wondering if I could tolerate the Zone if it turned pink instead of neon blue, I jogged upstairs to hug Milo.

He sniffed haughtily but agreed to eat the fish I chopped up for him. Bill had spoiled him by sending fillets home when he had leftovers. I wondered how Bill was doing in his zombie state and hoped he could somehow sense he had a luscious babe taking care of him.

Saturday night and I ain't got nobody wormed its way through my head as I nuked frozen Chinese. The image of a head dancing without a body loomed in my overwrought imagination. That's the reason

I should never watch musicals. Tunes stay inside my skull, circling and warping and driving me battier. Sleep wasn't happening with my mind on spin cycle.

I needed to eat before I headed out hunting for trouble, but, remembering my new toy, I dug the tablet out of my bag and turned it on. I could tune in and see what was happening. Seeing the low-battery signal, I realized I'd need a charger. Dang. I should have stolen that, too. Schwartz would be so mad at me. But there was plenty enough juice to get in and change the password to something a little smarter than my name.

I explored its contents while I ate, but I'm no chemistry major. I'd need Paddy to explain the head honcho's documents and programs. I plugged in a USB drive, backed up the tablet, then cleaned out the crap. My pretty new toy had built-in 4G, so I downloaded my e-mail program on Acme's dime.

I checked Facebook to see if I had any messages. None. I started fretting about Themis, my theoretical grandmother, who hadn't left me any messages in a while. When he was in hell, Max had said he had knowledge she was alive and living on another plane of reality, not that it was really proof to me. I'd never met the woman, and she didn't exist in any database that I could locate, other than a Facebook page for Themis Astrology and Tarot.

But I'd been receiving creepy messages from the Universe, like *Saturn is the planet of justice. It comes around every twenty-eight years to dispense karmic reward and punishment.* I wouldn't be twenty-seven for a few months yet, so that just felt like bad math on the planets' part and I was trying not to worry about that one.

Themis only seemed to drop by when I disturbed the universe's vibrations with my fury. Could she be one of the zombies Acme had nuked? Idiotic to worry about someone I'd never met, I knew.

I took a hasty shower, returned the tablet and the USB drive to my bag, and jogged over to Andre's carrying Milo over my shoulder. I reminded myself once again that I needed a bigger carryall for my pet. He had grown way past kitten size.

No one answered the door, so I let myself in. Milo preferred to take the stairs on his own. We clattered down and were met at the bottom by Cora.

"Where've you been, girl? Andre is about to send out the National Guard. Calm him down, will you? I've got to get home." Without explanation, Cora departed by the stairs I'd just traversed.

I hoped he wasn't sending out the Guard for my sake, but I dreaded finding out why our über-cool amoral leader was on the warpath.

I checked the room where I'd last seen Sleeping Beauty. She was still there, with Julius mournfully holding her hand. On another cot lay Sarah, still zonked, still with chimp appendages. I could have used some of those z's she was piling up, but I wanted to be able to wake up after. I studied her with concern, but for the life of me, I didn't know what to do if prayers to Saturn Daddy didn't work.

"Where did the other patients go?" I asked Julius.

"Andre moved them into the warehouse, where the

med students can look after them." With expert ease, Julius flipped Sleeping Beauty onto her side and began massaging her back.

My bet was that he'd been doing this for a while. I didn't know whether I had any right to question it.

"Have you eaten? Do I need to cook something?" There was a task I knew how to take on. I'd never nursed a patient, but I'd fed the famished hordes before.

"Lack of food may be part of Andre's problem. Find out what has him roaring, and then we'll sort things out." Julius has the patience of a saint, and his unhurried response proved it.

"If Andre and I tear each other's throats out, you might regret waiting," I warned.

He sent me a beatific smile and let me go. I wish I'd had a father like him.

The warehouse was on the other side of the street, accessible by a tunnel at the end of the bomb shelter. I trotted over with Milo at my heels.

I had to follow the sound of voices once I reached the top of the stairs on the other side. The warehouse was a rambling place. Andre used the loading dock as a garage for his Mercedes sports coupe. But off to one side were doors leading to offices and storage rooms and I had no idea what else. Not hearing any shouting or gunfire, I figured it was safe to explore.

I located a high-ceilinged room lined with shelves of supplies. Cartons had been stacked along the walls to clear a place for an infirmary filled with cots. Along with Leibowitz, there must have been a dozen zombies, with the med students moving among them, checking pulses, making notes, administering IVs. Where in heck had they found IVs? Suspecting illegal pilfering, I didn't ask.

Andre was on the phone, leaning against a stack of crates as if he didn't have a care in the world. His silk shirt was filthy and looked as if he'd never completely buttoned it all day. He had pink glitter on his tight trousers. His usually styled thick black hair had fallen across his brow. And even though he appeared cool and unruffled, I could tell he was breathing fire. I'm pretty much the only one who generates that reaction.

He glowered at me, snapped off his phone, and, in a voice that thundered doom, said, "Call off your boyfriend now or he's dead meat."

I came all the way over here for that old argument? I was asleep on my feet and didn't need more crap. I glowered back, said, "Good luck with that," and, turning on my heel, walked out.

Hell, I'd just strolled through a Magic lab. Andre didn't have nothing on me.

8

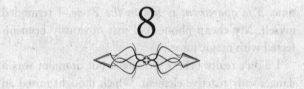

Knowing Max and Andre were growling at each other left me feeling like a bone caught between two dogs. Yeah, the Zone had to be hazardous to our health. But most of the people living and working there would have no lives at all otherwise. Where would a kid who turned invisible live outside the Zone? He'd be reduced to a life of crime. And Sarah? They'd have her in a zoo.

"Damn it, Saturn," I muttered, "if you really wanted to give me power, you'd give me fairy dust so I could just make everybody happy."

My head in a muddle, I stomped back to Julius's kitchen, dumped a bunch of cans into a casserole dish with some chicken I defrosted from his freezer and a

bunch of noodles, and shoved the concoction into the
microwave. I threw some frozen rolls into the oven.
I'd learned creative cooking while traveling around
the country with my mother. I couldn't guarantee
the result would taste good, but it had the maximum
number of calories and nutrition and served to distract me from Andre and Max.

My phone kept ringing—chiming church bells this
time. *The apartment is not in the Zone,* I reminded
myself. My cheap phone had just obviously been infected with magic juice.

I didn't really believe in magic, but uranium was a
dangerously reactive element. Which thought raised an
unease that had been niggling in the back of my mind
all day—what was in those pink particles? Of course,
for all I knew, we'd all be blown sky-high before we
had to worry about pink-particle contamination.

Once I had the casserole cooking, I checked my
caller list. Max.

I really, really couldn't afford to offend a senator,
no matter how weird he made me feel. And I owed
Andre a lot, as well, so I at least owed him an argument with my ex-do-gooder boyfriend's conscience
in an effort to keep the Feds from condemning the
rest of the Zone. Still, it was hard wrapping my mind
around Dane as Max—which was probably why I
was avoiding him.

With a sigh, while my casserole cooked, I settled
into a comfy chair in Julius's front room and called
Max back. I sure hoped no one was tapping his line
or recording his calls, because they'd wonder why a

powerful senator was talking to little old fractious me.

"Justy, I need you over here, now!" he shouted.

Okay, that was a surprise. I stared at the phone a full minute before returning it to my ear. "Why?" I asked cautiously.

He sounded immensely weary this time. "Because I asked you to, please?"

Wow, it surely must be serious for Macho Man to use the *p*-word. "Can I tell Andre that you're not shutting him down?" I'm a tough negotiator.

"I can't shut anyone down," he said with disgust. "I have to stay as far from my family's freaking plant as I can these days. Acme is a conflict of interest—you *know* this. I just wanted Andre to tell me what the hell was happening and if you were all right."

The Max I knew would never give up, but I really didn't know this Dane/Max person. Heck, I didn't even know if souls inhabited brains or if he still had Dane's brains or how in hell he was dealing with this weirdness. I grimaced as the microwave bell dinged. "Okay, let me feed a few people. Where should I meet you?"

"In Dane's condo. Hurry, will you?" He gave me the address and we signed off.

I wouldn't be human if my pulse didn't beat a little harder at the thought of visiting a hunky senator in his luxury tower, but I had no intention of being anyone's secret girlfriend. Max couldn't parade me to embassy dinners, and I can't stomach politicians, so we were so far from compatible as to inhabit different universes.

But Max had once been a friend. I could be there if he needed me.

I delivered the casserole and rolls to Julius, letting him work out how to feed whoever was hanging out in the warehouse.

Relieved that I no longer had to waste my evenings studying, I took Milo back to my place. Saturday night and now I had a date, of sorts. I glanced at my usual threads, removed the cotton T-shirt, found a fancier bra, donned a satiny shirt with my jeans, and considered myself well dressed. I added a leather jacket—after all, it was September and I was riding a Harley.

With my lion's mane from the devil, I didn't have to worry about helmet hair. I just snapped my hair into a clip I could take down when I got there. I wasn't into bling, so Max would just have to take me as he'd found me.

I tried not to be too nervous when I drove up to the security gate at Dane's place in Bethesda. The towering condos, ornate fence, and elaborate fountains screamed money, but the Vanderventers had million-dollar lines of credit at Tiffany. They could own homes like this all over the world.

I was just having difficulty picturing my biker Max living like this. He used to crash in a dive even more pathetic than my old one.

But it wasn't my scruffy, curly-haired Max meeting me at the door once I was buzzed in. Senator Dane Vanderventer, with his stylishly coiffed chestnut hair, greeted me, wearing gabardine trousers, a quietly elegant tailored shirt, and a loosened silk tie.

We stared at each other uneasily. The senator was a little taller than Max had been, a little leaner, but he was still one good-looking dude, with broad shoulders and narrow hips and piercing blue eyes. His dimpled chin was even more impressive than Kirk Douglas's.

"Lookin' good, Justy," he murmured as I removed my jacket.

The voice didn't sound right, but the words were pure Max, and a shiver crept down my spine. He was the only one who used that nickname. Once upon a time I used to fling myself into his welcoming bear hug when he said that. I wanted to do so again. But it wasn't the same.

Nervously, I resisted any such impulse. Hugging my elbows, I glanced around at the designer-decorated pad. Neutral tans and browns with splashes of black. Fat suede cushions, leather recliner, a huge flat-screen TV hidden behind a faux painting over the fireplace. It was obvious a man owned the place but didn't really live there. No beer cans.

Gathering my wits, I dropped my jacket over the arm of the couch and sat down, crossing my leg over my knee and peering up at him as if I belonged here. "Okay, I'm here. I'm creeped out. It's been a rotten long day, and I don't want to fight. What do you need?"

In a familiar Max gesture, he ran his hand through Dane's styled hair, disturbing the wax or whatever it is politicians use to maintain that polished image. A hank fell down over his forehead, and I almost smiled.

I used to tease Max about the curl in the middle of his forehead.

"I need sanity, among other things," he said bluntly. "Dane was a lying, cheating bastard. I'm still trying to pry his girlfriends out of my hair. Currently, they're threatening to go to the media and tell them what a horse's ass Dane is. I've told them to go ahead. I'd rather not even run for dogcatcher if it means putting up with their histrionics."

"Histrionics, that's good," I said, knowing he was just venting and that he didn't need me for this. "That's a Max word if I ever heard one. If you used it on his bimbos, they know you've flipped out."

A corner of his mouth twitched upward. "Yeah, after I blocked one girl's calls, she threatened to call my grandmother to tell her I need psychiatric help. Dane didn't mess with two-bit bimbos. These morons actually thought he'd marry them."

"How many are there?" I asked in awe, trying to imagine dangling more than one expensive high-society babe on a string, even with the honkin' big Tiffany credit line. D.C. really isn't a very large world.

"Three," he said with disgust. "He gave *friendship* rings to all of them. Who the hell gives people friendship rings anymore?"

"Your cousin," I pointed out unhelpfully. "And you didn't drag me over here to chitchat about your social life. You can handle that on your own. What's really up?"

Instead of answering, he picked up a remote and flicked on the fireplace. Neat trick, like summoning the devil with a finger snap. I admired the dancing flames.

"Take a closer look," he suggested. "Tell me if I've really flipped out. I don't want to check myself into the nearest funny farm unless necessary. Maybe Dane was experimenting with hallucinogens and they haven't completely left his body. But we've both seen hell, so it's not as if we're dealing with reality as we used to know it."

I'd only seen hell in the mirror with Max blocking the view, but that had been vile enough. I got up and walked across the huge living room to look closer at the flames. Expecting to see horns and a devil's ugly grin, I didn't see anything, at first.

But the twisting flames weren't normal. Flames should flicker. These wound around each other as if attempting origami. They whispered furiously instead of crackling. Maybe it was my guilt talking, but I could swear a voice inside my head was saying, *I'm going to kill you!*

"Not liking your fireplace, Max," I said, backing away. "Did you feed it magic pinecones?"

"It's gas. I don't feed it anything." The senator stood well behind me, arms crossed while observing the warped flames. Satisfied I was seeing what he was, he flicked off the remote. "Come look at this."

He led me through a dining room that could accommodate a state dinner and into a kitchen that would comfortably house a catering crew. Granite counters, marble floors, probably gold appliances for all I knew—they were all hidden behind mahogany cabinetry. I could have fed the entire Zone from there.

Max ate takeout. I could see the leftover Thai cartons still sitting on the counter.

He opened a panel under the gas burners of the stove and turned one on. "I thought I'd heat a can of soup earlier. That's when I called you to confirm I'm not bonkers. It's one freaking thing too many. I think Dane was the devil incarnate."

The stove flames performed the same bizarre dance as the ones in the fireplace, more frantically this time. They almost seemed as if they were trying to form an image. A whispered *Get me out of here!* was painfully familiar, though.

"That's what you said," I murmured. "Provided I'm actually hearing what I think I'm hearing."

Dane/Max hurriedly flicked off the stove. "'Get me out of here,' right? So I'm not imagining it? Dane has a haunted stove?"

I rubbed my nose with the heel of my hand and tried to dispel the itchiness. I didn't like any of this. A few months ago, I'd contemplated running away to Seattle to escape this madness. But I had no guarantees that Max's form of hell wouldn't follow me.

"You know who that sounds like, don't you?" I asked, because I had to spell out craziness.

Max ran a hand through Dane's hair. "The stove sounds like Dane," he said unhappily.

"Yeah, my thought, too. Wonder if we could get voice analysis?" I asked, sarcasm intended.

If Dane's demonic soul was still alive beyond the veil . . . Max and I were likely to be crispy critters any day now.

So not liking the idea of a real hell. Maybe we were both zonked on crazy juice.

"When did this start?" I asked, grasping at straws.

"Hard to say. I've been trying to ignore the weird gas logs, and I don't spend much time in the kitchen. But I think the voice is getting stronger, and both the stove and the fireplace in one night blew my mind. I just wanted to be certain I wasn't losing it."

"Is there any chance we've slipped into some kind of alternate universe?" I asked, returning to the front room and searching for a liquor cabinet. "Or better yet, could we theorize, since we never knew hell existed until you hit the wall, that we've freaked out, slipped over, gone around the bend?"

Guessing my direction, he opened a sleek, shiny wood cabinet and produced a bottle of vodka and another of Scotch. The Max I knew would have had beer. I opened the concealed refrigerator. It only had juice. I chose orange.

We were standing entirely too close. His expensive shaving cologne cried out for sniffing, and his loosened tie begged for release. I backed off as soon as he filled my glass.

"Post-traumatic stress?" he suggested, eyeing me with just a hint of longing that he disguised by filling his own glass. "We fried our brains?"

"We fried more than our brains," I pointed out, avoiding temptation by pacing.

"Oh, crap." Max threw back his whiskey neat.

"Yeah, that's kind of what I said that first time you appeared in my mirror." I'd harbored a lot of pent-up anguish these last months. I wasn't very tactful in opening the floodgates now. "Andre tried to tell me it was grief, that I was in a state of denial, but I doubt you're grieving over your cousin."

"Here I am, a walking, talking freak, and I'm *still* not buying Dane in hell." He scrubbed his head some more before pouring himself another drink.

"That's because you helped put him there, and you don't like the guilt. Talk to me about guilt sometime." Dane might have had the original Max murdered, but I'd been the one to damn Max's soul to hell instead of letting him go to the light or whatever he should have done. That guilt never went away, even though—and perhaps because—I was glad to have him back.

He sent me an undecipherable scowl and threw back a bigger gulp.

I was liking the unpolished image he was achieving. Maybe if I got him out of the silk tie and into bike leathers . . . But he was a U.S. senator. He had to play the part, if only for national security. Explaining that hell existed and that he'd once been a denizen would be hazardous to the public health. I didn't know if I was being a responsible citizen by keeping my distance or just acting on my usual caution.

"Sell the condo," I suggested. "You told me you could only see through my mirrors. Maybe he can only see through his flames."

"Or mine," he countered grimly. "This is his body, after all. He's probably still connected to it somehow. If we buy that's Dane in the fire, then we have to assume he's attached to this body. My memory of hell is pretty diluted, but I remember the mirrors. They were my link to you, since I didn't have a body anymore."

Because it had burned up in the fiery crash I'd brought down on him, right.

"I don't suppose you made any good connections down there, did you?" I asked gloomily, not expecting an answer to my sarcastic question.

"Only dead ones, unless you count your grandmother. And that only happened because Themis made the effort. If I believe in the impossible, then I guess I can believe she's a psychic or a medium or whatever and can talk to the dead." He paced the designer carpet.

"If Themis is so psychic, why doesn't she contact me?" I asked grumpily. "I have a lot of questions for the old bat."

"Which is why she isn't contacting you," he said annoyingly, happy to change the subject. "If she's anything like you, she'd rather act than explain. I had the sense that she was restricted to one place, though. She's old. Maybe she's in a nursing home somewhere."

"Nursing homes have phones. She left notes on my door. And this is a ridiculous conversation. Don't turn on your stove or your fireplace, and you'll be fine." I finished my screwdriver. I didn't dare have a second one, since I was biking home.

"Not if Dane wants his body back," Max said gloomily. "If I could take his, there must be some way of him returning."

Only if I wished for it. Struck with horror by this thought, I sank back on his fancy couch and buried my face in my hands. My gift-of-the-devil hair fell forward in a thick, silky mane.

"It's me," I told him. "Maybe I'm a *Satan's* daughter, after all. Maybe Themis has it all wrong. Saturn has nothing to do with anything. I sent Dane to hell, and now he wants me to bring him back like I did you."

Over my dead body was a very real possibility.

9

My old Max would have hugged and kissed and comforted me as I rocked back and forth in horror. Dane/Max hovered helplessly. We both sensed that we were bad for each other in too many weird ways, and until and unless we figured them out, life would be simpler apart.

Nothing like knowing you can't have something to make you want it more.

"I blame it on the Zone, Justy," he said wearily, tucking my hair behind my ear. "There's some weird stuff going down at Acme. I don't think blue goo and green clouds are helping whatever's warping you and everything else down there."

Max knew about winking statues and crowing weather vanes because he'd used me as a spy for months, back when he was an environmental activist trying to find a way to shut down Acme. Or maybe it was just to screw up his family's income. He hadn't really explained himself to me at the time.

Fortunately, I'm equally closemouthed and hadn't told him about the real weirdnesses, like Sarah's shape-shifting or Cora's snakes. Just as Andre didn't know for certain about Max. I was Keeper of the Secrets.

"That's not what Themis says," I pointed out, digging my fingers into his fancy leather chair rather than reach out for him. "The Zone has nothing to do with my bizarro shit. She says my asteroids are in the seventh house and Saturn is aligned with Mars or some such garbage." But Max was totally right that Acme was screwing with the neighborhood. I just didn't want to tell secrets that weren't mine to reveal.

"Believing in psychic old ladies could be another chemical reaction," he warned. "I was there when the tanks first spilled. I was between jobs, working in the office. My family wouldn't let me go back afterward, but I knew the company had been playing with some dangerous new material. We could both be polluted."

Dangerous new material, like magic elements. Yeah, tell me about it. Magic or a tool of Satan, which would I rather believe? Pink confetti looked like Disney magic to me. Maybe the devil was filming a show-and-tell on How to Destroy a Planet.

"I bet Dane didn't work down there," I pointed out. "So who do you want to believe is polluted, him or you? For all I know, Acme opened a gate to hell." I didn't think any environmental scientist in the world could begin to explain the Zone, so I saw no reason to muddy the waters with questions. But I gave him a small bone to chew on. "Paddy says Acme is still experimenting with the new element. Did you know he's actually sane, or is that a new development?" I cocked my head at him with interest, preferring this topic to my damning hobby.

"With Paddy, it's hard to tell." He poured a second glass of whiskey for himself but didn't immediately drink it. "He's Dane's father, Gloria's only son, but he doesn't communicate with the family as far as I'm aware. His number isn't in Dane's cell phone. Dane's mother ditched Paddy years ago. Last I heard, she was in France. She's not in his address book, either."

Dane/Max shrugged and continued. "Since my—Max's—grandmother still owns half the firm along with Gloria, she was the one who asked Paddy to hire me, but I'm pretty certain Paddy never contacts the MacNeill side of the family anymore, either."

The MacNeill side was Max's side. Paddy's cousin was Max's mother. Referring to one's original self in the third person was a trifle confusing, although it was even weirder for me to hear him refer to Dane that way, since physically, in my eyes, he was now Dane.

"I think I'm too tired for this," I said, rubbing my eyes. "You have an inside track on the grannies. Why don't you give them a visit and see if either one spills the family secrets? Let's blame our predicament on Acme and see how that flows."

"If we're going nuts and hearing Dane in flames, it's Acme's fault?" he asked with a hint of amusement, almost sounding like my Max. "And you still want to go back to the Zone?"

When he put it that way . . . I stood up and pulled on my jacket. "Yeah. Because even if the people living in the Zone are nuts, they're nuts in a positive way. They're good people. I like them a whole lot better than your greedy family. It's only when Acme steps into the picture that trouble starts. And maybe, just maybe, I'm meant to be there to keep Acme from hurting anyone else."

He frowned dubiously. I knew I couldn't ask Max for more help. He was a senator who needed to keep his job.

"You just keep your bimbos from blackmailing you, and I'll try to keep your family from killing you—again." I stood on my toes and kissed his handsome cheek, enjoying his solid masculinity in the only way I could. "You're a good man, Charlie Brown. Talk to the old harpies. Tell them the anesthesia from taking out the bullet messed with your memory and see what they tell you. Let me know if you learn anything, and I'll return the favor."

He let me go, although I could tell by his fisted hands that he was having difficulty keeping them off me. Old habits die hard.

If driving home with the wind in my face was my idea of a Saturday night date, I decided I was better off staying in with Milo.

I'd spent a few miserable weeks the previous May dodging Vanderventer's security goons. The habit was almost ingrained by now, especially after seeing Dane in person, so to speak. I didn't take a direct route back to my place. I steered the bike down dark alleys and waited for traffic to flow by. I didn't spy any tails.

Out of curiosity, I swung the bike behind the empty warehouse across from the town house where I made my bed. I knew a locked chain-link fence protected the entrance to Andre's lair, but I couldn't just waltz up to his front door at midnight and expect entrance.

I wanted company, and I wasn't above climbing a chain-link just to see what happened. Unlike Acme's goons, Andre probably wouldn't shoot me on sight.

I really should have gone home to Milo, but it was freaking Saturday night. I'd had a bad day and had spent the evening nobly resisting a hottie, and I was hornier than hell. Bad phrasing, but I wasn't in the mood to edit my thoughts.

To my surprise, the fence lock opened when I yanked at it. I shoved the gate open a few feet, rolled my bike through, and, keeping an eye on the shadows, closed it again. With Dane's evilness gone, I shouldn't have needed to be afraid, but caution had been my motto for long enough to become habit.

My headlight beam caught Andre leaning against the wall of the loading dock, appearing for all the world as if he'd just stepped out of a 1920s speakeasy for a smoke. Except Andre didn't smoke. So what was he doing out here?

He'd apparently showered off the glitter at some

point and donned a loose pale blue shirt and dark trousers. If he'd had a fedora and a coat swung over his shoulder, we'd have had the setting for a film noir.

"Don't you ever lock your gates?" I chirped, parking the Harley and switching off its light.

"Not when I know you'll just climb over. Did you get your senator boyfriend out of our hair?" He sounded more bleak than snarky.

Andre owned the world. He had no reason to be gloomy. I climbed up to the dock beside him, leaned against the wall, and admired the few stars visible above the roof lines. They say misery loves company.

"Dane has his own troubles. He doesn't have time for us these days. And no, I don't tell him what goes down here any more than I'll tell you what he's dealing with. Is there a reason we're standing outside?"

"Because you won't go to bed with me?" he asked, back to the usual snark.

"I'm thinking of becoming a nun," I taunted. "In Clancy's world, sex is too complicated, especially when the men are sneaky, deceptive, lying bastards."

"My parents are very much married," he said gravely.

"Your parents didn't give you the name Legrande," I countered. Were we just doing our usual boy/girl dance here, or was he offering more? Given the mood I was in, I needed more.

"True." He caught my elbow and opened the door to the warehouse before I could react. "We're not equipped to deal with nearly a dozen comatose patients. We need to send them where Acme can't find them."

"None of them are coming around?" The news was bad, but at least the subject was safer than anything personal. Although his strong grip on my arm didn't ease the hormone dance.

"See for yourself." He led me back to the room that had been cleared for the patients.

I gazed at the array of cots in dismay. Thank goodness it was September and not too hot or cold. I doubted the hundred-year-old warehouse was insulated or thermostatically controlled. It certainly wasn't sanitary.

Tim was sweeping the floor with a long broom and raising puffs of dust. He'd placed a vase of flowers near Nancy Rose's cot, which nearly broke my hard heart.

Apparently the med students had divided into shifts. Only a female one was on duty. I had some vague notion that medical residents worked abominable hours, so I was amazed and grateful that any of them found time for us.

Leibowitz lay there like a beached walrus with that ratty mustache. Not a single malevolent twitch from his cot.

I studied Nancy Rose. Mid-fifties would be my guess. Threads of frost in her mousy brown hair, jowls starting to sag, a bit on the plump side. She just seemed to be sleeping. I swallowed a lump in my throat. Tim thought of her as a mother figure. He needed her. I tested her pulse. Beating regularly as far as I could tell. Could she really be sick already?

The baby doc joined us and read her chart. "High white-blood-cell count, an indication of infection, conceivably cancer. Compromised breathing. Normally, I'd order more blood tests and pictures of her lungs. If her lungs are infected, they could be depriving her brain of oxygen and causing the coma. She probably ought to be hospitalized."

Damn. Not good. What about the others?

I counted ten beds in all. Out of their filthy clothes, the homeless patients mostly seemed unshaven and in need of a good barber. And they all appeared old enough to be my great-grandparents. Odd. I knew the homeless encampment contained all ages. Why did only the old ones turn toes-up? "And the others?"

"Minor contusions and lacerations from the fighting," she said. "A few bad hearts, possibly a diabetes case, the usual ills of age. Lack of insulin in the diabetes case might cause a comatose state. High blood pressure might in others. They all should have tests run."

I thought about the other half-dozen patients we'd seen at Acme, all similar to these. "Sixteen people in one small area can't concuss, have strokes, and fall victim to high blood pressure over a span of a few hours."

"The causes of coma are too numerous to list, but agreed, having sixteen people fall into one in the space of a few hours does suggest external poisoning interfering with blood or oxygen flow. These people reacted more strongly than others, possibly because some agents strike the elderly and ill harder, possibly for reasons unknown."

I bit my tongue to prevent a sarcastic *magic* from escaping. Paddy's euphemism for the new element could start a full-scale panic or turn us into a laughingstock. The latter seemed more likely.

"They need more medical help than we can provide," the lady doc concluded.

"I know a few people in the medical community," I admitted. "It's been years since I've talked to some of them, so I make no promises. But if we can ship them out to hospitals in surrounding states, will they be safe from Acme?"

"Tricky, unless your people are willing to lie about where they found them. Only a few of the patients have IDs. They're all apparently indigent except for Mrs. Rose and Officer Leibowitz." She checked the florist's IV. "They'll be turned away almost anywhere."

We'd have to take care of Sarah and Sleeping Beauty ourselves. A warehouse was no place for the others. I began mentally listing some of my mother's more dubious friends. Most of my college buddies knew better than to do anything for me, since I'd gotten them expelled, but I could ask around. I'd spent a year in a hospital. I could summon names.

"They may be fine by morning," Andre suggested. "But if not, start prioritizing them. We can't justify keeping them from Acme if we only kill them ourselves."

The doc nodded and returned to her rounds. Andre

caught my elbow and dragged me on. He had a bad habit of manhandling me, but he knew I could take him down if I objected.

Apparently, we both needed the physical contact for the moment.

"Acme sent street sweepers through the Zone," he said grimly, clambering down the stairs to the tunnel under the street. He picked up an automatic weapon that had been leaning against the wall.

I glanced warily at the gun. Had he grabbed it when I'd come through the gate? He probably had security alarms and cameras everywhere.

He stopped abruptly to open a door in the wall. The light level was low in here, and to me, a tunnel was a tunnel. I hadn't considered storage closets.

He shoved the weapon inside, and I caught a glimpse of a whole array of heavy metal before he slammed it again.

Andre had an arsenal prepared for war. I was trying really hard not to freak. Gun and conspiracy wing nuts who stockpiled weapons against the apocalypse seldom turned out well.

Biting my tongue about the weapons, I followed him across the street through his hidden tunnel, contemplating street sweepers. "Are they sweeping with big machines or little Roombas, and how do they keep them working?" I'd never seen anyone cleaning the Zone's streets before, so it sounded highly suspicious.

"They don't. The robot vacuums keeled over or rolled into the harbor. They've got people out there now with brooms."

Keeling vacuums were normal in my world. Sweeping in the Zone was the anomaly. "Better they kill people than machines?" I asked dubiously. "Why bother sweeping at all?"

"Paddy says the particles could be dangerous. He couldn't say whether they'd blow up or turn everyone in town into a zombie."

"The *particles*?" Crap. I'd been ignoring my fear all day. I didn't want it confirmed while I was down and just about out. "The pink confetti stuff?"

"Ashes from the new element," he confirmed, switching a light off in the tunnel as we entered the bomb shelter. "We've been washing it down the drain, into the sewer system, into the harbor, no telling where. We could be sitting on Chernobyl."

I tried to whistle but my mouth was dry. "It wasn't a big explosion," I argued, half running to keep up with his long strides. "A few dust particles here and there can't wipe out dinosaurs."

I'd trailed confetti uptown, through the city, into the courthouse. Police cars, ambulances, all would have carried them to parts unknown.

"Too late to stop the spread now," he said fatalistically. "Those of us living here face constant exposure. We can try, but we can't sweep it all up."

"We could all become Sleeping Beauties?" I asked facetiously. I was too tired to imagine all the ramifications.

He shot me a frown. "Sleeping Beauties?"

"Like the lady you've apparently been hiding. Is she one of Paddy's magical element experiments?"

"You won't quit until you find out, will you?" he asked, stopping in the bomb shelter.

"You'd rather I never asked questions? Went my own way, kept my head down?"

"You'd take my head off if I said yes."

He was right about that.

Without warning, he jerked me into the infirmary, where they were keeping Sarah and Sleeping Beauty. Neither appeared to have moved a muscle since I'd seen her last.

Andre led me to Beauty's side. I could see the resemblance even before he spoke.

"Mary Justine Clancy, I'd like to introduce you to my mother, Katerina Montoya. *Mi madre, esta es* Tina, the Zone's very own Alice in Wonderland. Or the devil's daughter, depending on how you want to look at it."

The woman in the bed didn't blink an eyelash. If I were the fainting type, I might have considered a brief bout of vapors.

Andre had a mother. And a name. And the *Montoya* rang bells as well.

Julius Montoya had written some of the law books I'd just finished studying.

10

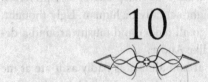

"Pleased to meet you, Mrs. Montoya," I said, patting Sleeping Beauty's limp hand and glaring at Andre. I'd had a few too many surprises over the last few months. I didn't appreciate this one.

His mother was a beautiful zombie. His father had been a distinguished judge and respected legal scholar. And Andre was . . . what?

Running a neighborhood for bizarro trolls. Neat little piles of evidence sorted themselves in the filing drawer of my mind, but this was real life and I had to deal with it in real time.

"How long have you and your father been taking care of her?" I asked after Andre adjusted her blanket and we returned to the main hall.

"Don't give me any credit. I was overseas at the time. Dad's been bearing the burden. When I saw her last, she was lashing me for joining the service, telling me to come home safely or she'd kill me, and weeping over losing her only son. Never a dull moment around the Montoya household."

He spoke with his usual sarcasm, but now I knew it hid grief. Andre wasn't all sharp edges, as I preferred to believe. He might actually be human. Ugly thought. I didn't want to go all tender and mushy around a deceptive criminal like Andre.

I bet guilt ate at him almost as badly as it ate at me for sending Max to his demise. Guilt, I was learning, is a powerful motivator.

"What do the doctors say is wrong with her?" I hadn't slept in thirty-six hours. Andre seemed as cool and relaxed as if he'd just risen from a long night's sleep, although I knew he'd been up as long as I had.

"They don't, not anymore. She had cancer. She was dying, with only months to live. I was in a battle zone. When I finally got my discharge, I came home to this." He started for the stairs. "I'm not sure if her death wouldn't have been better for all of us."

I could hear enough anger and pain in his voice to accept his story. "You came home to a zombie Sleeping Beauty and no explanation?"

"Experimental drugs, I was told. Old news, Clancy. Go call your friends. See if we can get the patients out of here before Acme comes snooping."

"You really think Acme will come after them?"

"Acme knows we're here. The cops aren't about to

protect us under these circumstances. They'll blame us for experimenting on sick people or something equally ugly. We always get the blame—not a good, upstanding, taxpaying corporation owned by a senator's wealthy, respectable family." Yup, definite snark in his tone.

"The zombies are mostly homeless bums," I protested. "Who would want them? Acme has Bill and bums of their own. They can play with their pink ash and try to figure out how not to blow things up. That's more than enough to keep them occupied." I trotted up the stairs behind him, fretting about Bill.

I really, truly did not want to go back into that death trap again if there was any other way of getting him out.

"Ask Paddy," was all he replied.

"I have to find Paddy before I can ask him," I grumbled, carrying on as if I wasn't shell-shocked. Maybe lack of sleep prevented a good panic. "Where did he go?"

Andre stopped and I almost ran into him in the dark. He grabbed my arms to steady me, held me a moment too long, and there was a heart-pounding moment when I thought he meant to kiss me again. After being good all day today, I really needed a kiss as a reward. Guns and mothers and pink ash flew straight out of my head. I tensed, preparing myself for . . . whatever.

"Good question, Clancy. Last I heard, he was at Acme with you and Schwartz. You might have to run another rescue mission." Instead of teasing me with full body contact, he released me and continued up the stairs.

He didn't like that Schwartz had saved the day. I didn't like the idea of running another rescue mission. And my hormones were in full-scale screaming mode.

"I'm a law clerk, remember? I can't do anything illegal." Two could play the snark game. "I'll camp on Paddy's doorstep. If he doesn't come home, I'll get Pearl to let me in and we'll see what he keeps under his bed."

"Go home, Clancy. Get some sleep. Tomorrow is another day." He pointed at the front door.

"Maybe I should go down and see if anything interesting is happening at Chesty's," I called over my shoulder as I departed. "Maybe Schwartz will walk me home!"

I really shouldn't have taunted a tiger.

Ticked at being abandoned for so long, Milo still wasn't speaking to me Sunday morning. I fried him a little bacon to top off his kitty food. My orange tabby Manx couldn't vent his anger by swishing his nonexistent tail, but he had attitude to spare anyway. He ate the bacon, turned his nose up at the healthy food, and leaped to his sentinel position in my front bay window overlooking the street. Everyone's a critic.

Checking in with the real world for a change, I signed into Facebook and almost fell over when I discovered a direct message from my mother. She was apparently now in some remote village in Peru where the Internet wasn't exactly common.

Mom's icon today was the Roman version of the goddess of justice, the blindfolded one holding a sword and scales. I'd already done my research and knew the Greek version of the justice goddess was Themis, and Greek Themis was a legendary psychic who didn't carry weapons or scales. So my grandmother thought she was psychic and my mother thought she was a sword-wielding Justitia. Swell. Where did that leave me? Any goddesses with law books in their hands?

Congratulations on your graduation, daughter. Perhaps you've taken a safer road than your grandmother in your search for justice. I cannot give you wealth, but knowledge is power. Wield it wisely.

She added a Web address, presumably as my graduation gift of knowledge. I wanted to check on our patients, but my mother communicated so infrequently, I couldn't resist wasting a little more time. I called up the website.

A discreet symbol of the Roman god Saturn holding his sickle was the only header on the site. The rest of the page appeared to be more message board than website. I couldn't find any place where I could leave comments should I want to. I didn't belong to their sekrit klub.

Another page gave me links to a couple of dozen websites—some in Arabic and Cyrillic and most of them with foreign domains. This was a pretty worldwide group. I recognized the address for the Themis Astrology and Tarot website and knew it held no surprises. Were these all Saturn's daughters? I was too excited and scared to hope.

Fat Chick in Canada's link was in English and caught my eye. I clicked on the address and called up a blog that seemed to be a dumping ground for rants about injustice. She had a blogroll down the side I didn't have time to follow.

The one item that struck me right between the eyes was the photo of Fat Chick. She was indeed large. Not obese, but Viking-warrior large. She looked to be about my age but she'd have made three of me. She held a sword in one hand.

The other hand was on the wheel of her chair. She was crippled.

Oh, wow. Oh, crap. She had waves of gorgeous red hair, brilliant blue eyes, a flashing white smile . . . and she was in a wheelchair. Shitcrapfuck.

Was this how Saturn punished bad judgment calls?

I was super-glad of my innate caution. I could have had two bad legs by now if I'd blasted everyone I'd wanted to blast.

So much for reality. The Zone was looking safer than my future. I looked out the bay window over Milo's head to the gray morning. No sign of green gas. I couldn't tell if any pink ash littered the square of yard in front of Pearl's house.

I didn't have the education necessary to figure out the explosive capabilities of Acme and pink ash, but I could at least attempt to move some of our patients to better medical facilities. I'd e-mailed my mother's dubious friends last night. Since it was Sunday, I didn't expect immediate replies. I wondered if I should talk to Max's biker buddies. If anyone knew how to dump unconscious victims, they did. But I wasn't certain our patients would receive the best of care in their hands.

Maliciously contemplating wishing Acme's management into outer space, worrying about ending up like Fat Chick, I used chewing gum to stick a message to Themis on my door asking if I would go to hell for visualizing punishment. She'd left me notes that way a few months back. I had no reason to believe she hung out in Baltimore, except the Zone was the only center of weirdness I knew, and even though I'd never met her, Granny rated high on my Wyrd Scale.

I almost wanted law school back so I could remember what it was like to have a sane day.

I couldn't call Jane at this hour on a weekend, so I e-mailed her asking if she'd heard anything more about Acme. Her story on the Internet news site might have broken sooner than anyone else's, but it didn't include any new information—like how Acme would prevent a nuclear explosion of zombie gas. I was a wee bit antsy about a repeat of yesterday or worse.

Next time, it could be nerve gas. Or Agent Orange. Would our new zombies be comatose forever? I needed information that didn't include chemical formulas.

I sent four-eyed computer geek Boris a request for a charger for the tablet. I could have ordered one online, but I'd never had a credit card. Now that I had a real job, maybe I should think about getting one. I needed a lot of things if I meant to tangle with Acme.

Restless, I decided to check upstairs to see if Paddy really lived there. I'd never ventured to Pearl's third floor, and I was admittedly curious. The old Victorian was sturdy, built with solid wood. The banister hadn't been polished in decades, but it was still smooth under my palm. These stairs weren't as worn as the lower ones. Perhaps the third floor had been mostly for storage.

The stairs ended in a six-panel door with no identifying marks. I rapped my knuckles against it, not really expecting to be heard. As far as I knew, Paddy winked in and out of existence like my granny.

I was about to turn away when I heard shuffling on the other side. I breathed a sigh of relief. I hadn't wanted Paddy to be harmed by our escapade yesterday, but the thought of returning to Acme to find him wasn't a happy one.

He opened the door and frowned in surprise. "I thought you were Pearl." He shuffled back into the apartment in old bedroom slippers, leaving the door open.

Looked like an invite to me. "Pearl can't climb the stairs anymore. I hope she's not still in the cellar. Should I check on her?"

"Don't believe everything Pearl says," was his ambiguous reply.

He had books and papers spread across every inch of the floor, and there were a lot of inches. I'd guessed right. This once must have been an attic. The floors were unvarnished wood. The walls were brick. Bare bulbs hung from the rafters overhead.

He had a good view for miles inland and toward the Zone if he opened the French doors to the tiny front balcony. Even from up here, the air was a normal gray fog color, raising doubts about the lingering effects of green gas.

But there were still a dozen or more comatose patients who hadn't come around. The cloud hadn't been our collective imagination. Even as I stared down, I saw little Roomba-like devices circling the street, sucking up dirt and presumably particles. Apparently, the machines worked this far outside the Zone. If Acme really was vacuuming the streets, I wondered what they were doing about the harbor. Employing tiny Nemos?

A plain door on the opposite wall blocked any view of the water. Someone had nailed shelves between the wall studs, from floor to ceiling, and Paddy had filled them with books.

The only furniture I could see was a top-of-the-line computer desk, chair, and equipment, with thick cables and several large monitors.

Milo sniffed around and settled down in front of the French doors to keep an eye on activities below.

I rummaged in my capri pocket for the USB drive I'd copied yesterday. "I liberated this from the head honcho's office. Don't know if it's useful."

He was flipping through a book on the desk but glanced up quizzically at my offering. His eyes were clear, and he seemed to be operating on all cylinders, despite his cryptic replies.

"Head honcho?" He took the drive and plugged it in without asking for more explanation. "You mean Ferguson, the one whose ID tag you stole?"

Okay, definitely operating on all cylinders. I was starting to enjoy myself. I could have a posse if Paddy was up to speed. "That would be the one."

"He's a pervert." He opened up the file list I'd copied, scrolling through. "I have most of this. The moron doesn't know the meaning of *password*." He clicked on one that couldn't have been labeled more obviously: private.

I had a quick glimpse of way too much gross nekkid anatomy, before Paddy deleted the entire folder with the push of a button.

"Maybe I should delete Ferguson like that," I muttered, not enjoying myself anymore.

"When we're ready to dispose of Ferguson, we can call the feds and have him taken out based on the contents of his computer," Paddy said, unfazed.

"You're almost as mean as I am," I said in wonder. "Why haven't you shut down Acme already?"

"Can't, for many reasons, as you've pointed out before. Besides, if I'd reported Ferguson, they would have locked me out permanently. Have you checked on our patients this morning?" He settled into his chair and started studying dates on the files I'd given him.

"I'll do that next. Anything else I can do?"

He glanced up in surprise. "You're asking?"

I shrugged. "I do that sometimes. Even surprise myself."

He snorted. "And then you do what you want anyway. Keep Andre from killing anyone. It's not healthy for him."

He returned to work as if I weren't there.

If I asked about Andre, it would imply I was interested. Not going there. If I meant to be a lawyer, I had to stay away from people who broke the law. Or thought they were above it.

That was a pretty dilemma for someone considering breaking, entering, and criminal trespass to retrieve Bill. I had justified saving Sarah because she was nuclear dangerous. But could I jeopardize my career for a gentle man who was just a friend? And then callously leave the others? Or was I trying to justify not going back to Acme's dungeon?

I let myself out. Milo trotted after me. He'd appointed himself my guard cat, but I'd seen him flung against a wall and almost killed. He wasn't invincible, but I couldn't convince him of that. He was as warped as any other being living in the Zone. Take my word for it.

Checking outside, still seeing and smelling nothing unusual beyond the mechanical critters sucking the street, I let Milo follow me next door. From this vantage point, I could see down Edgewater to the Zone's business district and ground zero of the barricaded harbor, with its rusted chimneys. Not a creature was stirring, not even pink ash.

No one answered the bell at Andre's place. As usual, the front door was unlocked. Since this and the warehouse were the only ways I knew to access our patients, I entered without invitation. Maybe Andre's security system sent him a Nuisance Alert message when I arrived so he could flip some magic switch.

If so, he didn't come out to stop me. I smelled burning toast from one of the kitchens, but as much as I liked Julius, I wasn't casting myself in the role of domestic goddess. I like to eat, and I'd learned to cook to prevent starvation. Just because I could didn't mean I was meant to feed the multitudes. I jogged down the cellar stairs with Milo on my heels.

Sarah and Katerina were just as I'd left them the prior night. They had fresh IVs. Katerina's lustrous black locks had been brushed. Sarah's frizzy mess had been pulled into a scrunchie to keep it out of her face. She was the same age as me, and her relaxed expression seemed almost innocent. I wondered if their brains were alive, and if they were conscious of anything, but I guessed we'd need MRIs to sort that out.

I tried to summon red rage for whatever had put them in here, but there were no direct correlations to any one person. I had no face to put to my whammy, and the rage didn't come.

"Why rage?" I asked Saturn. "Why can't I be filled with joy and happiness and just wish people better?" Enamored of this new notion, I concentrated on happily anticipating that the patients would rise and be well.

As usual, the Universe ignored me.

"Zap, you're better," I said, somewhat desperately, concentrating on them opening their eyes. Nothing.

More and more, it looked like Satan, not Saturn, guided me. Satan wanted minions, and Sarah and Katerina weren't what he had in mind.

I didn't want to be around if Sarah was startled

awake anyway. She had strangled several large men with her chimp hands. I didn't stand a chance against her. But she was the only other Saturn's daughter I'd met besides my mother, and I'd kind of hoped she might have a few things to teach me about our strange condition—if only by bad example. It hurt to watch her lie there, helpless. If her defective moral center could be fixed, she could save the world. Or some portion of it.

I wandered on. The other rooms of the bomb shelter were unoccupied. The theater was still a mess following the moving of the seats, but things were settling back to normal.

I proceeded on through the tunnel and up the stairs to the warehouse, with Milo trotting ahead. With no windows in this back part, the warehouse was dim even in daytime. I'd remembered a flashlight, since I wasn't as familiar with the light switches as Andre was. I picked my way past snow shovels and old tires and down the hall to the infirmary.

We had a male med student today. He was making frantic notes on a chart and text messaging at the same time. His red curls stood on end as if he'd run his fingers through them a few times.

"Can I help with anything?" I asked.

He glanced up, looking perplexed and just a little lost. I hoped the pink ash and gas cloud hadn't fried his brains.

"They've all improved overnight," he said in bewilderment. "I don't know if Christy was tired or these old gauges were faulty, but . . ." He wandered over to a microscope set up in the corner. "It's not normal."

An uneasy shiver crept down my spine. "It's the Zone," I said casually. "Equipment doesn't work right down here. Some kind of electromagnetic field."

"That's why I'm using this." He gestured at the old-fashioned microscope. "I had my roommate bring it over. No mechanical parts, just mirrors."

Well, I knew for a fact that mirrors could be windows to hell, but I bet that wasn't the case here. "And this proves what? They all still look dead to me."

"They're all healthier than they were yesterday!" he shouted, obviously losing his cool. "Insulin normal, blood pressure down, white-blood-cell count decreasing."

"Yesterday's readings were probably screwed up," I said consolingly. "It was kind of frantic here with the gas and all."

Nancy Rose was better? That seemed promising, in a screwball kind of way. Hope was a good feeling, one I wasn't much used to.

He rubbed his hair and nodded dubiously. "That might be it. These obviously aren't ideal conditions."

I was thinking we needed to get the baby docs and the patients out of here pretty quick. Once word spread that pink gas might cure all ills, we'd be inundated with media and feds and who knew what all. If they found Sarah and Katerina . . . we could have World War III with magic gas. What happened in the Zone *really* needed to stay in the Zone.

My grim thoughts were interrupted by a roar that

sounded as if the roof were being ripped from over our heads. We both glanced up and watched the beams vibrate. Tornado? In Baltimore? Earthquakes didn't last more than a minute or so, did they? This noise wasn't ending.

"Is there a helicopter pad up there?" the doc asked warily.

"Not that I know of." Since the warehouse was only three stories high, the roof wouldn't be ideal for rotating blades. I had visions of them taking out telephone poles and electric wires and frying us all, but my mind takes a chaos path pretty frequently.

"It sounds like a helicopter," the med student insisted. "I served in Afghanistan. I know helicopters."

Helicopters. Very Bad Sign that we had a war zone already. Nasty snakes twisted in my gut. I glanced around at the helpless patients. If Acme meant to eliminate all evidence of their gas attack . . . I didn't think those were medical evacuation helicopters up there.

"Let's get these people out of here!" I shouted over the racket, opting for caution. "Into the tunnel."

Andre would kill me for revealing his secret passage, to say nothing of his mother, but I'm more into that "United we stand" motto than exclusivity.

My logic ran along the lines of . . . I was pretty damned certain the army hadn't come to save us. I couldn't abandon our patients to goons with helicopters. Instinct said the tunnel was easier to guard than a hulking empty warehouse full of plywood-boarded windows. Conclusion: *Run!*

The doc didn't need to be told twice. I didn't know

if it was altruism or medical science he served, but he was totally with the program. He unhooked the IV of the first patient. Grabbing Milo and shoving him in my messenger bag, I raced the gurney down the hall, through the warehouse, and to the tunnel door. Paddy, Julius, and Tim met me there with grim expressions. My guess about unfriendly helicopters was apparently correct.

I wondered where Andre was but didn't have time to ask. Loud thumps on the roof warned that the invaders were dropping jackbooted troops. Crap. We couldn't move fast enough.

I debated visualizing our patients in outer Siberia, but whether that was a good or bad idea, I was pretty sure that exceeded my limits. Maybe I was only allowed so many visualizations, and then I'd die. I'm a lawyer, not a believer in fantasy. I needed a damned rulebook. So I resisted the fantastical and relied on good old human know-how.

Paddy and Tim raced for the next patients while I debated carrying some old guy down the tunnel stairs. I weigh 110 pounds soaking wet. A forty-pound backpack is more than I can manage.

Guessing my plight, Julius flipped a switch to unleash a primitive flatbed elevator, lowering it from the ceiling to the warehouse door. Thank heavens. I wheeled the gurney on. Julius hit the switch, and it took me past the stairs to the tunnel under the street.

Julius disappeared into the darkness above, leaving me alone in the dark, empty passage.

We could easily fit ten patients under the street

without entering Andre's secret bomb shelter. I played Charon, rowing the patients from the warehouse above to the darkened tunnel below. The loader was slow. Gurneys were still lined up at the door when the first shouts emerged from the warehouse.

Where the devil was Andre with his machine guns when we needed him?

A couple of old men and a few nerds didn't stand a chance against storm troopers, if that was what Acme had sent. My panic button started flashing madly.

As I rolled another gurney to the flatbed, a camou-flaged soldier type with a weapons belt and automatic at his shoulder rushed through the garage end of the building. Alarm blossomed into full-out panic. The soldier's boots hit the old wooden floor like thunder. Ignoring me, he grabbed the first gurney he saw. Un-fortunately, Tim was pushing it.

Tim did his best, he really did, but he's a teen and even slighter than I am. The moment the trooper tried to sling him away, Tim faded out. Disappeared. Van-ished. The trooper jerked with surprise—long enough for Julius to step out of the shadows and bash him with a snow shovel.

I'd watched enough westerns to know when we were outgunned. The pounding of more boots over-head and through the garage warned we'd only chopped one tentacle off the monster.

I tried counting heads, but I knew Leibowitz's big body hadn't been loaded onto the elevator yet. There were probably others left behind.

We simply didn't have a choice. With a sick feeling

in my middle, I hauled the gurney onto the flatbed and yelled, "Get in here now!"

I couldn't tell if Tim obeyed. Julius and the red-haired med student did. I didn't know where Paddy was, but he played crazy really well. They'd leave him alone. I slammed the door. Julius rammed a bar across the door, protecting Katerina his priority, and we cranked the flatbed down.

After we rolled the gurney off, I left the elevator positioned halfway up and unhooked the cable, blocking the stairs in hopes it could add to the obstacles, but they were already battering at the steel door above.

Steel doors. Andre had prepared for an invasion. How did he know these things? Or was he really that paranoid?

"Tim, you with us?" I cried as we ran the gurney down the tunnel to join the others.

No reply. Terrified for the little brother I'd never had, I prayed he had the sense to find a good hiding place. I tried to reassure myself that Tim could stay invisible for a really long time—but Acme would love to get their hands on him if they discovered what he was.

I heard the troopers beating at the steel door—followed by a muted explosion and automatic rifle fire as they tried to blow it open.

11

Andre's arsenal! While Julius rushed ahead to the bomb shelter and his wife, I stumbled down the tunnel looking for the door I'd seen Andre use.

I wasn't a trained soldier. But I'd die protecting Andre's mother and a woman who could damn all of Baltimore to perdition. The med student, a few zombies, and I were the only obstacles left between the concealed bomb shelter and armed thugs.

That justice gene is a real pain. I found the weapons closet.

The steel door at the top of the stairs buckled but didn't crash in.

I really wanted one of those old rifles from the westerns. I'd watched enough that I was familiar with their use. I didn't even know how to turn on an AK-47. Or if they had switches to turn them on. Color me clueless.

I flashed my light inside the closet, and my eyes bulged at the extent of Andre's secret cache. Andre was simply not right in the head.

He had *grenades*. Even I knew how grenades worked. I did not know how much they'd blow up, however. I could bring the whole tunnel down.

Milo fought his way out of my bag while I stared in dismay at the array of assorted death beams. He knocked over a few rifles and a shelf of handguns, then dashed after Julius. The med student continued to shove his patients out of the line of fire.

"Go get 'em, tiger," I called softly after my cat, praying he was fetching Andre as he had in the past.

Then I grabbed a rifle and checked for bullets—it was loaded, thank goodness, since I had no idea what kind of ammunition it took. I had time to hunt for a safety lock, line up more rifles on the wall beside me, and tuck a handgun into my waistband. I would probably shoot myself before I shot anyone else, but with all those innocent people behind me, I knew I would go down fighting.

I had too much adrenaline flooding my brain to think straight. I debated visualizing a lion on the flatbed, but hungry lions might find me a better snack than troopers in bulletproof vests. Besides, I didn't want a beast shot in my defense. Damn, this was difficult. *Focus, Clancy.*

It was liking trying to take a law test with a blood alcohol content of .25.

Wondering if self-defense counted as justice, I frantically pictured a stone wall between me and the soldiers. Before I was ready, the steel door burst open and a volley of automatic rifle fire shot puffs of dirt and old concrete at my feet.

They were shooting at comatose patients! Not to mention me. Red rage colored my vision.

Pieces of concrete bit into my bare legs. Their bullets were real. Panicked and furious, I started firing. For all I knew, bullets bounced off the advancing troops. They kept on coming. "*Damn you to—*"

I hadn't finished my curse before I was shoved aside. I landed in a heap on my butt while Andre grabbed one of the hulking big automatics from the closet.

Automatic fire in a tunnel isn't fun. I wanted to send them all to hell, but now that I'd been abruptly interrupted mid-curse, I realized the penalty for using it might be worse than dying. I didn't know that those guys were evil, or even guilty enough to justify a death penalty. Damn. For all I knew, they thought *we* were the criminals. Making these kinds of life-or-death decisions calcified my brain.

Hunkering down on the cold floor of the closet, nursing my bleeding wounds while a shirtsleeved Andre battled half a dozen soldiers, I got focused. I closed my eyes and pictured a rain of bullets and rocks and dead rats falling on the bastards. Better to scare them into heart attacks than to give the devil his due. Or end up in a wheelchair. Or hell.

A low rumble forced my eyes open again, and I gaped at the sight at the end of the tunnel.

Miraculously—or maybe not quite miraculously, given the echoing rounds of gunfire—the tunnel ceiling was cracking, shedding clouds of dust and rumbling like thunder. The troops stopped firing and threw nervous glances over their heads. Before they could retreat, the roof caved in, and a cloud of dust and rock filled the far end of the passage.

I stared, wondering if I was seeing a burial ground. Had *I* caused that?

Looking blurred around the edges and sleep-deprived, Andre froze in place, watching to see if anyone crawled out of the rubble. I'd never been so glad to see someone in my life—my soldier warrior. And I had to send him away.

"Tim and Paddy and more patients still in the warehouse!" I shouted over the screams and sounds of falling rock. I didn't think a rat could squeeze through that avalanche of debris. "I'll keep watch here."

Andre nodded, threw a second weapon over his shoulder, and raced back the way he'd come.

To my surprise, when I glanced back, Schwartz had joined him. I doubted if Studly Do-Right approved of illegal weapon caches, but he took the gun Andre shoved at him and followed him back into the well-lit bomb shelter.

I leaned against the wall, watching the dust settle. I held a rifle and pretended I was Wyatt Earp and knew how to use the damned thing.

The screams had stopped. I had no idea if I'd actually hit anyone with bullets or rocks or dead rats. Notice I didn't conjure live ones. When I focus, I really focus.

I conjured an avalanche. I was a menace to society and to myself. I shivered, watching the dust settle and wondering if we'd find dead bodies under there.

Maybe all those years of watching westerns had rotted my brains. Maybe I really thought I could produce justice just by wishing. Or by shooting someone, which is what they mostly did in westerns.

I didn't want to shoot people or end up in a wheelchair. I'd hated being lame. With my arms crossed over my bent knees, I buried my face and tried to control my breathing. I wanted to be a lawyer, maybe a judge. Vigilante justice would not accomplish that. It was far more likely to land me in jail.

I might have shot a man today. I'd certainly intended to. Of course, I'd almost sent them all to perdition. They could have families. I had no way of knowing if they were really bad guys. As in any war, the enemy was just faceless strangers in funny suits. They'd probably been told national security was at stake. So they were stupider than me. Didn't matter. They shouldn't have to die for someone else's war.

It was just too easy to react, much harder to think and do what was right. *Why me, Saturn?* I mentally screamed. *I want rulebooks or I'm not doing this anymore!*

No one burst out of the rock heap in an attempt to reach us. The red-haired med student eventually poked his head out from wherever he'd been hiding. Once he'd ascertained he wouldn't be shot, he kneeled down to check my bloody legs.

"Need to clean these out, but I don't think you've been shot," was his assessment.

I didn't know if I should risk sending him with the patients to Andre's now less-than-secret bomb shelter. We'd left all the IVs in the warehouse, so he couldn't do much. I counted six gurneys down here. We'd left four behind, including Officer Leibowitz's. Tim's doing, I was sure. He had managed to rescue Nancy Rose, but he despised Leibowitz.

I handed the student my rifle. "If you've been in Afghanistan, you know how to use this better than I do. Shoot any rats coming over that wall."

He checked the closet and found an automatic more to his liking. I left him to it.

There was no point in asking his name, much as I appreciated his aid. He was normal. I wasn't. He'd go on to lead a wealthy suburban life. I was tied to the Zone in ways even I couldn't understand. I needed familiar boundaries and people who accepted my weirdnesses.

In the bomb shelter, Julius was with Sarah and Katerina. He had turned almost as gray as Andre. He was a genial, gentle man. He shouldn't be exposed to this shit. I hugged him briefly, just because, and he hugged me back before shoving me away.

"Keep an eye on Andre," he said urgently. "He's reached his limit."

Okay, that was the second time today I'd been warned to look after the King of Cool. Except he wasn't so cool lately. I didn't really want to know what Andre's limit was. I nodded and trotted off, not certain what to do next. Visualizing a helicopter to Hades probably wasn't justified, but I thought I heard it still hovering. Andre and Leo were out there somewhere, waiting to take it down.

Milo met me in Andre's kitchen. I picked him up and hugged him and let the sadness roll over me.

Maybe I should have kept the rifle. But visions of me shooting everyone who crossed my path while shouting *Damn you!* kind of put me off on gun toting. The tunnel collapse had been horrifying. I wanted to shut out the memory. I still didn't know if I'd killed anyone.

I'd probably stand a better chance of not joining Satan if I stuck to commandments like "Thou shalt not kill." My mother hadn't brought me up in church, but I liked to read, and the Bible had acquired the status of an important, forbidden book in my rebellious youth.

Once I was upstairs, I heard the helicopter clearly. I'd lived in a lot of places but none of them had ever been a war zone, so I couldn't distinguish between hovering and taking off.

Cautiously, hanging on to Milo, I watched out the front window. The big porch prevented me from seeing the sky. Andre and Schwartz could be anywhere, but the warehouse would be their goal. I studied the seemingly vacant block of buildings across the street. Not a sign of life inside.

I'd been drugged and kidnapped a few months ago. I had no burning desire to put myself in the unpleasant path of danger again by going outside to see more.

On the theory that this house had an attic like Pearl's, I jogged up the stairs, past Tim and Julius's apartments, to an open door. I stepped into an infirmary more modern than the one in the tunnel—Sleeping Beauty's abode, I assumed.

I set Milo down to explore. Not wanting to leave a trail of blood across the pristine floor, I took advantage of the hospital-like facilities. I hastily washed my legs, wincing as I applied alcohol on my way to the balcony.

Unlike Paddy's hideaway, this attic was completely finished, with skylights and murals on the walls. Sun flooded in through French doors adorned with lacy curtains. They'd certainly provided Katerina with a happier abode than the usual nursing home.

With my legs pocked like the victims of a bad razor, I stepped onto the balcony and scrutinized the scene below. Two unmarked white vans rolled down the narrow alley behind the warehouses—did they carry the patients we couldn't rescue? Milo wrapped himself around my ankles and kept silent watch with me.

I clenched the rail in alarm at the sight of two figures covertly working their way along the flat roof of an empty store on the far side of the warehouse. I glanced up, but the helicopter was well away.

If that was Andre and Schwartz, they were prepared to tackle any army left behind.

I wanted to believe the troops had departed with the helicopter and vans, but I wasn't willing to wager my life—or Andre's or Schwartz's life. If there were soldiers left in the warehouse, I didn't know them, couldn't see them, and couldn't visualize them into another dimension. But I really disliked the idea of Andre being involved in another shoot-out.

And Paddy and Julius were telling me to keep him from killing anyone. I didn't know what was with that, but I was on board. *No killing.* I needed to clear the warehouse of enemy soldiers before anyone got hurt.

Just as my brain started to create an olfactory bomb of every nasty smell I could recollect, the plate-glass windows and front door of the warehouse burst into the street from the force of camouflaged troops crashing through them. A second later, the building went boom.

Oh, hell. Oh, shit. Frantically, I switched gears to protective mode. How could I save anyone from a bomb?

Remembering the pink iceberg I'd created to protect Ernesto, I pictured a safety shield between Schwartz and Andre and the exploding warehouse. Unfortunately, I couldn't do two things at once. While I tried to protect Andre and Schwartz from erupting bricks and boards, the troops rushed straight across the street—to the house where I was standing.

I had no idea if the shield trick had worked. All I knew was that Andre and Schwartz had disappeared, and the menacing troops aroused a rage so red that it might explode my skull.

They'd blown up my friends!

No more doubt about guilt or innocence. I wanted

to crush soldiers. I considered opening up the street to bury the enemy, only the med student and patients were in the tunnel under their feet. I tried imagining a wall dropping down around the house but nothing happened.

Shit. Not a fine time to learn my limits. Or even understand them.

Milo tried to shove me toward the door, but I couldn't run away without trying to defend Andre's home. This house offered the only other access to the bomb shelter and the patients. I'd already lost four patients, including Leibowitz. I had to protect the others. How did I keep out armed soldiers?

Before I could summon a solution, Andre reappeared. He crossed the roof of the office building beside the bombed-out warehouse, weapon in hand, working his way toward the front. Thank Saturn or his guardian angels, he was alive! Except he'd see the soldiers in the street any second, and war would ensue.

Shit and triple shit. The rage factor decreased enough for me to think again. How did I keep a lunatic from killing everyone in sight? I was operating on overload. Adrenaline coursed through my system like a hallucinogenic drug.

Justice. Concentrating so hard that I forgot I was a sitting target out here on the balcony, I shouted to the Universe, "In the name of Saturn, I command justice against thugs who blew up a building and attacked the injured. The punishment for such harm . . ."

I didn't finish the sentence aloud but visualized the

penalty. I was feeling mean, but the only image forming in my mind was that of big bad soldiers pushing
baby strollers with screaming toddlers, changing dirty
diapers, and singing incessant nursery rhymes for a
week.

Damn, Clancy, is that the best you can do? I could
almost hear Andre's voice in my head. But it wasn't
easy balancing the scales of justice and trying to save
lives—and maybe Andre's soul—at the same time.

The acrid stench of the explosion still burned in my
nasal passages and stung my eyes, but I grabbed the
rail and watched the street for a miracle.

Andre released a hail of automatic fire from his position on the roof. I hadn't visualized stopping Andre.
Damn.

The troops in the street looked startled, broke
ranks, and ran like rabbits—to a nursery school somewhere, if there was any justice in the world. Let them
nurture instead of destroy for a few days.

Thank you, Saturn.

The red-rage juice drained out of me. Sliding to the
floor, I couldn't even look up to see if Andre had left
bodies in the street.

12

It wasn't quite noon yet on my day off, and I was
completely wiped already.

Milo licked my face but I didn't have the energy
to view whatever chaos Andre had generated on the
street. I wanted to wish myself into a quiet law library,
but I was pretty sure now that the red-rage juice provided the energy for my visualizations and I couldn't
wish myself anywhere without it.

Lying on the balcony, watching smoke drift by, I realized that if I'd made copies of the case the judge was
working on, I could have taken the file over to the uni-
versity law library today and worked on it on my own.

Back in the good old days, that's exactly what I
would have done. I'm goal-oriented.

But my mind was apparently being controlled by a planet. Or Satan. Or insanity. Depending on the day of the week, maybe. I no longer thought like my old self. I thought like the Avenger of Justice or some other dingbat instead of a type-A legal beagle.

Maybe Max was right. Maybe I needed to move out of the Zone and its environs.

I was thinking of taking a nice nap when I heard voices in the attic. Invisibility would be a neat trick if I could pull it off. Maybe I'd ask Tim for pointers.

"Schwartz *is* the law," Andre shouted. "He's gone off to write a report, a freaking report, when Acme just blew up my warehouse and sent armed troops after my fucking family! The line was drawn and Gloria crossed it."

"We're not hurt. Calm down and be sensible. Where's Tim? Did he get out of the warehouse?"

I recognized Julius's soothing murmur. I also recognized that Andre had reached a plane beyond reason. I waited to hear about Tim. If Tim had been hurt, I'd probably go all red-ragey again, but I just didn't have it in me otherwise. I lay on the balcony and clung to mellow.

"The kid's not stupid," Andre yelled at his father. "He sneaked out and bashed one of the van drivers. He drove off with two of the old guys, but the other van got away with our people. Do you want to be responsible for whatever the hell they're doing to them up there in that frigging Frankenstein lab?"

Well, I could say the same about Julius's infirmary and Paddy's weird attic, but admittedly, neither of them had gassed a neighborhood and gone to extreme lengths to hide the fact that their chemicals had knocked people comatose.

Tim was safe. He hadn't been dragged into Acme's dungeon. No one was shooting at us. My mellow stayed mellow. I wondered if Tim had rescued the van with Leibowitz inside and if he'd done it while invisible. Not having to worry about him, I could breathe again. Andre's curses weren't all in English. I amused myself by making up translations. *Vaca* was cow, wasn't it? Cow-fornicating bastards?

"I'm just asking you to wait, clear your head," Julius said. "Check on your businesses. See if anyone is feeling any effects from the gas. Don't do anything hasty until you've had time to cool down."

"If I don't act now, the storm troopers will be back. Do you want to move Mom out of here? Put her in a nursing home somewhere?"

The silence was telling.

"I rest my case."

The snapping of locks and slamming of cabinet doors followed.

I waited for Andre to notice me through the French doors, but he apparently really was in his own world. I glanced up and saw Julius standing in front of me—deliberately?

"You can't confront Gloria," Julius said firmly. "Acme provided your scholarships at her behest."

Yup, deliberately. He was telling me where Andre was headed. Andre had told me once that his father had once worked with the Vanderventers. Pretty closely, apparently, if Gloria had provided Andre with a scholarship.

Julius was protecting Granny Vanderventer. Or Andre. I wasn't sure Gloria needed or deserved his friendship. But going after Gloria wasn't smart.

Controlling stockholder of Acme Chemical, Gloria Vanderventer had bloodthirsty goons out the wazoo, I knew from personal experience. They killed first and asked questions later. I figured the rotting corpses of her enemies composted her rose gardens. Or maybe since Dane's departure, she'd taken up knitting baby booties.

I stretched out and annoyed myself by wondering if I'd killed anyone today, and if I'd be rewarded in the morning. But I'd avoided damning people to hell, so maybe not. My, my. I yawned. Milo settled on my tummy. Now that I'd publicly blown up my boyfriend and sent him to hell, unseen deaths were reasonably anticlimactic. Or so I'd like to believe.

Andre slammed out of the attic. Julius followed. I could stroll on home, check my e-mail. I really needed to figure out how to find Themis one of these days. My mother's friends could have responded about body dumping by now.

I knew I wouldn't do any of the above. Really, I was too predictable.

I needed food if I was going to take the next step. Waiting until both sets of angry feet pounded down the stairs, I dragged myself off the balcony. Milo tagged along at my heels. Noticing a stout canvas tote bag hanging on the back of the door, I appropriated it. Milo needed a larger mode of transportation. I dropped him in. He poked his head out.

"I don't like war," I told him conversationally. "Do you think I could wish for peace on earth? Visualize ammunition melting?"

He gave a kitty snort. Yeah, that was my thought, too. My brain was too fuzzed to even picture the sandwich I intended to make. Maybe those old gurus got it right by living the hermit life on top of mountains where they could concentrate without interference. Unfortunately, I'm not much into masochism.

Besides, from what I'd learned so far, I needed a personal connection before I could zap someone. I'd wanted to find the invisible thief so badly, the Universe had to throw Tim at me or I'd probably have exploded. All my other visualizations had been of a similar category—highly emotional and directly related to me and mine. Imagining impersonal warehouses around the world full of melting bullets was simply beyond my capacity. Achieving world peace would probably require blowing up the planet.

Maybe the *Why me?* question was answered by *Because I'm rational.* But for how long?

Sirens were screaming down the street by the time we reached Julius's kitchen. The outside world tended to ignore the Zone, but an explosion had probably tripped a few seismic waves. I found Tim in the kitchen with a sub bun in hand, loading on every piece of processed meat and cheese he could locate in the refrigerator. I took tomatoes out of a hanging basket and sliced onto his chemically enhanced protein bomb. He shot me a nasty glare, but he needed veggies. I added some basil leaves and lettuce. Andre kept his father's kitchen well stocked. A pity Julius had never learned to cook.

Tim slathered on mayonnaise. I added mustard and bean sprouts and cut the bun in half. He took his half and peeled off all the veggies.

"You'll get scurvy and rickets if you don't eat your fruits and vegetables," I warned. "Your hair will fall out. Your bones will crumble."

"Bunny Bread builds strong bones and muscles," he countered, but he slapped one tomato back on before biting off a chunk bigger than he was.

"I told Andre only to buy his father brown bread. You're eating whole grains. Want to go for a bike ride?" I nibbled my sandwich. It needed onions, but I didn't have time to peel them.

"Can I drive?" He knew I owned a Harley and didn't mean a Schwinn.

"Doubtful, unless you've had lessons." I headed down the back stairs, still nibbling.

He didn't laugh at my bad joke or the grammar correction. "How will I learn if I don't have a bike?" he complained through a mouthful of bread.

"You need some driver's ed first. Maybe there's a motorcycle school." Of course, given that he'd just driven off in one of the vans, he already knew the basics. "Where'd you leave the van?" I asked.

"One of the medics took it away after I delivered the patients," he said resentfully.

All the patients were in the tunnel now, not far

from Andre's mother. I got it. The goons would be back and this time, they could blow up the street. Stopping a company with helicopters and troops wouldn't be easy. Andre was probably right to go for the Gorgon's head.

The question was, would Andre behave rationally or just blow Gloria off the map?

Andre in a rage could terrorize small countries. After being warned all day not to let him kill anyone, I apparently wasn't the only one fearing for his sanity. I ripped off a bite of sandwich and did my best to act as if I wasn't panicking.

Avoiding any lingering results of the explosion— like fire trucks parked in the street or cops looking for witnesses—Tim and I took Andre's back door and the alley over to Pearl's fenced-in backyard where I kept my Harley. *Max's* Harley. U.S. senators don't tool around on bikes. His loss.

I added calling Max to my to-do list. If Dane started showing up anywhere besides his gas appliances, I wanted to know about it. If I had to keep fighting the souls I sent to hell, I'd rather become a hermit.

"Where are we going?" Tim finally had the smarts to ask.

"You hid from the goons in the warehouse, didn't you?" I asked, to confirm my suspicion. "You're learning to control your little trick?"

"Sort of," he said warily, finishing off his sandwich before donning the helmet I handed him. "I went out like a light when that guy tackled me, though."

"Disappearing when attacked is an instinctive defense. Disappearing at will and staying invisible is a little more difficult." I strapped on my helmet and tucked Milo and his canvas bag into the bike's leather pouch, where he'd be safer.

This conversation would have had me checking into a mental ward six months ago. Since Max's death and my emergence as some kind of freak of nature, anything seemed feasible. And the kid needed someone to teach him that he was special, not weird. The Zone had its positive side. I needed to reinforce it.

"I walked past Leibowitz last week without him seeing me," Tim bragged.

"You're scared of Leibowitz. Disappearing when scared is still pretty much a defensive action. Remember the time we visited Senator Vanderventer in the hospital and you pulled his hair? Were you scared then?"

"You bet your shit I was. You do scary things." Horny male adolescent climbed on the bike and grabbed the bar instead of the hot babe.

I do not lack self-esteem. He'd just proved his sexual orientation.

"And you still haven't said where we're going."

"Just for a Sunday drive in the country," I said cheerfully, roaring the bike into action. I didn't want him getting scared and winking out on me before we got there.

I didn't turn the helmet radio on, so Tim couldn't question me further. I'd taken Sarah with me the last time I'd planned on terrorizing the Vanderventer homestead. That hadn't worked so well. My latest theory was that Zone inhabitants were survivors because they had an accelerated flight instinct—except the Zone had perverted that instinct into invisibility and shape-shifting instead of running. Sarah had shifted into a chimp the instant Gloria's guards had turned on us. Tim would go invisible.

And I'd be left standing all alone. Again.

Maybe I'd stop and call Max and tell him to give Dane's granny a visit today. But if Andre was heading in Gloria's direction, I feared I'd really have more trouble than I could take on. Having Dane/Max and Andre under the same roof might amuse Granny Gloria, up to the point that Andre aimed his toy guns at her grandson. No love lost between those two.

It was a lovely September day. It would have been nice to linger. A few trees along the mansion-studded roads of Towson were just starting to show color. Maple tree crowns flared with the occasional bright orange and red in the sunlight. Even as I roared down the center lane, I could feel Tim swiveling to take it all in. This was a world of luxury and beauty, just half an hour's drive from our blighted rusted-metal-and-blacktop environment.

I geared past the court building and wondered guiltily what the pink ash might have done to the inhabitants. I'd not seen any reactions beyond those of the comatose patients yet. Maybe it took a large quantity of ash and a compromised immune system. The baby docs had said their patients hadn't been healthy, which might have been why the homeless camp had taken such a hit. Bums didn't get good medical care. Neither did poor people with no medical insurance, which equated to just about everyone in the Zone, but odds were better that young people were stronger.

I hoped Julius or Paddy had gone down to help the gun-toting med student and his patients, because I didn't have time for them. Apparently I was more interested in preventing Andre from getting his head blown off by Gloria's goons than in protecting comatose patients. I made a lousy goddess, domestic or otherwise.

Sorry, guys. I hit the pedal heading out of town.

Since Andre had obviously known Gloria Vanderventer since childhood, he wouldn't have had the same difficulty I did in locating the mansion hidden down one of a thousand and one narrow lanes in this gazillion-dollar district. I'd only been here once. I remembered her mansion as being on top of a hill overlooking all the luxury homes that had usurped the countryside over the last century. Gloria had the last remaining estate-size acreage in the neighborhood.

I knew better than to drive through her gates this time. Despite the idyllic, tree-lined country lanes, her place was guarded by security cameras and black-suited thugs with cell phones and walkie-talkies and probably AK-47s just like Andre's. Gloria really didn't like surprise company.

I glanced in as I putted past the main ironwork gate and noted Andre's Mercedes sports car in front of the house. Despite the hair-raising speed with which we'd traveled, we didn't have much time.

I pulled down a side lane, out of sight of any cameras, and halted the bike near a grove of bamboo. "Work time," I told Tim, unfastening my helmet.

I knew better than to believe Milo would stay safely with the bike. I threw his bag over my shoulder. Milo and I would just have to adjust to the idea of short life spans.

It didn't seem to matter that my rational brain said that visiting Gloria again was a very bad, awful idea. That other overdeveloped lobe where my conscience dwelled said Andre and the other Zone inhabitants had been run roughshod over more certainly than any small farmers shot out by cattle barons. It was John Wayne time.

"Are you scared enough to wink out yet?" I asked carelessly when Tim had his helmet off. "Can you get over that wall?"

He flickered just seeing the high stones.

"I'd give you a boost, but I'm afraid the cameras might catch me," I said apologetically. "They probably have Wanted posters all over the place with my head on them."

Well, maybe not, if Gloria was stupid enough to believe I'd actually saved her grandson. Since Dane had kidnapped me off her back lawn just before he got shot, I was betting she'd ask questions after tying me to a cannon, but maybe she wouldn't shoot first.

"What do you want me to do once I get over?" Tim asked with intelligent suspicion.

"There's usually an electronic lock on those things." I nodded at the wrought-iron gates. "Looks like there's a pedestrian gate. This side will require a key code, but I bet just a button opens it on the inside. Push that to let me in."

Tim bravely switched out. The boy took clothes and all with him. I admired that ability. I couldn't see how he scaled the wall, but after a while, I could hear the click of the electronic security pad at the guard-house, and the pedestrian gate slid open.

I probably wouldn't set off any alarms, but the cameras would see me. I was just hoping a person on foot wouldn't attract too much interest. Guests, servants, delivery people must walk in and out all the time.

"How do you know how these things work?" Tim whispered as I joined him.

"I have a broad education," I told him. The real story was much too long to tell and involved my peripatetic childhood with my tree-hugging, lawbreaking mother. One didn't save the whales by owning the keys to places like these.

I'd learned from the best how to protest injustice. I was just taking a different route than PETA and Greenpeace.

Watching the shrubbery for black suits, I boldly jogged up the drive toward the Mercedes with in-visible Tim raising dust at my side. If I told myself I was just visiting Andre's car, maybe I could pretend I wasn't flaming insane. Maybe I could blow the horn and bring him running.

I spotted two black suits crouched behind the rho-dodendrons bordering the mansion's spacious gallery.

They were watching the door, not us. Not promising for Andre if they were about to storm in after him.

I stuck out my arm to hold Tim back. He bumped into me, and I grabbed where his bicep should have been.

I disappeared.

13

I freaking disappeared.

Even I couldn't see myself. I held up my hand. Nothing. I was a ghost. No wonder Tim was terrified of his own shadow. He never saw the damned thing!

I tugged him behind a yew hedge, ducked down, and released his arm. Once I wasn't touching him, I reappeared again. Tim didn't.

"What the shit?" I whispered. "Tim, you still there?"

I thought I heard a sound vaguely like *arrghh*. Then he flickered, glanced at me crossly, and winked out again.

"Don't do that," he finally said.

"Don't do what?" I had every right to ask. "I just touched you."

"It felt like electric shock waves," he grumbled. "I almost lost it."

"People touch you all the time, don't they?" But then I smacked my head. People couldn't touch him if they didn't see him.

He thought about it. "Not when I'm out," he finally said. "Nancy Rose pats me on the head, but that's only when she can see me."

Wow, that was a lonely existence. Every kid feels invisible at some time or another, but his problem won the gold cup. "What about Milo? Can you pet Milo when you're out?"

Had Milo disappeared with me? I glanced down at the sack, but my cat was eyeing a mockingbird in the tree. I was pretty sure sack and clothes and everything had winked out. Milo didn't seem too concerned.

"I guess he vanishes when I hold him," Tim admitted. "It would look kind of goofy if people saw him floating in thin air."

"Cheshire cat syndrome. Right. Okay, I'm going to touch you again. This is freaky, but Andre could be in some deep shit, and we need to sneak into the house without getting shot. You won't run and leave me stranded, will you?"

Of course he would, but I had to take the chance. I couldn't tell if he nodded. I just gave him a moment to brace himself, then waved my hand around until I found his arm. I hoped it was his arm.

He muttered ouch. I peered down and saw . . . nothing. Not even Milo. I patted his head to be certain he was there, and he bumped my palm. Okay, then. Here, but not here. Interesting.

I could think of a lot of things I'd like to try while invisible. Entering Gloria Vanderventer's house was not high on the list, not while thugs with guns lingered in the bushes. But duty was duty and Andre had been there when I needed him. I had to return the favor.

"C'mon, let's see what the Big Boss is doing. I've always wanted to be a ghost." Fateful words, even if I did say so myself. I had no idea how long Tim could sustain invisibility for both of us.

Sardonically amusing myself by imagining all the situations I could be in when I mysteriously rematerialized in the middle of a group of stressed-out guards swinging weapons, I led a shivering Tim past the boys in the bushes and up the stairs. The boards creaked. That ought to give the guards something to worry about.

The door wasn't fully closed. Maybe they'd think a breeze had opened it. I couldn't hope they'd flee ghosts unless I rattled a chain and went boo. Probably not even then. Thugs with guns lack imagination.

I heard shouts the instant we entered the three-story foyer. Atriums echo. That's about all they're good for, especially when constructed with marble floors and only columns to serve as walls. I wondered when they'd last played a symphony in here.

Still grasping Tim's skinny arm, I tilted my head

back to scan the upper halls circling the atrium. Opry-land Hotel was more subtle than this joint. Architecture with carved niches containing fake Grecian statues was so over, like maybe since the Renaissance. Wicked bad taste.

Andre's shouts carried clearly from the upper tier. "Gloria, money is not worth whatever your chemists are doing! Sell your shares, manufacture something legitimate, but shut the lab down!"

He and La Vanderventer were on the third circle of this particular hell. Three of her stooges stood behind her. Andre was miraculously unarmed.

I had to stare to make certain my eyes weren't deceiving me. After Acme had blown up his warehouse and terrorized his family, Andre hadn't come gunning for bear? I'd driven all the way out here to save him from killing and he really thought Granny was just a granny and he had no self-defense?

Damn, but men are so spectacularly dense when it comes to women. I was pretty damned certain this granny had plotted Max's demise with the help of her evil grandson not too many months ago. She'd certainly condoned my kidnapping from her back-yard.

The stooges behind Gloria wore black suit jackets, probably covering an assortment of weaponry. *Dammit, Andre, did you come looking to get killed?*

I clenched a fist in fear. Andre and I didn't always approve of each other, but the man had saved my life and given me a job when I'd needed it, and I'd occa-sionally caught glimpses of decency behind his cynicism. I was growing attached to the devil. I didn't want him killed.

Besides, I feared I'd have to do something ugly, like give the devil his due, if the guards started shooting. For now, the men kept their hands at their sides, so I couldn't justify wishing them to perdition. And I wasn't angry enough to visualize.

Like a Hollywood star from the twenties, Gloria was wearing something silky long and flowing. Sheesh. And she wore her age well. Slender, her golden hair artfully coiffed, she stood regally stiff, as if Andre were no more than a beggar at her feet, although he stood half a foot taller. I'd have liked to shoot her just for that.

This was Paddy's mother. I swear, she appeared young enough to be his wife. Or he looked too old for his age. Whatever. I was betting Granny Themis didn't look this good.

A fantasy about old witches running the world formed in my irrepressible imagination before Gloria brought me abruptly back to the moment.

"The laboratory is working on a product that can revolutionize the world," she replied with just the right amount of self-righteous, flag-waving disdain. "America can be strong again. It will return us to our superpower days. You cannot expect me to stop experimentation because of a small accident that even the EPA says caused no harm."

She sounded convincing, but I'd been there when her vans dispatched all evidence of what the gas had actually done. I'd seen the comatose victims she'd hidden from the cops. I was not the blind, deaf, and dumb EPA. Or the bribed and threatened Tweedledee and Dum. Take your pick.

Besides—pardon my bragging—I had some experience with superpowers. They were scary and prone to boosting the arrogant stupidity of the people wielding them—witness my standing here now thinking I could actually save the day. Superpowerdom required intelligence and rationality, and the human race—while not actually lacking in both—prefers emotional meltdowns to thinking.

Superpowerdom in the hands of lying villains was not a place I wanted to go.

"The gas caused no harm?" Andre asked mildly.

I recognized that ominous tone of nonchalance. Mr. Cool was back.

Even from down here, Andre looked laid-back, like he'd just stepped off a yacht, with his thick black hair slightly windblown from the convertible, his naturally bronzed, aristocratic features, and his nose a perfect patrician beak. He wasn't wearing an ascot, but I'd have bet that billowing shirt was silk. He'd hooked his suit coat over his shoulder, and I swear the man was wearing a vest. Some dark, satin embroidered thing, straight out of a *Maverick* episode where the Jim Garner character pulls a derringer and shoots the boots out from under the bad guy.

"No harm at all, Andre," Gloria said grandly. "If you're concerned for your family, why don't you move them out? We'll campaign for industrial zoning and clear out the neighborhoods, and you can enjoy life instead of fretting about a lot of lazy bums who will never amount to anything."

I dug my fingers into Tim's arm and he grunted. If she was referring to the entire area around the Zone, I was not a lazy bum. Neither were my friends. We're weird maybe, but not lazy. Not by a long shot. She talked about us as if we were cockroaches. That's the mentality generated by power, the arrogance of the privileged elite who sincerely believe they know best, though they never descend to the streets to meet or know us.

I'd have liked to shoot her right then, but I'd have had to justify offing just about every rich, powerful bitch in the country. Not good for my eternal health. Maybe I could visualize them scrubbing floors on an empty stomach so they would know what it felt like down here.

"You would tear down a community, throw people out of their homes, for what, Gloria? Magic gas?" Andre's tone remained cool, but his words were edgy enough to make the goons straighten and pat their coat pockets. Definitely holstered guns.

"It's not *magic*," Gloria said irritably. "My son spreads those ridiculous rumors for his own purposes. It's a new element, and Acme is the only company in the world to have it. I should think you of all people, Andre, would understand the importance of research."

Yeah, because it had certainly helped Katerina Montoya. *Comatose*, the new fountain of youth. I rolled my eyes and almost missed the most important part of the action. The boss man was fast and way too clever. From this distance, I couldn't see what Andre held, but it looked more like a tiny aerosol can than a weapon.

"Then if green gas causes no harm, you won't mind if I use it in here?" he asked conversationally. "It creates a splendid rainbow effect when applied properly."

Before anyone could jump him, he sprayed a pink and green cloud into Gloria's face.

Tim was muttering, "Shit, shit, shit," and I was thinking pretty much the same.

Beautiful, charming Gloria erupted like a Fury. She came out swinging and punching, no different from the bums back home when the first gas attack hit the streets. Man, I'd never seen an old lady box like a pro. That had to hurt. She had Andre by the shirtfront and was pounding his face as hard she could with her tiny little fist.

A chemical weapon that caused violence, *sweet*. Not.

Apparently unfazed and a hundred times stronger, Andre pried Granny loose and stepped out of reach before she could grab his hair and launch him over the railing. I swear, she was that mad.

Now what the hell should I do? Andre had started this. I couldn't punish Gloria for what he'd done. Justice was a real bitch.

The goons swarmed closer, trying to work around our raging virago to grab Andre. Gloria swung at them, too, calling them names that would make a sailor blush and smacking them around like punching bags.

"Geez," Tim whispered in awe. "She's a berserker."

Viking warriors notwithstanding, I dragged Tim across the impressive foyer in some idiot hope that I could persuade Andre to move his ass. Gloria was doing such a good job of keeping her guards occupied that he could have sprinted out of there, but it seemed as if the boss was doing the gentlemanly thing and trying to prevent the mad old bat from flying over the railing.

That was some powerful gas. Superpowerdom, my ass. Drop a canister of that in the Mideast and I'd save myself the trouble of blowing up the planet.

Before we could reach the bottom of the stairs, a shot rang out. I froze and jerked my gaze back to the third floor.

Gloria had grabbed a gun from one of the goons and was shooting wildly.

This was seriously not good. Andre had his back to us. I couldn't see what he meant to do, but he was wisely not tackling her. She was aiming at her own guards because they were wrestling with her, trying to prevent her from knocking them into next week.

The shot was apparently the final straw. One thug swung a blow to her jaw, in some dim hope of putting her out, maybe. Just like Nancy Rose after being bashed in the head with a chair, Gloria didn't go down. Instead, she backed out of reach, shrieked in fury, flung her arm up in the air, and discharged the weapon. The force of the discharge unbalanced her, and she fell backward . . .

Toward the railing.

Time slowed. I had a distinct impression that Andre

tried to grab her, but he'd backed too far away when she'd hauled out the gun. The goons didn't even seem to be bothering. Maybe they were waiting for her to fall unconscious so they could tote her off to bed. Or an asylum.

She fell against the railing with arm still upraised. She didn't stumble and collapse on the floor but rammed the rail with the momentum of all her weight. The wood cracked and tilted, and the force of her swing tumbled her over. Backward.

Her head hit the marble floor a million seconds later. Dropping pumpkins would have been less messy.

"Damn you to hell," I muttered without thinking, horrorstruck by both the blood spatter and the awfulness of dying in such gruesome ignominy. How could this ever be explained to her family?

Unable to drag my horrified gaze away, I watched in astonishment as the burning fires of hell blazed red in Gloria's dead and staring eyes. To my revulsion, it was as if her Botoxed and plastic face momentarily melted, morphing into a fiendishly blackened skull. And then there was nothing but blood and brains.

I had the urge to hurl.

Even Tim gagged and quit saying shit.

Andre stared over the railing, his usually amused expression transformed to one of horror. I didn't know if he'd seen what I'd just seen or was even realizing what would go down next. He was simply seeing an old family friend and suffering regret. He had worse to worry about.

I released Tim's arm for a nanosecond. Andre's dismay at seeing me was gratifying. I pointed firmly at the rear of the house, then grabbed Tim again before he could slip out of reach.

I dragged him in the direction of what ought to be the kitchen. My fine legal mind was ticking wildly. I would make a very bad witness given that no one had seen me until after the fact. I was pretty certain it would be better if the police didn't know Tim and I had been trespassing while invisible. And if someone wasn't calling 911 right now, I would. This was not the Zone. No way in hell was the death of Gloria Vanderventer getting swept under any rugs.

While the goons above were shouting at each other and into cell phones, security crashed in from every door. We didn't have much time. I stepped out of the way of two guards barging in from the rear, stuck my invisible foot out, and let one trip and the other fall on him. I needed amusement, and these guys or ones like them had harassed and kidnapped me a while back.

Andre was a bright boy. He was right on my heels. He dodged before the guards completed their tumbling act, then stepped over them.

He refrained from shouting my name. I was still invisible, but tumbling Keystone Cops gave him the evidence that I was damned well there. He intelligently locked the kitchen door behind him.

Once in the kitchen, Tim eagerly strained toward the refrigerator.

"Cameras," I hissed. I'd been spied on by Vanderventers enough to be familiar with their love of security equipment. They'd have Andre entering the house on video but not Tim and me. I doubted they had cameras on the private third floor, more's the pity.

I glanced around, found a slightly open closet door, and dragged Tim that way. Pantry, bingo. Even security guards got hungry occasionally, or wanted a smoke break. I smelled cigarettes as we stepped inside a closet almost as big as my kitchen.

I released Tim and let him rummage for Cheetos. He was still invisible but I could see boxes and bags wink out as he shuffled through them. I don't know how the boy could eat after the spectacle we'd just observed, but I doubted any of us was operating on rational. If I thought about what I'd just seen, I'd gag and freeze in horror. So I blocked it out.

Andre glared at me when he joined us, tugging the door almost shut. "I'm not even going to ask," was all he said. "I think I'll just wring your neck. You have no business—"

"Call 911." I interrupted his tirade. "They're up there getting their shit together, and it's not going to look good for you."

Grimly recognizing the truth of that, he produced his phone and called in a report. Putting his phone back in his pocket, he ran his hand through his glorious hair. "I meant to kill her," he declared defiantly. "If it came down to her or my mother, Gloria was going out."

"Wise choice. Did you see what I saw?" I was curious. Maybe I was the only one who could see men in hell, but it sure seemed as if Andre had sent Gloria there.

I couldn't see Tim's reaction, but Andre stared at me, waiting for explanation. Shoot, he hadn't seen what I'd seen.

Well, either I was crazy, or I'd just seen my very first demon. And watched her die. If demons were running Acme . . . that explained a *lot*, including magic gas. I shuddered in horror.

14

I'm a lawyer, not a priest. I don't read about demons much. I always thought they were fairy-tale characters, like witches. So it wasn't as if I could positively identify red burning eyes and crispy-black features. My brief brush with Max in hell was my only basis for my very weak conclusion. Until I had a better word, *demon* worked better than *not normal* or believing I was crazy.

I waved away the horrific image of demons on earth and returned to our very scary reality. A woman had died. There would be repercussions beyond the immediate, but we didn't have time for more than that. I sure wasn't going to waste time mourning a Vanderventer.

"The guards weren't doing anything but their jobs," I warned Andre. "Granny essentially killed herself, and that's your story. Stick with it. Give Tim that damned can so he can disappear it when we leave here. I don't know what's in that gas, but we don't want the police getting their hands on it."

Or the world, but that was well beyond our concerns right now.

Andre handed over the tiny can. Since I couldn't see Tim, I shoved it in my bag with Milo, who had remarkably just watched instead of roaring into bobcat mode. A bag of kitty treats rattled on the shelf. I got the message and helped myself, feeding them to Milo for his good behavior.

"How am I going to explain her rage?" Andre asked, rationally enough.

I grinned evilly. "You need a porn pic of Dane. That would send her around the bend. I don't suppose you can arrange that? The police will understand protecting a U.S. senator if you decline to reveal it. They won't like it, but it's better than a can of pink rage."

Surprisingly, he answered, "I can get some of Gloria with the pool boy. I just can't produce them now. Protecting a senator's grandmother ought to be enough, right?"

Oh, ugh. Not going there.

"Burn something on the gas stove," I suggested. "Say you came down here and burned the photo because you didn't want the world to see it."

"You should be a novelist," he said sarcastically.

"Now get the hell out of here. I hear sirens. If I get locked up, I need you out where you can help my dad."

I hated abandoning him. I knew the police routine well enough to know it wouldn't be pretty, especially with a hugely wealthy, respected society matron involved. But he was right. He didn't need hand-holding.

Amazingly, I wrapped my arms around Andre's neck and planted a big one on his cheek. For a very brief moment, his arms closed around me, and he hugged me as if I might be someone valuable. Even special. That didn't happen often, and I treasured the ridiculous idea.

I kissed his cheek again, then stepped away. "We have your back. Just get your story together and stick to it."

He nodded, tugged my ritzy new hair, and departed to burn paper on the stove. I waited until an expensive box of chocolates returned to sight, and grabbed the air near it. I caught Tim's arm and, invisibly, we slipped out the back door.

As we hurried down the delivery-entrance drive toward the road, I called Schwartz to tell him what had happened. He was a lieutenant now. He probably didn't have jurisdiction out here, but he'd know best how to protect Andre. He wasn't happy. He even used a swearword. But he was a Zonie now, whether he liked it or not.

"You can stay out if you like," I told Tim when we reached the bike and I released his arm. I didn't know if he could even turn himself back on. We'd seen some pretty scary stuff, and Tim was, well, timid. "Even if someone notices me, you won't be involved." I handed him a helmet. It disappeared when he took it.

"Just don't grab for me if I take a bend too fast!" I shouted, bringing the Harley roaring back to life.

The disappearing trick was highly entertaining, but a seemingly riderless bike would cause wrecks all over the freeway. Malicious mischief was only my style if the parties involved were nasty. Really, I'm a boring gnome in normal life.

We careened back to the row of Victorians that constituted home. Before we reached my place, I slowed down and gaped at the sight of a six-foot guy in camouflage jogging down the hill with a toddler stroller in hand and an infant strapped to his broad chest. I hoped he had been one of the storm troopers and let myself smile with a tiny bit of triumph. Muscles could be put to better use than destruction, and the toddler was laughing in joy at the speed. If only all our problems could be solved so peacefully!

In hopes that this was a benefit from Saturn Daddy, I properly offered up gratitude at the sight.

Back home, I parked in my normal spot by Pearl's shed. Tim was still scared and thus invisible. Maybe I'd gone a wee bit over the speed limit, but really, he had no cause to shake in his shoes.

An ugly thought belatedly occurred, and I glanced down at the bike, then over to the helmet that reappeared when he hung it on the seat. "Did we just ride here on an invisible bike?" I asked. I didn't think so. I'd been sort of watching the gauges.

"Until today, I never disappeared anything as big as you," he complained. "I can't disappear Harleys any more than I can vanish buildings."

"I'm not any bigger than you are." By much, at least. No Viking blood ran in my veins. I'd been told that my mother's family was from Iran, although she'd been born in the U.S. I'd never met her parents—unless you count the weird messages from Themis. I didn't know my father, but he sure hadn't passed on any tall genes.

"Yeah, but you're different," Tim concluded.

I sighed. The boy had a point. Hadn't I wished myself invisible a little earlier in the day? Saturn or the Universe or Satan usually gifted me with my wishes when I sent someone to hell. Did that mean I'd buried one of the troops in the tunnel with my avalanche? And the way I'd been cursing, I'd probably sent him to the devil. Damn.

I'd have to quit cursing.

It had been a long, strange day. And it was far from over. I left Tim to take a nap or do whatever it is teen boys do when no one can see them. I had to warn Julius that all hell was about to break loose.

And call Max! Man, how could I forget? Gloria was Dane's granny. And Paddy's mom. Ugh, I hated to be the bearer of bad tidings, although in this case, I didn't think Gloria would be universally mourned.

I punched in the senator's number as I jogged over to Andre's house. He didn't answer, and I got voice mail.

"Ding-dong, the witch is dead," I singsonged

into the machine. Rude of me, I know, but Gloria had not been what she appeared, and I'd hated her for a long time. Max had once stupidly thought she was interested only in shopping. After she'd had him killed, he'd had to open his eyes. Dane's eyes, because Max's big beautiful brown ones were gone forever.

"I thought I'd warn you before the media and cops cornered you," I continued. "Get your PR guys over to Gloria's, pronto. Never say I don't do anything for you. Smooch, big boy. Call me if you need to know more." I hung up.

I caught Julius and Paddy in the process of carrying Katerina back to her tower. They needed Andre's muscle. I didn't think they'd have it soon. Setting down Milo's bag, I shouldered the lower half of the stretcher next to Paddy so we could keep her semi-straight going up the stairs.

"Is Andre all right?" Julius asked worriedly, huffing only a little.

"Maybe I should wait until we put the lady down before talking," I stalled, trying not to gasp from the effort of lifting the weight. "He's fine," I said hurriedly when the stretcher sagged. "Long story."

I didn't know how much to tell them. They didn't know what I was, and since I didn't really know myself, I didn't want to say too much. So I couldn't mention invisibility and demons and all the parts I wanted to discuss. I had to stick to the real and the legal, like the good little lawyer I was supposed to be. Especially now that I knew Julius had once been a judge.

Instead, in lieu of conversation, I asked, "Who was the bonehead who gave Andre the cloud can?"

"That would be me," Paddy said wearily. "It had to be done. My mother hasn't been right in the head for years. I'm not sure senility can explain it. If anything will slow down Acme's dangerous experimentation, it's removing Gloria. What happened, do you know?"

The cloud can was still in my bag with Milo. Well, still in the bag. Milo was following us up the stairs.

"I know what happened," I said grimly, my shoulders aching from the weight. "You need an elevator in here."

"Normally, we don't carry much up and down the stairs," Julius said, breathing heavily as he shouldered open the door at the top.

"Well, maybe we won't be gassed again, so you won't need another bomb shelter run." I hadn't given much thought to anything except how Andre was faring, but I needed to consider all the other ramifications of Gloria's demise. Removing a demon from a chemical factory could only be good, I decided—unless, of course, I was crazy.

We swung the stretcher to the lovingly carved bed with its downy mattress. Sleeping Beauty didn't move so much as a finger when Julius expertly rolled her between the fine-woven sheets.

"Explain now," Paddy ordered curtly. "Where's Andre? We can't let that can loose into the world."

"Yeah, that was kind of my thinking. It's in my bag downstairs. Julius's bag," I corrected, remembering lifting it from the knob. "I'll go get it." I trotted back down to the kitchen. The bag was there. The can was not.

I'd told Tim to disappear it. Maybe he'd come in and taken it. I dashed back to the second floor and pounded on his apartment door. No answer.

Praying Tim had the can, I returned to the attic and handed Julius his canvas tote. "I think Tim took it. I told him it needed to stay disappeared. But he's not in his room. He may have gone to the shop to water the plants."

Paddy frowned but said nothing.

Julius waved away the bag. "Keep the tote. I'll talk to the boy whenever he comes in. Where's Andre?"

I checked my watch. After three. It had been over an hour since I'd left him. "Probably still giving his statement to a few dozen cops. And when they're done, they'll bring in a few dozen more. We won't be seeing him anytime soon. I've called Schwartz. I'm hoping he'll let us know if we need a lawyer."

Julius rubbed his forehead and sank into a cushy recliner. I bet he spent a lot of nights sleeping in it.

Paddy helped himself to the floor. He seemed at home there. "Did the cloud work?"

"That depends." I glowered at him. "What was it supposed to do?"

"We didn't know. I just siphoned some from the tank that didn't blow. I figured if Acme was experimenting on us, we should return the favor."

"You had to know he'd go after Gloria!" I shouted. "You had that can ready, knowing Andre would go after your mother. You planned this!"

See, even in my anger at injustice, the legal instincts kick in. He was talking premeditated murder. Almost. And I was the prosecutor. I really didn't want to prosecute Paddy for murder. He had given Andre the can. He had to have expected her to go berserk. Was that murder?

"I had no idea what the gas would do, and I did not tell Andre to use it on anyone," Paddy argued wearily. I wanted to believe him. "What happened?"

"You killed your mother," I said bluntly.

Both old men instantly appeared older, more tired and gray, with new lines etched in their skin. I hated causing them pain, but a woman had *died*. My instinct was to seek justice, no matter how wicked she'd been.

"She was a lovely woman once," Julius said, almost apologetically. "Very gracious."

"Until my father died and she sold her soul," Paddy said, surprisingly. "I thought at first she was just working too hard, learning how to run the company. I don't think he left her in as strong a financial position as she'd expected. I tried to help but I'm a scientist, not a financier." He gazed into the distance, as if trying to remember—or decide how much to reveal.

"My cousin Cynthia's husband steered some government contracts to Acme," he finally continued. "Since Cynthia's father left her some Acme shares when he died, Mike had a family interest in keeping it running."

Sleazy former Senator *Mike* MacNeill was Max's father. Dane had stepped into his political shoes after MacNeill pulled some shady deals—probably using his influence to get Acme government contracts. Mike's illegal activities were likely why Dane had had to place all his assets in a blind trust when he ran for Mike's seat.

"We hired new management," Paddy continued. "When they brought in the new element, my mother suddenly became obsessed with the company." He ran a shaky hand through his hair.

"Gloria was always good to us," Julius said wearily. "I wasn't earning enough as a prosecutor to put Andre through private school, but she and Katerina's mother were old friends. Gloria saw that he received scholarships. The Vanderventers probably helped me get appointed judge. And when I vacated the bench to care for Katerina, she hired Andre to work at the plant after he came home and couldn't settle down."

"PTSD," Paddy said, as if repeating an old tale. "Andre went through hell overseas, fighting two wars and terrorists. He just needed time to get his head straight. He would have been fine."

"But that's when things started turning sour," Julius argued. "In return for giving Andre a job, she wanted me to use my influence in favor of a rezoning to shut down Edgewater and the neighborhood."

I listened, keeping my big mouth buttoned. These old guys were spilling secrets Andre would never have told me.

"That was back before the chemical flood, when Acme first obtained the magic element and needed to expand." Paddy nodded in agreement. "That's when it all went south." He glanced up to me. "What happened today?"

Damn, I'd hoped they'd keep talking.

"Andre sprayed the gas in the can," I said slowly, waiting to see if they would exhibit any understanding of what that meant. Both watched me with curiosity and nothing more. "Gloria went berserk."

They turned to the woman in the bed. One whispered, "Damn." The other just sighed.

15

Before I went home, I jogged down to the tunnel to check on our patients. Milo found a cushion in Andre's place and appropriated it, declining to come with me.

The med students were now ensconced in the theater with the more ordinary zombies. Tim hadn't rescued Leibowitz but had brought two more of the homeless guys. Since yesterday, the baby docs had decided the new healthiness of their patients had something to do with the IV nutrients. They were excitedly talking about getting grants to study homelessness, disease, and nutrition. So maybe something good would come of the gas, should the victims ever awaken—though that wasn't looking likely.

With Katerina back in the tower, Sarah slept in lonely splendor in the official infirmary. Cora glanced up her from her smart phone when I entered. "Thank goodness! I gotta pee!"

She dashed out, leaving me to wonder what I was supposed to do. I could only stare sadly at a woman who had led a harsh life, one who'd not had many opportunities before Acme took her out. I hoped Julius would massage Sarah and keep her IV filled as he did for his wife, because we couldn't risk the med students in here. And I knew nothing about caretaking.

I sank onto Cora's seat, feeling useless, tired, and hungry. I wondered if Themis had answered my chewing-gum message. I hadn't been back to my place to find out.

Strangely, I wasn't as concerned about the question I'd asked as I was worried about Themis. As far as I knew, she could be part of my whacked-out imagination, but I had a hankering for a grandmotherly role model, I guess. I didn't want her lying comatose in Acme's secret labs.

My only other family was my mother, but she was in Peru. Which meant that, with Sarah out, I didn't have a lot of mentoring happening on this Saturn's daughter business.

"I'm fine," a throaty voice with a hint of humor said out of the blue. Or was that out of the pink?

I almost fell off the stool I was perched on. I'd thought I was alone. I glanced around the antiseptic steel office. I *was* alone. Except for Sarah.

I stared, but I could have sworn she hadn't moved.

A hospital white blanket still neatly covered her chimp appendages. Besides, Sarah had one of those baby-sweet, whispery voices. What I'd heard had sounded like a cigarette smoker's husky alto.

"Hello?" I said tentatively, wondering if IV stands could speak. "Who's there?"

"Your *madarbozorg, aziz.*"

The voice seemed to come from Sarah, but not an inch of her frizzy beehive stirred, although her lips might have.

Madarbozorg? The foreign mouthful almost seemed familiar, but I couldn't translate it.

"Visualizing is an unusual gift, *aziz,*" the voice spoke again, a little more distantly, as if too many words were difficult to project. "Use it for harm, and justice will be served. Use it for profit, and you will pay."

I'd asked Themis if I'd be punished for visualizing. I hadn't been specific. "Themis?" I asked tentatively. I still didn't know if she was crazier than me, but Max had assured me that these weird messages really came from my grandmother. Of course, he'd been in hell at the time.

Sarah's eyelids flickered. For a moment, I thought I saw black irises instead of Sarah's blue. I held my breath in anticipation, and then Sarah morphed entirely to monkey form right before my eyes.

I fell backward, knocking the stool over in my haste to escape.

Sarah was faster. Emitting a chimpanzee cry, she leaped for my neck.

Did I mention the chimp had strangled two strong men?

She wrapped her long arms around my head and her legs around my waist. I was strangling simply from the stench of unwashed chimp when Cora returned, waving her fancy phone at me.

"I believe this one's for you," Cora cried, before screeching to a halt inside the door, her eyes widening. "Rather you than me," was her helpful comment.

Apparently regaining some of what passes for her sense, Sarah loosened her grip but continued to cling.

Eyeing her warily, Cora held up the phone so I could see it past Sarah's hairy head. "If the Zone has spread all the way up here, Andre's gonna shit bombs."

Since Andre was probably sitting at the police station, that was an attractive image. I studied the text on her screen. *Sarah's mind is intact, what there is of it. Sad girl. Themis*

Shit. I reached around Sarah's furry body to grab the phone. I hastily texted a reply asking where Themis was but all I got was a Wikipedia page showing *aziz*—Persian for *dear*.

"I'm moving to Seattle," I told Cora, attempting to pry Sarah's legs loose from my waist, but she clung like a terrified Muppet.

"Yeah, that's what we all say," Cora said with a shrug. "But we never do. Reality sucks, y'know?"

Since Cora just assumed the Zone was messing with us, I didn't even begin to try to explain that Themis might exist. No way could I explain that she *might* be my grandmother and might have used Sarah as a vehicle to communicate—even I hadn't worked out all the ramifications. Didn't want to, to be frank, especially with the result clinging to my neck.

If I'd translated Themis's visualization message correctly, it meant that all I was going to get out of this Saturn gig was grief. If I conjured up a pot of gold, I'd end up paying for it one way or another. *Shit*. Still, she hadn't said I'd go to hell if I visualized bad guys pushing strollers. There was no harm or profit in that.

I left the tunnel carrying Sarah around my neck. I supposed I should take comfort that one of the zombies had wakened, and that it had been dangerous Sarah. That was one less burden to haul around, in a manner of speaking, since I now had to carry her physically. Except now I had to wonder if Themis could wake all the zombies or only daughters of Saturn. I suspected the latter.

With a sense of relief, I carried poor Sarah back to my apartment while debating justice and my place in the scheme of things.

That Nancy Rose and the others were growing healthier by the minute didn't exactly justify gassing a rich old lady in hopes she'd improve, too. I didn't know for certain that Gloria was some kind of demon. I didn't even believe in demons. But she'd certainly been dangerous. Did that justify Paddy's offing her? Or letting Andre gas her?

"Really, Saturn?" I muttered as I climbed the stairs. "Do I have to get involved now that Gloria's dead and the world is a better place? Can't I just say, 'Amen, and so it goes'?"

Sarah bobbed her head in agreement, which made me uneasy. I didn't really want to agree with a serial murderer on this one.

The message I'd left on my door was gone. I didn't think Schwartz had been here to take it, but maybe Paddy had. Or maybe Themis had made it disappear in a puff of smoke. I set Sarah on the floor and let her toddle off to explore. Her chimp shape embarrassed her, but it was just us girls here. She knew where to find the bananas, the only food of mine she'd ever consented to eat.

I mulled over what I'd learned and what I should do as I stir-fried veggies. I didn't see Gloria's face in the gas flames of my stove, thank goodness. I didn't hear from Max, either. I'd tried calling Schwartz to find out what was going down, but he didn't have time to talk to me.

Sarah reappeared as Sarah while I was opening the tortilla package. She'd helped herself to one of my sundresses and a cardigan I never wore. Her missile-shaped breasts strained at the cotton that would have covered my more modest assets.

"Welcome back," I said cautiously.

She looked at my vegetables with disinterest and opened the refrigerator. "I had the strangest dream," she said as she rummaged. "I was down at Chesty's, sitting at the bar with Bill and a lot of ugly old men and a woman who said she was a florist. I was wondering where the regulars were. Then this strange

Gypsy woman showed up talking gibberish. And then I woke up in your arms."

"Don't make too much of it," I said warily, pondering a dream including our unconscious patients. Could Sarah have known Bill and Nancy Rose were gassed before she clocked out? "You got gassed and were out for a few days." How much should I tell her?

"Gassed?" She emerged from behind the refrigerator door holding peanut butter and apples.

I didn't precisely trust a woman who would kill her mama in return for prettier legs, but she was the only Saturn's daughter I knew. I kept hoping she might impart a few secrets. So I dumped my veggies into a tortilla, added some feta, and gave her a brief, expurgated version of events.

"Paddy and Julius clammed up after I told them how Gloria died," I finished up. "I didn't tell them she turned into a demon before she departed." I waited for any insight Sarah might offer.

She ate her apple, core and all, and licked peanut butter off her fingers. "Mama said the devil's demons walk the earth," she offered, shrugging. "And that we'd join them one day. But she didn't do anything cool like turn black when she died."

So very not useful—unless I wanted confirmation that Sarah had killed her mother. "Have you ever visualized punishing someone who does bad things?" I asked, hoping for a real discussion.

She studied me as if I were queer in the head. "Why? Isn't it easier just to wish them dead?"

Well, no, but maybe that was my legal training.

And now I had to worry that I could just *wish* someone out of existence.

"I don't think killing people is our purpose," I gently pointed out, not wanting to get on her wrong side. "If it was, after a while there wouldn't be any more people in the world."

She frowned a little, as if she were really thinking about it. "I don't think I'll ever go any farther than Baltimore," she concluded. "I don't think anyone will complain too much if I eliminate a few jerks. It will be a nicer place to live."

"Save it for the real bad guys, at least," I admonished. "Where would we be without Ernesto?"

She nodded as if she'd taken my point. "Thanks for lunch. I'd better get back to work."

I didn't think Chesty's would be open on a Sunday afternoon, but heck if I meant to stop her. Maybe, if the world was really lucky, the pink particles had improved her morals, if not her brains. Milo and I watched her go. I think even my cat sighed in relief. Maybe we should let her loose in Acme—our very own neutron bomb.

I needed someone to help me through the murky maze of right and wrong so I'd know what to do next.

Julius had been a judge and Paddy a research scientist at Acme when the last chemical flood occurred. Paddy, at least, had to have known Gloria's going berserk if gassed was a possible reaction.

He'd probably expected her to go comatose, like the others. Point to ponder, if I were judge and jury. A real jury wouldn't know enough about weirdness to believe the argument—a point Andre had made previously. I might be the only person capable of judging Zonies.

Thinking I might have to adjudicate friends as well as enemies made me itchy. If I refused the duty, would I get punished?

"If you don't give me the rulebook, you old bastard," I told my invisible daddy, "then you have no right to judge me!"

While I waited to hear from Andre and Max, I kept my ears open. No more helicopters broke the Sunday silence. I kept hoping for another stroller sighting, but I'd probably have to go further inland, where there were real neighborhoods. I had an aching need to know I was making things better instead of worse.

I needed to ask Julius if he'd found Tim and the canister. That thing was a dangerous time bomb waiting to explode.

Finishing my tortilla, I settled down with my new toy computer. The tablet would be lousy for word processing, but it had built-in Internet access, which I assumed Acme was paying for. And it was fast, far faster than my cheap netbook. The tablet still had power, and Boris had left a message saying he was delivering a charger to Chesty's.

I could probably go over and usurp Andre's computers now that I knew how to get into them, but I liked keeping my mail and Facebook private. My page is under Mary Clancy, so people who don't know me really well can't find it.

I opened my e-mail, hoping to find answers to my

requests regarding body dumping. One of my correspondents was a doctor who worked with a hospital in Massachusetts. He said he could admit a comatose patient for a limited time, but after that they'd go to a state-run nursing home.

As if to exacerbate my worries, I thought I felt the ground shake. I froze, but I didn't feel it again. Someone really needed to get back inside Acme and find that damned machinery and turn it off. I was a lawyer, not a rocket scientist. I had limits.

I needed to talk to Andre. The Zone *needed* his leadership. Things went seriously wrong when I took up the reins, as I'd learned the hard way. I was a loner, not a leader. Besides, I had to go to work in the morning.

Could we drop Nancy Rose off at a local hospital and have someone ship one of the old guys to Massachusetts? Would it be safe now that Gloria was out of the picture? Could I believe she was the only force of evil at Acme?

I glanced at my computer clock, but the digits weren't changing any faster. Antsy and worried, I called Jane the reporter to see if she'd learned anything interesting about the gas.

"No story," she told me with disappointment. "I earned brownie points for breaking the news, but Acme's press release merely says a worker cleaning a tank accidentally released some chlorine, causing a few residents with asthma to go to the hospital. I haven't located any of those residents, so I assume they've all gone home."

"Hogwash," I said wearily. "They didn't have asthma, it wasn't chlorine, and Acme hid anyone who keeled over at the plant, not the hospital." I didn't mention the ones we'd rescued. Jane has an overdeveloped sense of curiosity. "But none of it probably matters now. Gloria Vanderventer died today. I assume new management will be stepping in."

At the back of my mind, I'd been wondering who that new management would be. Paddy? He was her son, so that would make sense, except everyone thought he was crazy.

"Gloria Vanderventer?" Jane asked, obviously taking notes. "The senator's mother?"

"I'm sure it's all over the news by now. I'll let you know what I can, but I'm still waiting for calls."

I signed off. Jane and her son weren't Zonies, so I needed to keep them outside the information loop. The *Baltimore Edition* was one of those cheap online deals, but if I wanted to work the media, she was eager.

I'd resisted as long as I could. After hanging up on Jane, I dialed Andre's cell.

He actually answered. I guessed that meant he hadn't been locked up yet.

"Just checking to see if you need a lawyer," I said carelessly.

"Not yet, but soon," he agreed. "The goons have decided to take me down rather than take the blame."

No surprise there. I'd had enough experience to see that coming. Always being the new kid in school, I'd dealt with my share of bullies over the years. They always threw the blame elsewhere. "Well, you have to admit, you squirted her," I said without sympathy. "They're only guilty of getting in her face and letting her have a gun. Where are you? If I need to swing bail, where do I get it?"

His voice, when he answered, sounded relieved. He probably hadn't been certain that I could actually be a friend when needed. "Checkbook in my office at Bill's. I'm at the Towson precinct. Ask my father to call one of his lawyer pals to try to keep costs down."

Andre had given me a car when I needed it, then fixed it up when he'd seen what a junker it was. He'd helped me in so many ways lately that I had to pay back some of what I owed. "I'll call Judge Snootypants. That's his bailiwick. I'll tell him I'm your lawyer. He'll get a snort out of that."

"Not if you call him 'Snootypants,'" Andre said with half a laugh. "Thanks, Clancy."

Andre suspected I could send the lying goons to another planet if I wanted. But he wasn't nagging me to do so. He respected my choices. I liked that in a man. We hung up, and I cranked the whirling gears of my mind.

I suspected Dane/Max as Senator Vanderventer was the reason Snotty Snootypants had hired me. I wasn't exactly the Ivy League sort the judge obviously preferred. Despite my joking promise to Andre, I couldn't persuade Judge Snodgrass to so much as answer a phone for a lowly clerk, even if he could be reached on a Sunday. It wasn't as if I had his cell phone number.

I didn't think Max would help me out once he learned Andre had killed Granny Gloria. Max had a serious self-righteous streak to balance Dane's evil, and he disliked Andre. Maybe Julius should talk to the judge, persuade him that Andre wasn't dangerous so he could bond out if charged.

No, it really needed to be Max the Senator. The whole world thought Gloria was his grandmother. If Gloria's grandson spoke up for Andre, whoever ended up with Andre's arraignment would listen.

I didn't think I could make that argument with a telephone call.

It was Sunday evening. Bill's bar would be closed. I called the bartender who was working in Bill's place and asked him if he could open up so I could get at Andre's checkbook. He'd been listening to the news and agreed with alacrity.

If I meant to vamp Max into doing me favors he didn't want to do, I'd have to dress the part. That was my biker Max inside the good senator's tailored suit. Max had never been into pearls and kitten heels. I showered and blow-dried my thick new hair. I hated mirrors, but I forced myself to glare into the steamy bathroom one to apply a bit of color. My mother couldn't afford braces when I was a kid, so I'd learned to live with my imperfect teeth. Men were more into breasts and ass, and I had enough of those to get by.

I could have sworn the mirror wavered strangely, and I stepped back, recalling the days Max had flickered in there. I really didn't want to see Dane or Gloria over my sink. Grimacing, I faced my ridiculous fears, applied lipstick and mascara, and made it to my closet without breaking glass. If I meant to arrive without resembling a two-bit messenger, I'd have to take my car and not the bike. So I didn't have to wear leather.

I wiggled into black spandex capris that showed off my nifty new leg. If I was going to hell for accepting gifts from the devil, then I'd get the most out of them here on earth. I completed the outfit with a matching microfiber tank top that painted itself to my curves. I topped it all off with a peekaboo tiger-striped gauze tunic that said, *Look, but don't touch.*

"Want to visit Max?" I asked Milo when I was done. He'd been watching the process from his post by the sliding doors to my deck. He kneaded his bed of dirty laundry on the floor, curled up, and closed his eyes. I took that as a good sign that he didn't think I needed his protection. He'd had a long day and deserved a kitty nap.

Apparently there was no rest for daughters of Saturn.

I stopped by the bar and picked up Andre's checkbook before hitting the freeway. Bill's bar was a sad place without Bill's big bulk behind the counter. I left more determined than ever to right what Acme had done wrong.

I preferred the solid Harley to my plastic Miata, but I had to admit, sporty red convertibles had more panache for driving up to million-dollar condos. Jaw set, I flashed my license, and the guard at the gate let me through. Max was thoughtful that way. Of course, he'd probably have my name stricken from the register after tonight.

He hadn't returned my earlier call, so he didn't deserve a warning of my arrival. I had a hunch he wasn't studying up on the latest congressional bill for screwing the taxpayers. The devil in me wanted to see what Max the Senator did on Sunday nights.

So I was playing girlfriend games. It happens.

I took a real live working elevator up to the top floor—marvelous how technology actually worked outside the Zone. My phone rang as I pushed the doorbell.

I checked caller ID. Not Max. I answered anyway.

"They've arrested Andre," Julius said wearily. "Charged him with first-degree murder. The press is crawling all over the Zone."

I had promised to curb the swearing, but a few epithets crossed my glossy lips. I'd hoped they wouldn't charge him so quickly, but Vanderventers owned this part of town.

Julius knew all that. It was the media in the Zone that he worried about. I took a deep breath and tried to sound sane. "Are they in your face yet?"

"At the door. I'm not answering. Schwartz is outside patrolling, keeping them to public places. They can't find anyone to talk to on a Sunday night. I just wanted to warn you."

"I must have escaped before they got the word. I'm over at Dane's, waiting for him to come home." Since the good senator obviously wasn't answering his door, I had to assume he was out. "You might want to try calling some of your lawyer friends, asking them who'll be arraigning the case. Get back to me if you find out."

"I don't have many friends anymore, but I'll see what I can do."

"Your books are still used in the classroom, Julius. You've earned respect. You'll get it. Do you know any lawyers who will take his case?" I sat down cross-legged in the hall and rested my back against the wall.

"I'll ask around, but the Vanderventers—" He caught himself, realizing I was sitting outside a Vanderventer door. "Paddy said he'll help if he can."

I thought about that. "Tell him to hold off. Until we know what's going down at the plant, it's better if his family still thinks he's cuckoo."

I wasn't convinced he *wasn't* cuckoo, but for now, he seemed saner than the rest of the world.

"Don't do anything rash," Julius said quietly, "but Andre may have a problem with confinement."

I grimaced. I didn't know about all of Andre's problems, but I could imagine his reaction should anyone push him too far. Heads would roll. Literally. Special Ops with PTSD—ugly.

"I'm on it." I hung up. Andre's checkbook weighed heavy in my bag. Andre wasn't poor by a long shot, but it didn't matter how much money he had if he got a judge who wouldn't allow bail. He could totally freak in jail, and then he really *would* off somebody.

It knotted my insides to ask for anything, especially from Max the senator. We were a few universes apart these days. He had his problems. I had mine. It would be better if the twain never met. But I couldn't let Andre down. The pincers of eternal conflict squeezed my skull tighter.

The elevator door finally clanked and slid open. There were two condos up here, so I didn't rush to stand. Damn good thing.

Senator Vanderventer stepped out with Glenys MacNeill, the late Max's sister, hanging on his arm.

I could almost hear the Max inside the senator screaming *Help*! as if he were still caught behind my mirror.

16

The devil made me do it, I swear. Even if he was wearing Dane's disguise, that was my Max that Glenys was drooling on. So it wasn't for the sake of Max's everlasting soul that I stood up and sauntered toward the couple stepping off the elevator.

I had on three-inch Ferragamos from the Goodwill store, and I was probably still half a head shorter than Glenys. Max's family wasn't small. I'd never let my size stand in my way. I smiled wickedly through my Luscious Ruby lipstick. I didn't just swing my spandex-clad hips; I rolled them like a hooker. I shook out my glorious mane. I stunned the Max I saw in Dane's eyes. He hadn't been around enough lately to appreciate the new me.

Glenys narrowed her eyes and clung more posses-sively to Dane's arm. Even if she didn't know the soul inside his body was that of her brother, the senator was still her second cousin, for pity's sake. Did the girl know no shame? If she had any brains or compassion at all, she would have recognized by now that the man who had walked out of the hospital a few months ago was no longer the same Dane she'd grown up with.

"Hello, Danny boy," I purred. "I'm not into three-somes, so if you want to get it on with the lady, I'll be moving along."

"You're that witch who killed Max!" Glenys cried in sudden fury, finally seeing through my vamp dis-guise. She dropped Dane's arm like a hot poker and turned her glare on him. "You're fucking Max's whore?"

"Oh, very pretty, Glenys. Such elegant language." I vowed again to quit cursing. It turned Glenys into an ugly bitch, even though she wasn't half bad, in an older-woman sort of way.

"I told you I was busy, Glenys," Dane/Max said apologetically. "I have several meetings scheduled for this evening. Tina is giving me background for one of them."

Oh, Max, you liar, you. But then, I already knew he was a liar, which was how he'd ended up cursed in the first place.

"Sorry, Senator," I said pertly. "It's hard to resist. Sunday is supposed to be my day of rest, and buzz-ing up to D.C. to be blown off by a booty call kind of tilted my wheels."

Max glared through Dane's blue eyes. I smiled boldly, as if I teased and confronted U.S. senators every day. Glenys narrowed her eyes in disbelief, but she made a nice turnabout. She patted Dane's arm, kissed his cheek, whispered a few sweet nothings in his ear. Then, after giving me a glare, she swung out.

She worked hard on that hip sway, but Dane/Max didn't even look. Brothers really don't notice sisters.

"Thanks, I think," he said, unlocking his door. "She's hatching some scheme to take over Acme now that Gloria's out of the way. She seems to think we'll inherit some of her shares. That's a distant chance."

"*Her* chance might be distant, but Dane has a good likelihood of inheriting," I reminded him as we entered his chilly apartment.

I kept expecting Harley parts and clutter. Max had been a mechanic with a very loose bookkeeping system and no interest in domesticity, but he probably had a cleaning service these days. And no engines to take apart. One more fine mechanical mind lost to white-collardom.

"Isn't it lovely that the buzzards are circling before the body is even cold?" I asked, rather than mourn what was no longer. Max was at least back here on earth instead of stuck in the outer rings of hell. For that, I should be grateful.

He opened the bar, poured himself a bourbon, and gestured to ask if I wanted anything. Figuring I needed a clear head for this argument, I didn't take him up on the offer. My Max would have been swilling cheap beer, my drink of choice. I didn't think there was any point in learning to swill the hundred-dollar-a-gallon stuff.

"The media is all over the story, by the way," he said. "Thanks for the warning. It gave the speechwriters time to spin a good 'we need to be with family' press release so I could dodge questions I couldn't answer." He sipped his drink and stared into the dead fireplace. He didn't realize I had the answers. After all we'd been through, he should have.

"Cold, Max. Does the family care at all?" I asked out of curiosity.

He shrugged. "Gloria alienated almost everyone over the past years. I'm not sure how Dane endured her. She's been demanding I visit, but my getting shot has its advantages. I worked that injury for months. I couldn't have for much longer."

I didn't know how to tell him that he'd been procrastinating over a demon. Had Sarah's mother been literal or metaphorical about demons walking the earth? I'd seen enough to vote for literal, even if they were disguised as grannies.

To be truthful, I was still a little restless from that sexual battle in the hall, so I wasn't as focused as I should have been. I didn't have the hots for the Dane standing there, but I still wanted the Max I heard talking. Listening to him ripped me down the middle.

"I assume you're here because of Andre," he said before I could summon a proper response.

"You were never stupid," I said grudgingly. I didn't like being so obvious. Oh well, time to lay it on the line. "Seen any more of Dane in the fire? Or do you want to turn that thing on and see if Gloria pops up?"

I picked up the gas remote and waved it like a wand at the logs, but I didn't push the buttons. I didn't want to see Dane any more than he did.

"Why should Gloria pop up?" he asked irritably. "*Andre* killed her. She has no reason to haunt me."

"Because she's Dane's grandmother, and she's probably dancing in the fires of hell now and realizing her grandson's down there with her instead of up here." I threw the remote aside like a hot potato just thinking about it. I much preferred the days when I thought hell was a figment of Bible Belt folklore.

Dane/Max struggled with his better self and, instead of saying something karmically nasty, resorted to trusting me for a change. "Do I want to know why you believe Gloria is in hell? Or is this old news?"

I hadn't told Andre about the Gloria-fiend I'd seen, but he had enough on his mind. And he'd never visited hell, as Max had. I could trust Max to believe me if I said I had seen a demon. Although he'd probably go ballistic if I told him I'd been at Gloria's house with Andre. Warped priorities. Still, I needed him to believe that Andre had done the world a favor.

"Long story," I warned. "Better take a seat. It's been a really bad day."

"Yeah, tell me about it." He sank into a comfy pedestal recliner and put up his feet, sipping his bourbon as if he'd been born to luxury. Well, actually, he had. I just hadn't known it when we were dating.

The opulence made me antsy. Or just hearing Max

made me horny. Whatever. I curled up on the couch and refused to look at him as I recited my tale of woe from the gas cloud on. I left out our battle over the homeless guys in the basement and that Sarah had been caught mid-shift. I just said we'd rescued a friend from the plant and verified that Acme was covering up their disaster.

I didn't want to tell him that I'd been invisible, so I glossed over my time at Gloria's by saying I'd been hiding, and that no one had known I was there. I didn't think Max would encourage me to act as a witness under those circumstances.

He rubbed his hand through his hair when I was finished, glanced longingly at the bar, and gallantly resisted. "Gloria turned into a demon?" he asked in incredulity. "Are you sure Andre didn't gas her into one?"

"Gloria had you killed!" I shouted. "Gloria and Dane were up to their stinking asses in crap. You know that. They're holding hostages in their dungeon! Haven't you found evidence of what they're doing at Acme yet? Or have you been too busy tossing bimbos to try?"

That brought him back to the Max I knew. He glared. "You never were one to win votes with your sterling personality and charm. I can't interfere in Acme's business. Period. You sure you want Andre to go free?"

"Damned right I do!" I was running out of steam now that I'd said my piece. I sighed and shoved my mass of hair out of my face. "You really don't want me running things in the Zone while working out of the judge's office in my spare time. Right now, the media is crawling all over. Do you want me zapping them?"

That ought to give him pause. I'd literally blown reporters away the last time they got in my way.

Since he had his stubborn face on, I continued my argument. "The Zone needs Andre, not me. So no matter what you think of him, we have to persuade a judge to bond him out. I'm not asking for money. I'm simply asking you to use your influence as Gloria's grandson. Say she had become senile and violent lately. Tell them Andre's story is credible, and that your mother's security guards are capable of collusion. Tell them anything you want. You know they'll listen."

"That burns, doesn't it?" he said wryly, unexpectedly. "I always resented Dane's influence. I'd always thought that if I'd had his power, I could change the world. It's not as easy as it looks from the outside."

"Cry me a river," I muttered. "You've got it a lot easier than the rest of us."

"In some ways," he agreed. "But every good deed requires payback. If I make a few calls, they'll expect favors in return. I swear, some of these guys have scorecards in their heads that date back decades. I'm thinking of creating a spreadsheet to keep up with who owes what to whom and why."

"Try deciding whether sending someone to hell is worth years of eternal damnation," I said. "I'm thinking if I visualize anyone else into danger, I'm cutting my life short here on earth. We're both walking on quicksand."

Max had been in hell when I'd done most of my mumbo jumbo, but he'd been aware on some level that I'd been throwing my Saturnian weight around. He seemed interested and tired as he fit my complaint with his little bit of knowledge. Apparently deciding he didn't need to know more, he nodded.

"You really think Acme has invented some kind of gas that causes violent reactions?" he asked, succinctly nailing down my case.

"That's the only conclusion we can reach. I figure they thought they were developing a weapon, but that's what happened as far as we can see. I'm no scientist, but even Paddy agrees."

I'd been hesitant about mentioning Dane's crazy-inventor father, but if Max would help me, I had to let him know that his new family wasn't entirely what they seemed.

"Paddy? And you believe a crazy guy?" he asked with rightful suspicion.

"I think he's crazy like a fox. Now that Gloria's not breathing the flames of hell down his back, he's making sense. You want that story, too?"

He shook his head. "Not right now. Let me make some calls before everyone's gone to bed. Does Andre have a lawyer yet?"

"Just me, for now. Julius is on it, but I have a feeling that the sooner I bail Andre out, the better off the world will be."

"That almost makes sense. Let me flip through Dane's call list and see what I can do. I hate making cold calls and not knowing if Dane's made an enemy or a pal of whoever is on the other end." He pulled out his smart phone and began scrolling through his contacts.

Not wanting to listen in on any uncomfortable discussions, I wandered around the big room. I really wanted to find his office and bedroom and see if there were any signs of my Max in Dane's elegant home, but I was too edgy. My nerve ends felt like they'd spit bullets if crossed. I didn't want to imagine Andre losing his cool in some crappy jail cell with perverts and drunks while I looked for a reason to hook up with an old boyfriend.

Because that was pretty much what I was doing: looking for excuses to trust Max again. It wasn't smart, safe, or entirely rational, just my hormones talking.

Luckily, my hormones weren't entirely engaged by Dane's slick good looks. So I was resisting.

By the time Dane put down the phone, I was back in control again. This was Dane the senator, not Max the biker. He had influence out the wazoo and appearances to keep up. A nobody like Tina Clancy didn't fit into that picture.

"We lucked out," he said. "Judge Snodgrass is an old friend of both Julius and Paddy. He's willing to take my word that Gloria wasn't rational. He can't get the charges dropped, of course. But the judge can put in a good word and have bail posted. I told him Andre had served with Special Ops and suffers from PTSD, so he's willing to see it done tonight."

Snodgrass was my boss. That Dane/Max had been

able to extract a promise from him with a single call pretty much proved the senator had landed my job for me.

I wanted to hug him for everything he was doing for us. He looked as if he expected it. I had a sad feeling it wouldn't stop with hugs. Dane's testosterone and Max's memories were a combustible combination.

He was still sitting in his recliner, so I leaned over, stroked his bristly jaw, and kissed him in gratitude. "I owe you more than one, Danny Boy. I've got a long ride to Towson and an early wake-up call in the morning, so let's not think whatever you're thinking, okay?"

"For saving me from Glenys, I'll let you go this time, Justy," he agreed wearily. "But I think we should both just take Dane's money and retire to the South Pacific."

"You might have a point." And I actually meant it, except I kept picturing my mother running from town to town all my life, and knew running from my duties would solve nothing. "But unfortunately, we're not cowards. So let's see where this road leads us."

"I've already been to hell. Can't be much worse," he said cynically, getting up to see me out.

I thought I saw him standing in his window when I drove away. Lonely didn't cover how either of us was feeling.

I drove the freeway to Towson with no traffic or monsters stopping me, only a few lumbering semis to dodge. And I could have sworn I saw another soldier in camouflage strolling down a lane with a screaming infant, but that could have been wishful thinking. Peace on earth, goodwill toward men . . . Lovely dream. I needed to focus on Andre.

I was only a newbie lawyer. Despite my license, I'd never worked the courthouse, and the only police action I'd seen had been from the wrong side of the bars. By the time I arrived at the precinct, figured out the Byzantine jail system, and sprang Andre, it was pushing midnight. As we emerged from the building and walked to the nearly empty parking lot, I noticed he had turned pretty gray around the edges. After all the warnings, I worried about him.

"You're not looking so good, Boss," I said. "Do we need to stop for anything before heading out?" We were still a good half hour's drive from the Zone.

"It's nothing, Clancy. Just take me home. How is everyone holding up?" He sank down into the passenger seat without fighting me for the keys, so I knew he was done in.

"Sarah is back. The bomb shelter is good, but you'll need a new secret tunnel. I have a lead on getting rid of one of our patients. Nancy Rose probably has insurance, so we could send her to a local hospital if you think Acme will back off now that the witch is dead. Still working on the others."

"Gloria was my godmother," Andre said without inflection. "She was a good person once."

We both sat silently thinking about how power corrupts. Or that's what I was thinking about. I wasn't sure what Andre was doing—until he spoke again.

"I'm not going to make it back. Just park in the alley and call my father. He'll know what to do. Stay on Snodgrass's good side if you know what's good for you."

He leaned the seat back and just like that, he conked out. No warning, just out like a light.

Like our comatose patients.

17

I'd been counting on Andre to carry his share of the load, and now he was as useless as the homeless guys in the bomb shelter. I knew this wasn't any ordinary sleep. A strong man like Andre checking out like that gave me cold chills. Being left out here alone with no backup had me pondering Seattle again. But I couldn't desert a friend, and whatever else he was, Andre was a friend.

Just to give me heart failure and to prove the Zone wasn't on my side, the road beneath my wheels began to rumble as I hit Edgewater. Streetlights swayed and one of the gargoyles took flight. Andre didn't stir. It was the wee hours of Monday and even Chesty's was closed, so no one ran screaming into the streets. Fatalistically, I waited for the road to open and swallow us.

The rumble stopped before I drove up the hill. I had to wonder if the pink particles were eating their way to hell and creating chasms beneath our feet. Or maybe the Zone had just sneezed. Maybe instead of worrying about rescuing Bill, I should be thinking about evacuating the area.

Thanks to Andre's comatose state, I had no one with whom to share my fears. I punched his arm. Hard. He didn't stir.

I tried erasing worry with grumbling as I parked in the alley and trekked upstairs to wake Julius. I'd gotten myself all tarted up and contemplated surrendering my nonexistent virtue to a schizophrenic senator to save Andre's sorry ass for what? And didn't it just figure that the first time I relied on a man, he conked out.

I started remembering the other times I'd counted on Andre and he'd disappeared. Maybe he had sleeping sickness. Maybe I should have one of the baby docs examine him. No telling what kind of disease he'd picked up overseas. I was back to fretting by the time I reached his father's apartment.

Julius only nodded sadly when I pounded on his door and woke him up. He thanked me for everything I'd done, assured me that Andre would be just fine, that I should go home and get some sleep. I hated that. I wanted to make things better. Stupid.

Too tired and shaken to argue, I went back to my place, hoping I wouldn't have a dead body in my car when I went to work in a few hours.

I needed anger to cover the pain, a trick I'd discovered in the course of my misspent youth. If I stayed angry long enough, it obliterated all softer emotions. Sometimes anger even crushed the fear, but that's when I got stupid. I was trying to avoid stupid these days.

Wondering if Schwartz was sleeping soundly in his bed across the hall, or if Paddy was up inventing ways to burn down the house, I unlocked my door and hunted for my cat. Milo was always glad to see me, even if he just needed me for a pillow.

A dog might run and jump into my arms and lick my face. Milo merely glanced at me disdainfully and circled his empty bowl. See, me and Milo were soul mates. All we needed was to be fed. I added some dry food to his bowl but didn't bother feeding myself.

I dropped my clothes on the floor in the dark and was pulling back the covers on the bed when I noticed the rectangular shape of my stolen tablet computer lying on top of them. I didn't think I'd left it there. I'm rather cautious with expensive machinery.

My nerves already rattled, I glanced around, but the sliding doors were shut and barred. I slipped on an old T-shirt and turned on a light.

Pressing the power button, I opened to a screen that read, *Rule #1: Visualization for personal gain will kick you in the butt in direct correlation to the extent of gain.*

It was signed, *The Fat Chick.*

The Fat Chick? The one in the wheelchair?

No e-mail address. The message was a damned wallpaper covering up my screen. Some screwup had hacked my tablet and replaced the background with— *a rulebook*?

I'd wished for a rulebook. And daddy dearest had provided? No, the Fat Chick. How had she accessed a computer I'd just acquired? And why? Or—horror of horrors—had this come from Acme?

I poked around a little but I was too tired to concentrate and couldn't see anything else that might actually constitute a real book instead of a modern translation of Themis's spooky warning. Frustrated, I turned off the light and went to bed. I had exactly five hours left to sleep.

Which is when it struck me—I'd been rewarded after midnight. Usually, my rewards appeared when I got up in the morning. Since I'd not been to bed, I'd received this one a little earlier.

Sending Gloria to hell had only earned me a stupid rule instead of bigger boobs or better brains? I needed to start paying attention to what I wished for. Or maybe since Gloria had already sold her soul, she wasn't worth much.

Early Monday morning, I stumbled out of bed when the radio alarm growled. It was supposed to play hard rock. The Zone—or pink ash—was apparently spreading its tentacles, but I didn't have time to work out this latest mechanical kink. I was nothing if not determined. For the last dozen years of my life I'd been working toward one goal: becoming a lawyer. If eventually having my own office meant serving coffee to Judge Snooty and his minions, so be it.

I also wanted to check on Andre, see how our patients were doing, and if Julius had retrieved the cloud can from Tim. I desperately needed to get in touch with Fat Chick, but all I had time to do was shower and dress. Dane/Max had used his clout to get me this job, and after last night, it was obvious that clout was exceedingly useful. I wanted my share of it.

Rather than disturb Andre if he was still sleeping in my car, I took the Harley to work. Unprofessional, maybe, but it got me through rush-hour traffic in record time, although it also earned me a fair share of middle-finger salutes.

No one at the office acknowledged my existence. It was almost like being back in law school. I scurried from one task to the next, asking only if people wanted cream and sugar, or both criminal and torte law cases. I made phone calls, ran errands, provided copies.

In the courthouse halls, I overheard whispered conversations about the unusual circumstances of the Vanderventer murder case. Apparently, lawyers like discussing gory details. And if they aren't gory enough, they make up more gruesome ones. The story was taking on a life of its own. And for a change, no one connected me with it at all.

Anonymity had suited me for years while I earned my degree. It didn't sit so well now that I'd had a taste of what I was capable of doing. I wanted to know what the establishment thought about Andre's case and Gloria's behavior and the Vanderventer fortune. I wanted in on those conversations so I could help.

I didn't need Tim to make me invisible. In here, I already was.

Seething with unhealthy frustration, I poured coffee.

I knew I needed to learn the courthouse ropes, and the judge's office was the best place to learn. I wasn't arrogant enough to believe that good grades and a few law books would make a lawyer of me, but neither would acting as a glorified secretary.

I kept my ears open, hoping I'd pick up the name of a strong defense attorney for Andre. Instead, all I heard were reasons for giving his case a wide berth. It seemed Andre was rumored to be a psychopathic nut job his father was protecting.

Okay, so chances were good that Andre *was* borderline psycho—except Gloria had been the one who'd gone berserk, not Andre. But the Vanderventers were wealthy, and Andre was an unknown factor. Odds were stacking up against him. I'd been the underdog enough to know how that worked.

It didn't help that Andre had actually produced pics of Gloria, once given access to a computer. It seemed Dane's glorified asshat of a grandmother had liked displaying her naked plastic assets around the pool boy—where the security cameras could see them. The courthouse gossip was ugly.

My frustration increased. Over lunch, I pulled out case law establishing precedent for Andre's situation and began preparing a defense outline. Of course, I had more inside info than the average dick, but the case was fairly basic: accidental death. Playing the witnesses was the key. If the witnesses told the truth, they wouldn't even have a manslaughter charge against Andre.

I could, of course, attempt to visualize the witnesses into honesty. I had no idea if it would work. And since it wasn't exactly punishment for evil deeds, I figured it would come under personal gain and the payback would be painful. I didn't want to end up a chimp or in a wheelchair. Caution had its uses.

I preferred sticking to the law. Andre was innocent. I had no reason to believe that justice couldn't be served legally this time.

I didn't have time to finish the outline before Reggie-baby demanded that I fetch a file from another office. He only had a year's experience more than me, and he was a year younger.

I'd had enough practice these past years to bite my sharp tongue and trot obediently off to do his bidding, even though my lunch break wasn't over. I'd spent a lifetime teaching good behavior to bullies by punching them out. I was an adult now. In this new environment, I had to use subtlety.

I politely delivered both files and coffee. In return, Reggie hugged me and tried to feel me up.

I was willing to put up with a lot, but sexual harassment didn't happen on my time card. Pretending shock and surprise, I accidentally tipped the mug, and hot coffee steamed his Lauren trousers. And probably his Calvin Klein boxers, but I didn't hang around long enough to find out. I left him yelling and yanking off his belt.

Giving me a glare that promised vengeance, Jill dashed off to the restroom for paper towels. I took her place at the front desk and answered phones while surreptitiously scanning the logs to see what cases the judge had on his agenda. Maybe I could study up and get ahead of Reggie. My eyebrows soared when I saw Vanderventer and MacNeill on the list.

As if the Universe had decided I needed a reward for scalding Ivy Boy's balls, the phone rang and caller ID gave me Paddy's name. Interesting.

Pretending I was snobby Jill, I answered with the office name.

"This is Padraig Vanderventer. I need to speak with Judge Snodgrass," he said stiffly, probably because he never used a phone. I was totally amazed that he owned one. They didn't work so hot in the Zone, so he was probably with Julius.

"The judge is in a meeting, Mr. Vanderventer," I said with a completely straight face. "If I may ask what this is in reference to, I can pull the files and have them waiting on his desk when he returns your call."

"Tina, is that you?" he asked with a heavy dose of ill humor. "Is that what they have you doing, answering phones?"

"Ah, what gave me away? And I was trying so very hard, too." So maybe it hadn't been Dane/Max who'd got me this job. Maybe Paddy had. Or Julius. They all apparently knew the old goat.

"No one in that office is ever that efficient," he said with irritation. "Snodgrass was my mother's attorney back in the days when she bothered to consult with anyone besides herself. She should have a will. The MacNeills are already talking to Acme management. I'd like to let them have the cesspool, but I need to keep my access to that building. Can you find the file?"

Jill and Reginald were standing over me, glaring. I admired the dark stain on Reggie's trousers, tapped a pencil on the log, and nodded briskly. "Yes, sir, of course, sir. I'll get right on it."

I hung up, brushed past them as if they were obstacles to be hurdled, and, without offering a word of explanation, proceeded to the file vault. Really, I could play the silly game of one-upmanship. I'm not much of a team player, but my competitive instincts are strong. I knew how to whip Reggie's ass. If he'd been smarter, he'd have learned to work with me instead of against me.

Since Jill thought I was working under the judge's orders, she let me alone. Assuming Gloria had dropped the firm after she'd inherited Acme, I hunted through the pre-computer files from that decade. I located a Vanderventer file, but it contained no will. I quickly scanned documents for anything interesting, but they mostly related to Paddy's father. He hadn't left a will, apparently, but everything he owned had Gloria's name on it. She got the lot. Bad estate planning. The taxes had probably sucked the Gucci right out of her purse.

I entered the file number into the computer to see if there was anything more recent, but as Paddy had said, Gloria went her own way once she had the estate in her hands. Notations of a few phone calls, several discussions and notes about a new will, stock exchanges, and land sales. There should have been a draft, at least, but there wasn't.

Control issues was my bet. She could have been given a draft, asked that it be stricken from her file, and never returned for a final to keep snoops like me out of her business. A bank could have had the documents witnessed and notarized without contacting a law office. If she had stored the final copy in a bank box, my assessment of the lady's intelligence would drop by fifteen IQ points.

As I'd promised Paddy, I placed copies of the appropriate files on the judge's desk along with Paddy's message, or the message he would have left had I not cut him off so abruptly. Jill and Reggie would pry, but there wasn't anything I could do about that.

As a bonus, Reggie didn't ask me for any more coffee. I returned to filing until almost closing time, when Jill came back to my cubbyhole with a peculiar expression on her face.

"Senator Vanderventer wishes to speak with you," she announced.

I didn't say a word or blink an eyelash. Nodding as if senators regularly called me, I picked up the extension and waited pointedly for Jill to get her ass away from my closet. With a scowl, she did, although I noticed she left the door partially open.

"Senator, how good to hear from you so soon," I said in my best professional voice, before I got up and closed the door tightly.

"You didn't answer your cell," Max said with irritation. "What is this crap about Gloria getting it on with the pool boy? I'll kill Andre myself."

"I can't take personal calls while on the job," I chirped. "So this had better be business. If I were you, I'd delete the footage from the security cameras around the pool. Otherwise, did you want Gloria's will, too?"

"Have you taken up mind reading? No, don't answer that," he said hastily. "Has the judge found it?"

"The judge wouldn't know where to look if you shoved it up his ass. I scoured the files. There isn't a will or any record of one being filed. That doesn't mean there isn't one somewhere else, just not here. I'm waiting for him to return. Want me to ask what he knows?"

"Yeah, or the next media blitz will be about the two families going at each other with axes, with me caught in the middle. Although I'm willing to cut Andre's throat, too, if pressed. My father and sister are already moving in over there. They seem to think the place is theirs, since anything I inherit goes in the trust. When did Paddy come back to his senses?"

"When Gloria died would be the best answer." Especially since I didn't know if the gas attack had anything to do with it. "The man's no fool, just not willing to fight his own mother or the forces of evil. Be careful, Max. It may be hard to believe, but I'm thinking the devil walks this earth, and Acme is his playground."

"That's almost ridiculous enough to believe. Talk to Snodgrass. Have him call me. I can't believe I have to fight my father and Dane's at the same time. I really don't need this right now."

Technically speaking, *Max's* grandmother, Ida Vanderventer, had inherited most of her husband's share of Acme. Apparently Ida had been letting her son-in-law sit on the board in her place. Ex-senator Michael MacNeill loved throwing his considerable weight around, and he and Gloria had apparently worked hand in glove. Paddy and MacNeill? Probably not so much.

MacNeill could be right. Gloria might have left her shares to him instead of Paddy. Or not.

I could hear phones ringing and voices in the background while Max waited for my reply. Senators were busy men. I sighed with regret. Talking on the phone, where I couldn't see his Dane disguise, was almost like having the old Max back.

"I'll do what I can," I promised. "I hope you have someone guarding Granny's house, because you'll have your family all over it shortly."

"The place crawls with guards," he said sardonically, "all of them looking after their own asses. Have the judge call me."

He hung up abruptly, leaving me with an image of

all the black suits walking around, glancing over their shoulders at their pretty tushies. An amusing image, enough to leave a smile on my face when the judge entered.

"Clancy, I need to talk with you," he thundered. He wasn't a tall man, but he wielded enough stomach to give him an air of authority.

"Of course, sir. Do you want a report on Senator Vanderventer's call, or should I just leave a message on your desk? It appears his grandmother hasn't left a will, and there's some consternation among the family."

He frowned, diverted from his tirade. "Gloria refused to leave a copy in the office or let me file one. You mean to say she didn't give a copy to anyone else, either?"

"Appears so, Your Honor. As I'm sure you're aware, she's not been entirely rational these past years." It wouldn't hurt to butter up Andre's case while I was at it. "The family needs to know who is legally responsible for the upkeep of the estate and various enterprises."

"Basic law, Clancy. Without a will, it's her direct descendants, Padraig and Dane. I don't remember her ever specifying anyone else. I'll give them a call." He went out shaking his head and muttering about giving millions of dollars to a crackpot who couldn't comb his hair. I assumed that reference was to Paddy. Dane's hair was never out of place.

My duty was done for the day. With my nose stuck higher than Reggie's, I sailed out of the office and hit the Harley. I really needed to see that my home was still safe. Somewhere along the way, the world outside the Zone had become alien to me. I needed the Zone's eccentricities to keep me grounded and provide the security I'd lacked most of my life.

And yeah, that was pretty pathetic.

18

I didn't take time to eat after I got home from work but grabbed a handful of Nutribars and munched while shucking off my office clothes and changing into more functional jeans. I didn't own an elaborate wardrobe and had opted for skirts for professional dress for years, but now that my leg was straight, jeans fit better than they used to.

I checked my tablet to see if any new rules had appeared, but Fat Chick's message still scrolled across the screen.

Themis had said, *Visualizing is an unusual gift. Use it for harm, and justice will be served. Use it for profit, and you will pay.* Was this how Fat Chick had paid? Was that how she'd known about Rule #1? I hoped whatever she'd visualized for gain had been worth the wheelchair.

Milo opted for action and followed me over to Andre's place. My former boss didn't keep regular hours, so I never knew where he'd be or when, even on a workday like today. I just wanted to know that he was back to normal.

As usual, no one answered my knock. I let myself in and decided to check on our patients first. I figured if Andre was around, he'd know I'd arrived.

I fretted over Bill, but to be honest, the thought of another assault on the dungeon scared the crap out of me. There was no way I could blow my way out of a subbasement without bringing the entire plant crashing down on our heads.

But I could hope that, with Gloria gone and Paddy moving in, Acme would do the right thing. Maybe. Eventually. So I wouldn't have to face the dragons in the dungeon.

Two of the baby docs were consulting over our homeless guys in the theater. One of them was the red-haired former soldier from yesterday. They'd set up a battery of equipment they'd probably borrowed from Johns Hopkins' supply closets. Someone had trimmed the patients' beards and hair and found clean hospital gowns for them.

I suspected most of these old guys were vets who would come up roaring in outrage if we discovered how to flip their switches. But they were polite pussycats for now.

"No news?" I asked when the docs glanced up. "I

have a taker for a patient if anyone wants to make a run to Massachusetts."

"Andre said it was okay to use this place if we can keep it staffed," the red-haired doc replied. "The study results are so phenomenal that we're using our off-duty hours to rotate. We can sleep here."

He indicated a couple of empty cots they'd set up. "It's working out. So thanks, but no thanks."

I shrugged. "No skin off my nose. Are you sure they're alive and functioning?"

"We can't do MRIs, but we've run EEGs." He nodded at the equipment. "Full electrical neuron activity detected. Their health is improving and stabilizing. We can't find any reason for the vegetative state."

"Side effect worse than the cure," I muttered enigmatically, thinking of the gas. "Shame. Anyone tried to come over the tunnel wall lately?"

The doc who had wielded weapons the other day made a note in his tablet and shook his head. "It's been quiet. Maybe now that Old Lady Vanderventer is gone, Acme will back off. If Andre really killed her, he did the world a favor."

"He didn't kill her. The gas did, one way or another. Is anyone feeding you?"

Both docs appeared interested. Red answered. "We've been foraging from our apartments but haven't had time for grocery shopping."

"Let me see what Julius has. I'm in the mood for tacos. That work?"

They didn't seem thrilled but nodded acceptance.

They'd never eaten my tacos. They'd not go back to pizzas again.

I jogged upstairs and to the floor where Julius and Tim resided. Tim's apartment was small and similar to mine, but Julius lived in spacious elegance, with a well-stocked kitchen. He never left the house, but Andre provided everything he could need and more.

Julius's face had gained a few more lines since I'd seen him last.

"Andre?" I asked first.

"Down at Chesty's. We still haven't found a lawyer willing to take his case." He led me back to the kitchen.

I tried not to breathe too deeply in relief that Andre had overcome his near-comatose state. Maybe I'd been mistaken and he'd just stressed out and needed sleep.

Julius and I bonded over food. He couldn't cook. I hated to eat alone. It worked. I talked while examining the contents of his freezer. "The courthouse is buzzing. I bet if you'd just go over there and schmooze a little, you could persuade them that the state doesn't have a case."

"I can't leave Katerina," he said sadly. "I'm too out of touch to schmooze anyway. We'll keep trying. Maybe the witnesses will change their stories."

"One of them slugged Gloria. One of their guns caused her to flip over. Nope, they won't be talking truth anytime soon." I nuked some chicken breasts to defrost them and started chopping veggies.

I wondered if there was any way I could do a

Marley's ghost routine and terrify the goons into telling the truth, but I just couldn't see how it would work. That's the problem with visualization—I have to be able to imagine it. Besides, I didn't want to end up in any wheelchair for misusing my power. I needed to spend more time on that website. And see if Fat Chick answered questions better than Themis or Sarah.

We were stuck between a rock and a hard place. I was too inexperienced to know the right lawyer. Julius was too out of touch.

We set that topic aside and wandered to the next. "What about the gas cloud can? Did you get Tim to cough it up?" I whacked chicken and flung pieces in a frying pan.

"He swears he doesn't have it. Could it have fallen out of your bag on the ride back here?"

Saturn preserve us, I hoped not. "If Milo didn't fall out, I don't see how the can could have," I said with a little more assurance than I felt. "Maybe it rolled under some furniture? I'll take a look later." I frowned, trying to remember my progress yesterday. I was pretty certain I'd come straight to Andre's back door before setting down the tote.

I was filling taco shells for Julius when Paddy arrived. The windows were open and the air was redolent of chicken and jalapeños, so I figured his nose had led him here. I already had another batch cooking for the docs, so I dished up a third plate. Tacos are easy and can be anything you want them to be when you have a stocked larder. I preferred veggies to beans and rice, but the men took everything. With extra cheese and a jar of guacamole.

"We need to search the mansion," Paddy said without preamble.

He'd spent so many years outside society, his manners could use some polish. Of course, if he'd been an engineer of some sort, maybe he'd always been socially inept.

"Right." I savored the first decent meal I'd had in days and slipped Milo a bit of chicken under the table. "Snodgrass says you and Dane get to fight over your mother's assets if no will is found, so the two of you have at it."

No way was I trying to explain to Paddy that his son had grown a conscience thanks to Max. I had enough headaches to juggle. I'd let the two of them work it out. First, they'd have to try talking to each other.

"The judge says I need an estate lawyer to file a probate claim," Paddy said gloomily. "I don't want that family gate to hell, but if I don't inherit the entire controlling share, Dane's trust executor will sell to MacNeill, and I'll be booted out. MacNeill is dangerous."

"Probate is easy. Even I can do that." I took another mouthful of taco before I realized both men were staring at me. "What?" I asked through my cheese.

The two old friends seemed to be communicating silently. Fine, at least I'd had a chance to eat before they crucified me.

"It might work," Julius said softly, tapping his fingers on the table. "We should probably talk to Andre."

I waited. They didn't let me in on the secret. Hurt but not wanting to show it, I rolled my eyes. Finishing my taco, I rose to put my plate in the sink and gather a tray of fixings for the docs.

They didn't mind talking to me when they wanted something, but I was excess baggage otherwise. Fine. I'd been on my own most of my life. I was good with that.

No, I wasn't. I'd hated being an outsider as a kid. It's a lonely existence. I'd enjoyed making friends in the Zone. I thought they'd accepted me.

I used to have Max, but he was out of reach now. Maybe Schwartz would like some tacos.

I even considered entertaining the docs with my presence when they fell gratefully on the grub. But in the end, I decided Mom was right. Knowledge was power, and I needed to brush up on mine. Loneliness was irrelevant.

Milo checked out all the patients a second time, then obediently trotted after me when I returned home. I swear, he'd appointed himself my guard cat.

Which is why I felt perfectly safe unlocking my apartment door and walking in without turning on the lights. Milo didn't warn me.

A dark figure rose out of the shadows and swung a bat at me.

19

My own baseball bat flying out of the night in my own damned home shouldn't have been happening. I had good locks. I practiced caution. But I'd been caught by surprise once in the last dozen years, and it had nearly cost me a leg. Since then, I'd learned to duck and roll.

I ducked. I rolled. I pulled my steel-reinforced messenger bag over my vitals.

I came up kicking. I caught my assailant squarely in the groin. Or I would have, except he was faster than me. He sidestepped and leaned on his bat, waiting for me to come at him again.

Which made absolutely no sense in the world of dirty fighting. My next move should have been to go at his knees, the goal being to bring him down and get my thumbs on his jugular. But that bat could bust my knees or my spine in the process.

Besides, I could smell him now, a woodsy aroma with a hint of spice. I sat up and leaned against the wall. "What in hell was that for? I get you out of jail so you can bust my ass?"

Andre returned my bat to its hiding place and settled on my aging couch. "Just testing your reflexes. You'll be needing them."

"For what?" I asked suspiciously.

"Just write it off to my bad dreams." He dismissed his weird statement with the wave of a hand.

"How did you get in?" But I knew as soon as I asked. I'd given a spare key to my landlady. Pearl would have been putty in Andre's hands.

"Proves you haven't learned the extra caution it takes if you're planning on staying in the Zone against all better sense," he said, not answering my question.

"Until you, no one has attacked me in my apartment," I grumbled. Make a prediction vague and broad enough, and eventually some form of it would materialize. Andre was a master at fuzzy prophecies. "It's only out in the real world that people come after me with guns and cameras."

"Don't believe that for a minute," he warned, leaning against the couch cushion, crossing his hands behind his head, and sprawling his long legs across the floor. "We have the guinea pigs Acme wants, and they've already proved they're willing to use force to get them. I don't want you to be our weak link."

I preferred having this discussion in the dark. I don't entertain and don't own much in the way of furniture. I wasn't about to sit next to Andre on the couch. I pulled down a cushion and leaned against the wall. "Sarah's the one who shifted before their wondering eyes. You're the friggin' moron who went after Gloria and ended up in jail. Anyone can be a weak link."

"Okay, then you're *my* weak link. I need to know I can trust you. I don't even know what you are or if you're here to help us or destroy us. And that annoys the hell out of me." Über-cool Andre did not express emotion, but the man sitting here in the dark was walking a thin edge, frustration being the least cause of his testiness. "How did you wake up Sarah?"

"I didn't do any damn thing," I said, matching his frustration. "Even I don't know what I am," I added with as much scorn as I could muster, "so you get to take me at face value, just like anyone else. And if you swing one more bat at me, your ass is grass. I get enough grief elsewhere. What do you want, Andre?"

"Besides you?"

His voice was low and sexy and there was a certain appeal to sitting here in the dark, my cat curling in my lap and a hunk of glorious male relaxing on my furniture. My gonads hummed in expectation. Some casual sex would do us both good. But I'd learned the hard way that there's no such thing as casual sex with someone you see every damned day. Or with someone who's mental enough to come after you with a bat.

"Swinging a bat at me is not how to get on my

good side, dipstick. Try another." I squashed hormonal hope, his and mine.

"I need a lawyer." It cost him to say that, I could tell.

I was still ticked by the bat and didn't intend to make this easy. "Yeah, I gathered that. Julius is in a better position than I am to find you one. Oddly, people regard you with suspicion. How many lawyers have you swung a bat at lately?"

He ignored my sarcasm. "My father went to school with half those old farts at the courthouse, and the younger ones learned at his knee. They watched me grow up. You really don't think I want a lawyer who used to dandle me on his lap?"

I snorted at the image. "You took bats to them, didn't you?" I asked. "They tried to butter up your father by playing ball with you. What did you do, beat 'em all out of the park?"

"Sometimes," he agreed, without concern. "I wasn't a polite child. But I freaked most of them out when I came home and decided Acme was to blame for my mother's coma. When no one would take the case, I pulled an assault rifle on them. They have reason to believe I'm psycho."

Well, yeah, he probably had been. Might still be now. But he also had a point. "Not helping your case, macho man," I said anyway, wanting more info than Andre is ever willing to give. "Someone give you Prozac? That's why you're so cool now?"

It was his turn to snort. "Hell, no. Gloria gave me a job at the plant to shut me up. Told me to snoop around all I wanted, see if I could prove Acme had anything to do with my mother's condition. I shut up, learned to play Joe Cool, and almost got fried in the chemical flood a few months later."

"Intentionally?" I had to ask.

"That's a question only the devil can answer."

Typically, he cut off the communication just as it was getting interesting by dropping to the floor next to me. Without warning, he swung one leg over mine and trapped me between his knees. I scrambled to escape; my cushion slipped, and I toppled backward. Milo had the sense to leap for safety before he was squashed by Andre's weight. Andre had me flat on the floor with his big arms propped on either side of me before I could manage a protest.

Okay, maybe the humming gonads were in control after all. I really liked his crotch pressed into mine.

He planted kisses behind my ear and along my throat, and I shivered in anticipation. So much for my much-touted determination. The man was dynamite. I ached for more. As a diversion from a touchy topic, his move worked much too well.

Not according to plan, Andre propped his weight on his hands and bulging biceps and continued talking, depriving me of more intimate contact. "Paddy pulled me out of the flood. It was a Saturday night. I don't know what he was even doing at the plant on a weekend. I didn't know about the Magic lab then, but I suspected it."

I didn't scramble away. Torn between wanting sex and his story, I waited.

He bent over and kissed my lips this time, frying

my brain before I could absorb the implications of Andre caught in a chemical flood. I wrapped my arms around his neck and drank in magic sex. Damn, but he was too good. I was hot and ready and so not doing this.

I grabbed his ears and yanked him out of my face. "Why are you telling me now?" I demanded.

Andre shifted upward, removing his ears from the imminent danger of my fingernails. He straddled my waist and cupped my breasts. I nearly creamed my pants until I summoned my damned rebellious self-control and tried to scramble out from under him. When he found the opening to my shirt, I located the pulse point on his arm and applied enough pressure to cut off circulation. Rather than lose use of an arm, he swung off me and leaned against the wall as I'd been doing earlier.

I hurried to sit up again. The battle of the sexes held new meaning when Andre and I went at it.

"We have to get Bill and the others out of Acme's lab before the place blows again," Andre announced, as if he'd just said, *Thanks for the quick lay.*

"Paddy can do that if he inherits, can't he?" I grabbed my cushion and scooted out of his range.

"There will be court battles and power struggles if Paddy tries to take over, but we need to see he has the chance," he agreed. "It just won't help Bill right now. I think there's more going on over there than even Gloria knew. I can't keep an eye on Acme from a jail cell. Haven't you felt the rumbles?"

Damn, I'd been afraid those mini-earthquakes

weren't my imagination. Andre knew damned well I couldn't abandon Bill to potential disaster. "What can I do?" I asked.

"Be my lawyer," he said without inflection. "Keep me out of jail so we can stop Acme."

He might as well have come after me with the bat again. Except I knew how to tumble and roll from a weapon. I didn't know how to avoid a responsibility so huge I figured it would crush me like a spider under a steamroller. I gaped in amazement, but I doubted he could see me.

"I don't have one iota of courtroom experience," I protested, shoving back to lean against the wall. "It's a murder one rap! I don't own a law library. I don't have a defense team of any sort. You're asking the insane."

"Not totally," Andre argued. "No one else will take my case, so you're a better option than nothing."

"Thanks," I muttered, neatly put in my place.

He ignored that. "My father's available to offer his expertise and experience. He just won't leave the house, so you have to be his face in the courtroom. He has the library and the contacts. And you have one advantage that no one else does—you understand the Zone and what's at stake. To anyone else, we're scum. They have nothing to lose if I go to jail."

I had enough conceit to entertain the idea with great glee. I could rub Reggie's nose in my dust. But I'm a realist as well, dammit. "You're putting your life in feeble hands, Legrande. If money isn't an issue, we can go outside Baltimore for representation."

"The Zone needs its own lawyer, Clancy," he said wearily. "Paddy needs someone to handle the estate's probate. We need to see that he has full access to Acme. We have problems that no normal lawyer can address. And you have the key to justice."

He had a point there, possibly in more ways than he understood. I pushed the heels of my palms into my eyes and tried to work around it. The legal system didn't recognize shape-shifters and snake conjurers like Sarah and Cora. It didn't understand dollar bills that turned to winking Georges or traffic lights that blinked purple. The law liked black and white and not the shades of neon that existed here.

And once I had enough evidence for a case, I could make my own justice—without court approval. Heady—*dangerous*—stuff. But I wasn't certain Andre fully comprehended that I could be his judge and jury.

"Julius is on board with this?" I asked, stalling. I'd seen that look Julius and Paddy had exchanged. This was their friggin' idea. They'd just had to run it by Andre first.

"I wouldn't have asked otherwise," he said, as expected. "If nothing else, it will give my father something constructive to do besides mope over what can't be changed. I wouldn't ask if I thought you couldn't do it. I wouldn't ask if I thought you would move on and have a life. But whatever you are, Clancy, it's not normal."

"You're such a flatterer." I pushed off the wall and snapped on a light. Andre appeared paler than he should have, but there wasn't anything wrong with the rest of him. Giving his bulging trouser front a look of regret, I headed for the kitchen.

"I can set up an office for you across the street," he called from the front room. "It's still clear from Zone interference and not too damaged from the explosion. You can have the latest equipment, access to online libraries. I can't promise you'll make a living wage."

Which would mean a huge step up for me, actually. With my own office and equipment, I could make more money than I was as an intern. It would be far more satisfying than serving coffee and answering phones. Although I'd have to answer my own phone. I couldn't afford a secretary.

I needed to cool off and quit thinking with my hoo-ha, which was twitching with a desperate craving for what Andre had started. I took a couple of cold drinks out of the refrigerator and returned to the parlor. Andre hadn't moved from the floor. His weird blue-green eyes were light against his dark lashes and regarded me questioningly, but he took the drink and gulped half the can while I settled back on my floor cushion.

He was wearing brown silk tonight, with the buttons half undone. Khaki trousers, so he was going for informal. I had a hunch that T-shirts and jeans represented his old life, and he was making a statement with his choice of business attire. I could dig that.

I sipped my drink and tried to settle my rampaging hormones. He could have taken my ribs out with that bat. He would practically own me if he provided office and equipment. I always looked gift horses in the mouth. I'd learned a lot of life lessons by watching westerns. I surely hadn't learned any from my nonexistent father or hippie mother.

"I can handle probate," I told him. "Traffic court, zoning violations, petty civil stuff, with Julius's knowledge, sure. A murder case, no way. I'd have to list Julius as senior partner just to keep the judge from throwing me out. The state's attorney would have to send all evidence to your father, let him make the inquiries we'll need into the background of the witnesses. . . . I don't suppose Paddy can give us any insight into his mother's state of mind or even on the goons she hired?"

Andre almost purred in satisfaction. I had to check that Milo was still asleep in the bay window to be sure they weren't one and the same. Andre finished off the rest of the drink in a few more swallows, then stood up.

"We'll set the office up in the morning. Paddy won't testify for me. He needs to stay neutral so he can have access to the plant. The new and improved senator might say a good word, if you provide incentive. I give you permission to spend whatever you need to investigate Gloria or anyone else. My father can handle the paperwork as long as you make the court appearances. Start with Paddy's probate, though. I'm still dubious of his new sanity. Let's get Acme settled before he dumps blue goo or pink fairy dust in MacNeill's coffee. Two murder cases might be pushing your limits."

That was the Andre I knew, back to being Boss of

the World and the reason we were not going to get it on. Ever.

I didn't get up to see him out. I was thinking I'd rather he'd hit me with the bat. Bumps on the skull merely rattled the brains. Andre was rattling my soul to the core.

He honestly asked the impossible. Licensed or not, no way could a law student step out of class and into a courtroom alone, especially on a case like this. I could be a freakin' genius for all I knew, but I really wasn't an arrogant idiot.

Except, with Julius as my senior partner . . . He'd been out of the world too long to realize the respect he'd earned in these past years of writing textbooks. His name would open doors.

If I could legally put Paddy in charge of Acme, we could rescue Bill and Leibowitz before the next disaster, knock wood.

I could hope I'd gather enough evidence to justifiably red-rage Andre's accusers into another dimension.

Damn, I was actually going to do it. I needed my head examined.

Instead, I unlocked my stolen tablet computer. Someone—presumably Andre—had left a charger and Boris's invoice on the table. I plugged in the tablet and began surfing websites, hoping to find knowledge in my mother's graduation gift. Looking for evidence that I wasn't out of my skull was probably a better description.

Computers are only a minor weapon in my arsenal.

I'm no expert. But from my first quick scan, I judged the websites listed on Saturn's page as amateurish. Themis only had a page advertising her services, with no obvious means of e-mailing her.

Fat Chick's page was little more than a blog. It contained links to sites containing everything from scientific analyses of obesity to far-left political diatribes to academic-sounding astrological advice. Unlike at Saturn's site, however, I could leave comments on her blog. Not many people did.

Words are another weapon I know how to wield. I pondered mine carefully. *Thx for the message, sister,* I typed. *Preach on.* I didn't have a cool tag of my own, so I simply signed in as Justy in D.C. No point in giving away everything, and D.C. wasn't that far away.

I didn't have a website—I'd have to hire Boris to set one up for the law office—so I just signed in on Facebook before typing it.

By the time I'd worked through half the sites on Saturn's page without learning anything except that the participants were as weird, and varied, as I was I had a direct message waiting on my Facebook page: *For real? You got the rule? Friggin' awesome! You have any for me?*

Oh, wow. I stared in incredulity at the seemingly innocuous words on the screen.

I'd found another Saturn's daughter? And she didn't have a rulebook, either?

I didn't know whether to sob or laugh. Saturn was a deadbeat dad.

20

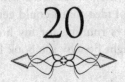

Tuesday morning, I'd barely rolled out of bed when my door knocker rattled the dishes.

"Emergency evacuation!" a stranger's voice shouted.

I froze. Had those earthquakes disrupted gas lines? I waited for the low rumble I feared would blow the neighborhood sky-high.

Nothing.

Milo growled from his nest at the foot of my mattress. Milo's growl is my paranoia alert.

Thinking on my feet, I jerked on jeans and a hoodie, shoved Milo in my bag, stepped onto my balcony, and shimmied down the support. I know that's not a normal reaction to a knock on the door, but my few attempts at normality usually got me hurt. After

Andre's lesson the previous night, I was taking security to new levels.

Hitting the ground, I pondered my next move. I could take the Harley and get the hell out, or satisfy my curiosity and sneak.

I sneaked. Maybe I should tell Fat Chick the next rule is: *Knowledge is power.* We could start a *Rules of Justice* handbook. Or a comic book. That was a pretty cool idea that I could get excited about if I wasn't always running for my life. Or someone else's. Which might be why the book had never been written.

I peered through a crack between the fence boards at the back alley. A plain white sedan blocked the nearest exit. If I tried escaping out the opposite end of the alley, I could be spotted and outraced.

I didn't think emergency personnel drove plain sedans or blocked alleys. *Not normal,* warned my suspicion-ometer.

With back alley escape blocked, the only cover between me and whoever was in the house would be the houses themselves and their overgrown shrubbery. Lacking Andre's nifty tunnel, I had no way of getting out of here, if it was called for.

Before performing any stunts involving the Harley and white sedans, I crept under the shrubbery between Pearl's and the house on the far side from Andre's, intelligently avoiding the hornets in the bushes next to Andre's place.

Another unmarked white car waited in the street. Very weird. Acme's goons usually arrived in fancy black Escalades. Cops would have used marked emergency vehicles.

Tim had been taking care of the potted plants on Pearl's porch lately. They were finally showing signs of life, but the greenery didn't conceal Pearl standing in bewilderment just above where I crouched. She was wringing her hands in her apron and talking to a tall guy in a gray suit and shades. He had the confident stance of a fed and not a shifty goon.

Another one stood on the steps of the neighboring house, speaking to one of the nameless and interchangeable med students. I shrank back into the bushes, hit Leo's private number on my cell, and willed him to answer.

"We have what appears to be feds evacuating the neighborhood," I whispered when I heard his tired *Whassup?* "Where are you and what do you know about this?"

"I'm on the shit shift and just about to head home." He sounded a little more alert. "I've not heard about any evacuation orders. No black-and-whites?"

"None. Which means someone's bluffing, right?"

"They have to have court orders to force you to leave your home. Uniformed emergency personnel can only suggest evacuation, not legally enforce it. At this hour, I'm going with intimidation tactics. They're after our patients."

I liked the way Leo thought. "Can you send us some cops? Or do you want me to do this my way?" I was already mad enough to conjure a gate to hell for thugs harassing old ladies. But evidence was still light on any other wrongdoing. Hell is a stiff penalty for being a bully, and I didn't want to end up in a wheel-chair. Guilt did not necessarily equate evil.

"I've got two cars in the vicinity. Give them ten. I'll be there in thirty." He hung up.

The brute who must have been pounding fu-tilely on my apartment door appeared on the porch, wearing the same menacing attitude of his comrades in arms. He glared at poor Pearl, who shook a little harder. Silver-haired and toothless without her den-tures, Pearl was harmless. I was sure, like everyone else, she had a story. That didn't justify scaring her half to death.

"No one's answering. It's a matter of life and death. If your tenants are asleep, we need your keys to wake them." Gray Suit stuck out his hand, using his authori-tative voice and appearance to pressure my landlady.

It occurred to me then that if these were Acme's goons, they didn't know to which house the ware-house tunnel led. What they really wanted was in Pearl's basement, without any witnesses to see what they were doing.

If these pretend feds were from Acme, someone be-sides Gloria had sent them, which meant Gloria might not have been the only ugly over there. Bad, bad news. We really needed to rescue Bill and the others from the plant before Acme turned them into Frankenstein monsters. Or turned them blue like the buildings. I only hoped it wasn't too late.

Schwartz had said ten minutes until his men could get here, but I could hear sirens screaming in the distance. I had to hope they'd been closer than Schwartz thought and that they were heading this way, because I was about to get obnoxious. Shoving aside the bushes, I sauntered onto the square patch of front lawn.

"Good morning to you, Mrs. Bodine," I called cheerily. I waved at the confused med student wiping sleep from his eyes on the other porch. "Bit early for visitors, isn't it?"

Pearl's jaw relaxed in relief. Paddy had said not to underestimate her, but she seemed happy to see me. The med student narrowed his eyes warily, which was probably the more intelligent reaction to my unusual gaiety.

"These gentlemen say we need to evacuate, dear. Something to do with the chemical cloud, I think?" Pearl said as I approached.

"A little late for that, gentlemen. We've all been exposed and we're all still alive." Milo leaped out of my bag to sniff trouser cuffs and growl. I never knew whether he was half bobcat or dog. I just let him do his thing.

The creep on the stair edged away from Milo. My cat's reputation probably preceded him. He'd nearly ripped the head off one of Acme's guards in the past. I used the cleared space to elbow my way to the porch.

"Federal orders, ma'am," the unfriendly guy behind Pearl snarled. "Mandatory evacuation."

Ignoring him, I patted Pearl's shoulder. "Leo is on his way. Why don't you fry up some nice crisp bacon while I talk to these pretty men?"

"Can't allow you back in there, ma'am," Unfriendly warned, blocking the door with his bulk.

"Unless you have a court order, you can't keep us out," I said, keeping the anger down and the cheer level up. "Legally, by blocking our access to the door, you are giving us no avenue of retreat, which means we can act in self-defense. So let's see the orders, boys." Legal educations are so very useful—at least mine would be, right up until the point I flung the creeps into the bushes.

"Orders aren't needed for an emergency evacuation," the scaredy-cat afraid of Milo countered. "These orders are straight from the top."

On the porch next to us, the med student was listening to our argument and conspicuously blocking his own door. On the other side, Andre's door opened, but no one appeared on his porch. Which probably meant Tim had come out to spy. Julius wouldn't leave Katerina's side, and who knew where Andre was. But knowing I had support just yards away, I managed to keep from losing my cool. There'd been a time when I'd been all alone, and my obnoxiousness got out of hand as a result. These days, I was enjoying company and going for sane.

"We don't have to comply with emergency evacuations," I countered. "Only a court-ordered one. I'll have to see your documents."

The sirens were screaming closer. The gray suits grew restless. Scaredy-Cat on the steps finally produced a packet of papers from an inner pocket and handed them over.

I was angry enough to contemplate ripping them up and flinging them in their faces, but med students and Tim weren't totally reliable bodyguards. Stalling until the cops arrived was the safest route. I bolted down the lid on my pressure-cooker temper and glanced through the bogus legalese, almost laughing at their feeble attempts.

"Very nice, boys," I said. "I could have done better and it would have cost you less, but these appear impressive enough to scare an old lady and a few exhausted interns. Probably wouldn't pass Julius, which is why you're not on his doorstep."

I folded the papers up and handed them back. "You said it yourself, the governor doesn't write up court orders in an emergency, and that's all these papers are declaring. Next time, try to remember who's ordering us out, use a little more imagination, and conjure better excuses. Now leave before we have you arrested."

Which shows where conceit gets you. I'd stupidly thought I could intimidate the intimidators, forgetting that goons carry guns. The one barring the door pressed one into my back.

"This official enough?" he asked, shoving me toward Scaredy-Cat.

Fury fully engaged. I struggled with the red rage, ready to damn them to hell whether they were evil or not. Except, for a change, I'd actually planned ahead and knew precisely how to do this using my smarts. I didn't need Saturn's powers or to risk my eternal soul.

Calculating the goon with the gun behind me wouldn't risk offing his pal, I fell forward and rammed both palms into Scaredy-Cat's chest. He was twice as big as I was, so I couldn't hope to knock him down, just throw him off-balance with surprise. While he staggered to regain his footing, I grabbed his jacket and located the bulge of his gun. I aimed my knee at his balls at the same time I relieved him of his weapon.

I'm not much on guns, and Pearl was in the way of a shoot-out, so disarming was my only intent. I flung the weapon into the shrubbery as Scaredy-Cat gasped and curled around his bruised junk. Saturn had fixed my lameness. That didn't mean he'd made my knees any less bony.

Milo shrieked his mighty roar and leaped for the guy with the gun. But my cat had to sail past Pearl, and his aim was off. He merely landed on the intimidator's shoulder. The goon shouted with pain as Milo ripped at his ear, but he didn't drop the gun. I had to act fast before my cat got hurt.

There were no water sprinklers to imagine raining on this parade. No pots of shit available. I did the best I could with what I had on hand—I called on the yellow-jacket nest I'd been giving wide berth all summer. While Milo ripped an ear, I envisioned enraged wasps and directed them at the intimidator with the gun.

When the right tools are at hand, justice can be swift. I needed to add that to the handbook.

I dropped to the ground, and Pearl had the sense to step out of the way as well.

Man, you'd think the intimidator had personally kicked wasp ass, I thought admiringly as a black, angry cloud rose over the rail. With a little help from my visualization, the furies of hell swarmed out of the bushes like all the plagues of Egypt. Yellow jackets hurt. Even Milo leapt to the rail and over to Tim's porch for safety.

With furious wasps swarming his head, the intimidator hurdled the railing, screaming. He crushed a few half-dead azaleas below and fled for the sedan. While Scaredy-Cat nearly fell off the step dodging angry insects, the main mass of the yellow-jacket nest followed on the gunman's tail. Pearl shrieked and ran back inside. The bugs didn't follow her. They stuck with the gray-suited goon.

With the wasps safely heading in the right direction, I straightened when the guy with bruised balls tried to run and kicked his knee, hard. He howled. That's when the cop cars screamed down the street, a little late for the party.

The med student and his suit merely stared and wisely stayed out of the way of the swarming insects. I figured Tim dodged back inside. He didn't like police or wasps.

I hadn't had my breakfast yet, and I get mean on an empty stomach. I just leaned against the porch rail, crossed my puny brown arms, and let the big men figure out how to handle the situation. *Innocent little ol' me couldn't have caused all this ruckus, right? They're all twice my size.* I shook out my glossy hair and smiled pretty for the men in blue.

Andre arrived in his Mercedes convertible right after the cop cars parked a fair distance from the raging insects. The intimidator was inside his sedan, but yellow jackets have a reputation for a good reason. They'd followed him in, and the ones on the outside were circling the car, hunting for new openings. The goon was screaming bloody murder and swatting too hard to turn on the ignition.

Scarcely giving the swarming bugs a second glance, Andre strolled toward me, both fighting a grin and wearing his stern, don't-mess-with-me demeanor. Two-faced shark, the bastard.

"I was thinking pancakes for breakfast," I called, remembering my bedhead and combing my fingers through my thick mane. That was usually all it took to tame it. Andre's appreciative gaze said the gesture worked. "Leo said he'd be here shortly. Want to join us?" I asked.

"Blueberry with antifreeze syrup?" he asked sarcastically. Despite my most excellent offer, he didn't take my arm and retreat to more pleasant environs. Instead, he grabbed the collar of the guy I'd just kneed and dragged him upright.

Now that the Zone's unofficial mayor had arrived, the cops warily climbed out of their cars. The yellow jackets stuck to the unmarked white sedan. The baddies weren't going anywhere in their vehicle anytime soon.

I nodded at the corner and called to the cops, "There's another car blocking the alley, if you want one that isn't under attack."

A pair of uniforms peeled off in that direction. The other pair separated, one taking Andre's prisoner, the other advancing on the frozen fool on the other porch.

So maybe that one really did think he was legitimately evacuating the neighborhood, which made him an even bigger fool.

"We think they're the same thieves who broke into the warehouse," I lied to the officers. "They were threatening poor Pearl and pulled a gun on me. I'll happily press charges."

Policemen didn't like the Zone because we were peculiar and our troubles seldom fell under normal laws. So I prettified the situation in terms they understood.

"What have you got inside that they'd go to this much trouble for?" one uniform sensibly asked, handcuffing my black-and-blue-balled victim.

I pulled the fake evacuation orders out of Scaredy-Cat's pocket and handed them over as evidence. "Green gas," I said with a straight face. "Evidence of chemical warfare and valuable only to Acme."

"Neighborhood dispute?" the cop translated wryly.

"You can call it that. We may not have evidence on the warehouse break-in, but we have witnesses who saw them attempt to enter our houses under false pretenses. Waspman pulled a gun. You'll find it in the yews. Just let me know what you need and I'll comply," I said with good cheer, hiding my fury. If I didn't have to work regular hours anymore, I could spend as much time as I liked testifying against bad guys.

This realization was a totally major development and walloped me upside the head.

By offering to take me on as partner, Julius was doing me a favor so large I couldn't comprehend the immensity. Without Judge Snootypants breathing down my collar, I had time to pursue justice legally, without interference from anyone, a hitherto unknown freedom. I wanted to pop champagne and dance, but I'd have to save it until I had Acme where I wanted them.

I wasn't pretending my new job would be easy. The walls I had to climb next were perpendicular and towered way out of my sight. But I stupidly preferred challenges to pouring coffee for twerps.

Andre stalked up the stairs to shut me up, apparently not liking the determination in my eyes. He wasn't fond of the law interfering in his territory, but that gun had been in *my* back, and I wasn't his territory. I glared back at him.

"Let's have those pancakes, Clancy," he said menacingly. "The men in blue can handle your prisoners, if you'll call off your wasps."

I appreciated that he understood who was in control here. "Anyone have a hose?" I called helpfully. "Just squirt them down."

I was still furious, but I hoped I had it under wraps. No one came after me with a gun or threatened my friends without consequence.

21

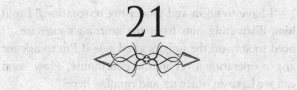

"If I open an office in your building, will I be placing Pearl and the others in jeopardy?" I demanded as soon as Andre and I hit my apartment. "I don't want them waking up to any more mornings like this."

"They woke up to green gas from Acme the other day," he said grumpily. "The ground is threatening to crack open and swallow us. They know this isn't a safe neighborhood. At least they're not dealing with gang shoot-outs and druggies on the corner."

I wasn't mollified. If I was to be a free agent, I didn't have to toe anyone's lines but my own. I had Acme in my sights. I had no idea if the gas cloud had been intentional, but I hated that they were experimenting with dangerous chemical weapons that had reached families up the hill as well as the trolls who hung around the Zone. Bill and Sarah had made their own choices, but kids didn't have that opportunity.

I didn't tell Andre that. He had a murder charge hanging over his head. That had to be his priority. He was peculiarly pale after his encounter with prison bars, but at least he was alive and not a zombie. I tried not to give him ideas by showing my relief.

"I have to go in and tender my resignation," I told him, distracting him from the morning's exercise. "I need to stay on the judge's good side if I'm to ask for any cooperation over at the courthouse. How soon can we have an office up and running here?"

He shrugged. "No difficulty. The warehouse needs to be torn down, but if we're careful removing them, the contents are still mostly available. I can salvage tables and bookshelves. I'll call Boris to set up computers. You just have to order whatever online services you need. Do you have a credit card?"

"You're kidding, right?" I mixed pancake batter and nuked frozen blueberries. "You know how much you didn't pay me. Hard to get a credit card without a W-2."

"Well, apply for one now while you still have a real job," he said snidely. "You won't qualify once you're self-employed. In the meantime, I'll give you mine. We'll have space cleaned out by the time you return."

Andre filled my tiny kitchen with his presence and his restlessness. I was still running on adrenaline. Pancakes were the last thing on my mind, but they gave my hands something more useful to do than running themselves through Andre's blue-black hair and seeking release for overstimulation.

I poured half a dozen pancakes on the old griddle on the stove and handed Andre a spatula. "Flip them when they bubble. I have to dress for work."

Rather than deal with the hyper sex drive between us, I left him to make his own blasted pancakes. By the time I returned to the kitchen, Schwartz had joined him, and Andre just about had pancake flipping under control. Leo was Norwegian big, and blond. Andre was Mediterranean dark, and sleek. Choices, so many lovely choices. I couldn't afford to take either of them.

"You two look good together," I said, grabbing a pancake off the top of a stack. "Have a nice life. I'm heading into town."

They were probably glaring daggers at my back as I dashed out, but Milo purred a happy farewell.

Instead of pouring coffee when I reached the judge's office, I prepared probate papers to file at the courthouse on Paddy's behalf. Reggie stayed out of my way. Once the judge finally put in an appearance, I cornered him in his lair and pleaded my case. I was determined not to be a loose-cannon superhero. I wanted the law solidly on my side.

When he learned Julius was taking me on as a junior, Snodgrass actually managed a smile. "I didn't know Montoya was still alive! What's he been doing? Have him give me a call, will you? We can catch up on old times. How is that lovely wife of his?"

Now I could see why Julius hated making phone

calls and talking to his old friends. It had to be painful to keep saying his wife was in a coma—and, ultimately, impossible to explain. The Zone had completely claimed him, even if he hadn't been otherwise affected by the chemicals.

"She's stable," I said noncommittally. "Opening an office near his home is the only reason he's agreeing to this. I'll have a commute to the courthouse, but I can do that more easily than he can. Padraig Vanderventer wants me to file the probate papers while I'm over here. I'm doing it on your time, so you can invoice him. If there's any problem, can you follow up?"

I knew how to play nice. I puffed his ego, said all the right things, and took care of business. I was no longer a twenty-year-old hothead egging the provost's office. Admittedly, I'd sent my boyfriend to hell in a fit of fury, but I'd learned from the experience and brought him back—sort of. I hoped I was mature enough to take on this next step.

After we wrangled an emergency approval, probate was mostly paperwork, collecting a million copies of Gloria's death certificate and filing them hither and yon. I was already hoping I could earn enough money to pay for a clerk. I'd developed a taste for action, and paperwork and errand-running no longer rang my chimes.

I writhed with my need to bring Acme down and rescue poor Bill and hunt for the missing cloud can. Maybe once Paddy was set free at the plant, he could stop whatever was shaking the ground and discover what was wrong with the pink particles. That was pushing my luck, I knew. But if he could just find the bad guys . . . maybe I could wish for the victims to be cured while I sent the bastards to hell. I still had a lot to learn about this Saturn business.

Max called after I'd tucked Paddy's documents into my messenger bag and was on the bike, ready to head home. I would have to buy a briefcase, I realized. Carrying legal papers in a messenger bag full of cat hair wasn't very professional. It would have been nice if I'd had a loving normal family showering me with congratulations and fancy briefcases for graduation instead of one that sent me links to strange websites, but I'd make do. My lack of family had taught me a self-sufficiency that had kept me alive all these years.

"Temporary probate filed," I told Max when I answered. "You and Paddy will share equally unless a will is found. Want me to set up a meeting between the two of you?"

I shouldn't be so malicious. I had no idea what the relationship had been between scientific Paddy and his son, the materialistic, greedy Dane, but I was pretty certain it hadn't been great. Throwing Max's social conscience into the scenario would bollix it up nicely. I didn't have to have my own family to understand the meaning of *dysfunctional*.

"I'd rather you sent me back to hell," Max growled. "Except I think you're right. I think Dane's in hell, and he's trying to kill me. The gas logs exploded this morning."

My concern was instantaneous. I gunned the Harley and prepared to turn toward his condo instead of home. "What happened? Are you all right? I don't want to be visiting you in a hospital room ever again."

"I'm all right. The fire department called it a malfunction and turned off the gas. I'm having the gas stove replaced with electric."

"Consequences," I sighed, turning off the engine again so I could hear. "I knew playing with fire had consequences. I just didn't know what they'd be. If I'm opening mirrors on hell, it can't be good."

I hadn't been visited by any of the other cretins I'd dispatched to their just rewards. But maybe the Vanderventers were as privileged in the afterlife as they had been in this one. An affinity for wealth and power sounded evil enough to entice Satan.

"You didn't take out Gloria, so you're safe," he said reassuringly. "I'll probably look for a Realtor, but I've got the condo under control for now. I am not ashamed to admit that I want no part of Gloria's hell house. Paddy can look for a damned will if he's not happy sharing. Andre might want to stay out of the mansion, too. Logic has even less purpose on the other side than it does in the real world. All that bottled-up rage, hate, and fear is pretty raw and gruesome."

"My expert on hell," I said dryly, hating to think about my bighearted Max suffering such horror.

And I was fretting because I realized that, technically, Andre had brought about Dane's death as well as Gloria's, even if they'd caused their own demises. My very own demon slayer—and if she could, Gloria would go after him.

I wasn't precisely innocent in Dane's death. I figured illogical rage would find me if it haunted the mansion. I didn't want any of us out there.

"Without a will, your trustees have to work with Paddy against your parents and grandmother for control of Acme," I warned. "Divided this way, neither of you will have a controlling share. And I suspect Paddy won't be satisfied until he's searched the mansion and found Gloria left no surprises that might blow up in his face should MacNeill get to them first. It would be better if he had witnesses."

"I don't think Paddy is ready to work with anyone," he said cynically. "Can you trust me to send out a team to help him?"

"You can try. Don't feel bad if Paddy rejects them."

I debated whether I should tell Paddy about the Dane/Max soul transference, but I still wasn't positive Paddy was sane, and I doubted whether Max wanted his scary secret spread to the world if Paddy talked. I'd have to play that one by ear.

We agreed on a time, and I roared home, enjoying the ride down country lanes struck with more autumn colors with each passing day. I wondered what would happen if I tried to plant a tree in Pearl's backyard. I would have to clear out the dead appliances and old sinks first.

I wheeled home, grabbed a sandwich, added Milo to his new tote bag, then trotted next door. Julius had crates of books stacked in the foyer, ready to be moved to our new office. I was already having second and third thoughts about Andre's grandiose scheme.

"Won't you need these?" I asked. "Wouldn't it be better if I just came over here when I need your library?"

"I have a photographic memory," he said with a shrug. "I've read these enough that I can recall what page each case is on. I've kept them up to date because I don't want to memorize ever-changing computer pages. But reading law and practicing it are two different things. I can tell you what cases are most applicable, but you have to decide how to apply them."

That sounded like more responsibility than I had the experience to handle, but I pretended I agreed. Maybe I could learn to hypnotize a jury before I went to court. In Andre's case, I was hoping we wouldn't get as far as a courtroom.

After learning there'd been no change in our patients, that the cloud can hadn't been found, and that Julius would give Paddy my message about probate, I shouldered a small box and crossed the street to my new office.

The block of buildings across from the town houses had been abandoned for years, as far as I could tell. The long brick warehouse that had been the site of our run-in with Acme's paratroopers gaped emptily, like a bombed-out relic of a war zone. The showroom windows in several of the other brick buildings had been boarded up. The four-story edifice the helicopter had landed on had been designed for offices.

That was the one Andre had opened for me. Guess we knew the roof was sturdy if a helicopter could land on it.

Entering the foyer, I admired the unboarded and

newly washed windows that let in the late-afternoon sunlight. The lingering odor of bleach explained the lack of any musty smell in the tile-floored entrance. Someone had been busy while I was at work. Desks, filing cabinets, credenzas, and chairs were scattered willy-nilly all over the lobby. The space still seemed enormously empty.

I wandered in carrying my box of books, wondering which cubicle Andre had decided was mine. Given that the place was otherwise empty, I hoped he'd chosen a room with a window, but his paranoia might demand solid walls.

Before I'd gone ten paces, a dozen people leaped from behind doorways and desks screaming and waving their arms. I nearly peed my pants until I realized they were shouting, "Surprise!"

Julius had warned them of my arrival, the old sneak. Tears of shock welled. I dropped my box and sat down on it so I didn't reveal how weak-kneed I was. I swallowed and stared in amazement at gold and black balloons erupting from some hidden gate, scattering upward to bounce on the high ceiling. Cora and Frank opened a foldout banner with gold lettering that shouted CONGRATULATIONS, SUPERLAWYER TINA!

I almost choked on a sob. A suspicious wetness gathered in the corners of my eyes. Boris the Geek was there, and some of the staff from Chesty's, and Ernesto, and Tim—totally visible and wearing pink-and-green plaid shorts. Sarah hung out in the back, a bit confused but wanting to be part of the crowd—just like me.

Andre emerged bearing a beribboned briefcase, the

kind I'd vaguely wished I'd had family to bestow on me. How did he *know* these things?

It was beautiful, supple, camel-colored leather with brass zippers and clasps and pockets for everything. And it was big enough for Milo and a laptop. Not that I had a laptop, but it would last long enough for me to acquire one. The tag said it had metal-reinforced security straps. My kind of bag. I hugged it. I actually hugged it.

I hated crying, but I was shaking from holding back the tears. Cora hung her corner of the banner on a nail and came over to squeeze my shoulders.

"You're officially one of the family, hon," she told me. "It's all about us down here. Most of the time, it's a bum job being us, but once in a while, we come through."

I nodded, missing burly Bill and even Leibowitz. *Family.* Ugly and mean, sometimes, but we were there for each other. I did cry then. I'd finally found a real home.

"We'll have to put her to work so she gets back to being mean," Andre said with mock disgust. "We're short a waitress at Chesty's. Want to help?"

"Obnoxious bastard," I muttered tearily, clinging to my beautiful briefcase and studying the office they'd been creating for me. They were putting me right in front, in the foyer. Insane.

But since I had no receptionist or partners, it made as much sense as anything. I could keep a protective eye on the houses across the street through the plate-glass windows.

"Does this place have tunnels, too?" I asked Andre while Frank broke out champagne—tonic water for Andre—and everyone crowded around with plastic glasses.

"You don't want to know," he said, snapping his fingers and demanding that we be served first.

"Oh yeah, I do. So either you show me, or I find them on my own," I murmured as Leo carried over three glasses.

"Paddy wants you to meet him over at his mother's estate," Leo informed me, blithely ignoring the under-current between me and Andre. "You can't have more than one of these if you're driving."

"Maybe we ought to move the party over there," I suggested, really not wanting to confront a fiery Gloria if there was any chance her demonic spirit could explode gas lines.

My suggestion met with enthusiastic approval, although as it turned out, most of the party had to work and couldn't go. So we drained the champagne bottles, popped balloons with pencils that Tim sharpened, moved furniture into a semi-official-looking arrangement, and then let Leo drive us to Towson in his old Ford SUV.

Us being me, Leo, Andre, and Frank, our Finder. If Gloria and the will were anywhere on the estate, we'd find them or they'd find us.

22

"You realize you're wasting time searching this place, don't you?" Andre said pessimistically as we drove up the private drive without being stopped by sinister guards. "She's locked her papers up at Acme."

"Is this one of your invaluable predictions?" I asked. "Should I be grateful you're not swinging a bat to test my reflexes?"

"I'm just warning you not to raise your hopes."

"You realize you're returning to the scene of the crime?" I countered with a veiled warning of my own. Remembering Max's admonition, I wasn't certain it was wise for Andre to be here, but I'd come up with no way to persuade him otherwise when he was in

Master of the Universe mode. At least I'd been able to lock Milo in the apartment before we left.

Leo pulled up behind a silver Lincoln Town Car I didn't recognize. Unless Paddy owned a car, I had to assume it was Max's team.

"The place is probably full of booby traps." Frank added his note of optimism. "You can't tell me the rich don't consort with the devil."

"Our resident communist," Andre said, climbing out the instant the Ford stopped. "Last time I looked, you weren't exactly poor, Frank. Made any pacts with Satan lately?"

"Keep your nose out of my bank account, Legrande." Frank slid out and stood beside him, gazing up at the enormous imitation Southern mansion. The crime scene tape that had been tied to the columns was tattered and broken now.

Frank was the kind of guy you'd blink and forget, really slight and kind of shadowy, which apparently gave him an advantage as a private investigator. "You'll have to dismantle the place if she really hid the will," he continued.

That was my fear. Someone who lived with terrorists for bodyguards would undoubtedly exhibit a higher degree of paranoia than either Andre or I did. Even without Andre's pessimism, I wasn't holding out much hope for this search. But Paddy was the heir. He called the shots.

Inside, Max's team was methodically working through desks and dressers, the normal places one might store a will or keys to a bank lockbox. If Gloria had stupidly stored the will in a bank vault, we were screwed until probate court had time to send someone official to the bank to audit the contents. Which could be the twelfth of never. Only one of many hurdles we could face.

Actually, now that I gave it some thought, Gloria would probably have made it as difficult as possible for anyone to take over Acme, giving any evil jerk-wads over there time to cover up whatever they were doing. Andre was probably right, curse him.

I located Paddy in the pantry, where Andre and I had consulted after Gloria's unexpected demise. I doubted he'd arrived with Max's people, but I had no idea if he had a car of his own. None had been parked out front.

"Any inspiration here?" I asked, scanning boxes of granola and pasta.

"She used to have hidden doors, like at the plant. Those guys in the Lincoln, can we trust them?" He ran his fingers along the walls he could reach.

"Yeah, I think we can. You and Dane need to have a talk. You'll find he's changed since he almost died." It seemed to me the contents of the shelves would fall off if the wall actually moved, but I jiggled shelves as if I knew what I was doing.

"He wanted to have me certified and locked up. No, thanks."

"I bet it was your mother who suggested that. Gloria was the one who was certifiable. And you didn't help give the right impression," I reminded him. "Dane needed a father's guidance. You gave him crazy.

It's a wonder Dane didn't think insanity ran in the family."

"Just bad chemicals," he said enigmatically.

"A new kind of drug?" I suggested, trying to pry real info out of inscrutable Paddy. It didn't work. He started on the next wall.

I went back to the Dane argument. "Consider that months in a hospital may have leached the evil or the drugs or whatever out of him." Still no response.

Fine. So I wasn't a mediator. "Is there a basement to this place? I think evil lurks in darkness." I gave up on the pantry, or reasoning with a formerly mad man. My thinking was that Gloria wouldn't have trusted workmen to build her a hiding place unless she killed them afterward.

And yeah, I know I was condemning the woman without really knowing her, but she was already dead. I could mentally vilify her and work out a little anger and fear without endangering my eternal soul.

Paddy pointed out a door near the back entrance but didn't seem interested in joining me. To each his own. I stopped at the camouflaged refrigerator and helped myself to an apple and a few grapes. The plentiful empty space inside the fridge didn't encourage grazing. Gloria must not have entertained much. Or fed her staff.

After appropriating a hunk of expensive specialty Gorgonzola, I opened the basement door and searched for a light switch. Damp, musty air flowed upward. The fluorescent bulb that flickered on was pretty pathetic for a mansion. I supposed the house had been built back in the dark ages when basements were for canned goods and root veggies and not of much interest otherwise. Living here all by herself, Gloria certainly hadn't needed the extra square footage.

Checking for cobwebs and finding the passage surprisingly clear, I trotted down the cement steps, wishing I'd brought Milo with me. Despite the prosaic mops and brooms hanging on the walls, the air here was almost sulfurous, adding to the general creepiness. It didn't look much like a place where a fashion model like Gloria would hang out.

I persevered, apparently in the belief that evil liked to lie low and hide in darkness and misery. Or in a place that stank like an oil well. Which had nothing to do with wills and a lot to do with my opinion of Gloria.

The stairs led to a small concrete bunker. One wall held an old wooden door. Like Alice, I couldn't resist opening it. On the other side, it was more coal cellar than basement. I stepped onto the hard-packed earth and gazed blindly into the dark. Gravel had been ground into the dirt, but I was glad I'd donned athletic shoes for this search.

I groped around for a switch to illuminate the vast space I couldn't see in just the stair light. Before I located what I sought, I heard a squeak and a flutter of wings, and something brushed my hair.

I went all girly and shrieked. Generally, I'm not afraid of rats or bats or I wouldn't have been down there. But despite all my other paranoid premonitions, I hadn't expected critters beneath a mansion, and this one startled the shit out of me.

I would have shut up faster, except a rush of more wings and weird squeaks flew past me, straight up to the house through the door I'd left open. So I kept shrieking and ducking while all hell swooped over my head.

"It's a damned cave down here!" Leo shouted a million years later, his heavy boots racing downward through the cloud of flying vermin.

Ludicrously, he held an umbrella. My hero!

In their haste to escape, the bats flooded the stairwell, miraculously missing walls and ceiling and flowing like water into the kitchen.

"Not normal," Paddy commented laconically once Leo and I returned to the kitchen. The room swirled with a black cloud of bats attempting to escape. We kept our backs to the walls and gazed around in awe. "Probably need to trap them."

While I was being terrorized in the cellar, Andre, predictably, had produced both an automatic pistol and a coal shovel to take a battle stance in a cloud of creepies. I should have known he had been carrying concealed to Gloria's booby trap. "A touch of PTSD, Andre?" I called. "Just a little overreaction?"

Squealing black uglies swooped all around him, swiping the kitchen ceiling and walls. Andre stood on the granite island, alternately swinging and shooting at the creatures like an old-time Western gunfighter. Except he'd probably have needed two guns for that.

He ignored me and knocked two bats out of the air with one shot. The man was good.

"Cellar might be safer," I said wryly, dodging ricocheting bullets and bat bodies.

Someone had sensibly shut the door to the rest of the house. I noticed Max's team wasn't in here fighting flying vermin. Of course, neither was Frank.

"Open the windows!" Leo shouted. "Let them fly out."

Seemed sensible to me, better than shooting the critters. But Paddy grabbed a lacy tablecloth from a drawer and stood blocking the back door, netting anything that came near him.

"Not normal," he repeated. "Andre, drop the damned gun so the rest of us can trap them."

One of Andre's victims fell at my feet. Paddy was right. The creatures weren't normal. This one had a face.

I shuddered and forced myself to study the oddly rounded eyes, snub nose, hairless cheeks, and tiny fangs. Contrary to my cowardly behavior, I knew a little something about bats. Occasionally, living in barns and abandoned structures with my tree-hugging mother could be very instructive. Bats are actually mammals. There are infinite varieties of bats. I didn't remember any of them having red eyes and humanoid faces. This dead one had the same black-rat appearance Gloria had taken on after she'd met her just reward.

"Demon bats," I muttered, not daring to say it aloud. Trapping them might be as dangerous as shooting them, I concluded. Creatures from hell were more my line of work than Paddy's.

Which meant this was my problem, naturally. I was still debating this Saturn/Satan dichotomy, but good or bad, I couldn't let a thousand miniature Hells Angels loose into the world. I just didn't know if I could actually send a bat to Hades or if I would be punished or rewarded for trying.

But if they were demons . . . I should try. The image of demonic bats escaping into the world on my watch easily raised my blood pressure to that level of rage where I saw red and could curse anything. Fortunately, for a change, I hadn't reached my usual state of incoherency.

"Saturn, damn these infernal creatures back to the hell from whence they came," I intoned under my breath, legalizing my normal, furious curses for the sake of clarity and on the off chance I was wrong about their origins. And stupidly trusting that none of the people in the room came from hell.

Of course, I had utterly no idea if I was serving justice by frying bats in eternal fires, but if there was any chance these really were demons or imps from Hades or whatever, I wouldn't let my friends be bitten by them. My posse might be a little oddball, but they were my friends. Demons were not.

The first victim of my curse fell and smacked Andre on the head.

"What the fuck?" He dodged and glared malevolently at the ceiling, firing off another round or two before realizing he was caught in a dead-bat downpour.

I guessed that confirmed the origin of the critters and that hell existed. Ouch.

"It's raining bats!" Leo shouted, ducking under the umbrella with me. "What the devil is going on?" That was pretty strong language for Leo.

I didn't want to explain that *I* was what was going on here. So I just asked innocently, "Maybe exposure to sunlight kills them?"

Not that anyone cared what was killing them.

Paddy darted back to the pantry. Andre swung his coal shovel like a baseball bat, apparently venting one whale of a lot of suppressed hostility by using furballs for targets. He was losing his sickly pallor and was almost back to his real self. Charming.

Within minutes, the floor was flooded with snarling, dying demonic bats. Even naïve Leo stared at the ugly creatures in horror. I assumed he hadn't heard my curse or he would probably have been staring at me like that.

I'd killed a horde of bats. I was feeling pretty queasy, too. I'd actually killed them. Cursed them. I wasn't just Saturn's daughter—I was some kind of blamed witch. At least my curse about infernal creatures hadn't sent *me* to hell. I'd better watch my language even closer than I'd thought. I wanted to emit a *damn* right about now, but bit my tongue.

"Gate to hell," Paddy muttered, emerging from the pantry as the waterfall of bats dried up. "She opened it."

Leo and Andre stared at him as if they were contemplating straitjackets. Me, I wanted to ask—*before or after she died?* Instead, I kicked a path through the oddly crunchy shells to the kitchen sink, where I methodically soaped my hands and arms.

"*I* didn't open any gates," I informed them, just in case there was any mistaking that pronoun. "It was already open when I got down there."

Andre and Leo turned their stares to me. I shrugged it off. Andre knew I wasn't normal. Leo sometimes suspected it, but I'd spent years learning to be a respectable lawyer, and I kind of liked to keep authority figures thinking that's what I was.

Paddy shrugged. "Burn 'em." He opened the rear entrance to an enormous screened porch complete with outdoor kitchen and gestured at the giant gas grill.

After my experience with Max's freaky gas, you couldn't have paid me to go near that grill. For all I knew, gas pipes were lines straight to the underworld. I aimed for a chiminea outside on the tiled terrace. Gathering some kindling, I set it smoking. I'd have preferred a flamethrower.

We had the kitchen almost shoveled clear by the time Max's team and Frank came in to see what we were cooking. Andre had nailed a bar across the basement door. Paddy had dissected a couple of the creatures, or tried. They crumbled at the touch of a knife.

Hunting for wills had gone by the wayside.

In between sweeping and shoveling furballs into the fire, I'd located some plaster patch, and Leo and I were politely filling the sieve Andre had made of the ceiling. I didn't have wood patch to repair the cabinets.

We hadn't had time to mop the floor. The team of proper suits and ties stared at the chaos of guts, plaster, and smoke with disbelief. Just another day in the Zone for us.

Except we hadn't been in the Zone. We'd have to ponder that anomaly and discuss it at some later time.

"No will here," Frank declared. Since he was our Finder, we were inclined to accept his word over that of Max's suits.

"That's because it's at Acme, I told you," Andre said. "Does Paddy need a court order to search?"

"As things stand, the MacNeills have the controlling share. If they object to a search, a court order could take weeks, even if we get Dane's agreement," I warned, not trusting Andre's weird predictions, even if they were right.

Paddy met my gaze. He had no intention of leaving Acme in enemy hands for weeks. Neither did I, not if it meant leaving Bill and Leibowitz and the other patients trapped as guinea pigs.

Shit. I knew what that meant.

23

Once we returned to our part of town, I didn't want to be left alone. The guys dropped me off to change out of my bat-smeared clothes, but, figuring I'd have nightmares of rat faces frying in hell, I agreed to meet them at Chesty's for a meal and maybe a pow-wow. I changed into a pair of battered leather pants and a billowy black silk blouse that hid my arms and not much else. The genie effect made me feel almost normal.

I sought the comfort of friends to cure my jitters. I walked down the main drag, avoiding the mobile Dumpsters lurking near the polluted harbor. Maybe they only danced under a full moon, but in my current state of trepidation I wasn't taking chances. As it was, the ground rumbled beneath my feet, and I started seeing bats swooping around the burned-out chimneys of the old plant. In his bag, Milo stiffened in alarm, not reassuring me.

Earthquakes seriously dampened any furious need to raid the dungeon again, except now I worried about Bill being buried in rubble. If Paddy didn't think he could find a will in time to rescue the patients . . . Like a rat in a maze, my brain frantically sought a way out.

The gargoyle on the florist's shop eyed me balefully. A whiff of sulfur rose from the sewer, but all else seemed as normal as the Zone gets. I'd worked at Chesty's enough to be more at home with murals of nudes dancing—literally—than in Snodgrass's stuffy office or the Vanderventer mansion.

Barely dressed waitresses waved greetings as I entered and headed back to the others commandeering my favorite booth in the back. Sarah didn't work here at this hour. She was too afraid of people. Or men. Or of being startled into a chimp. But I was glad she was back from zombiedom. She didn't deserve whatever green gas had done to her.

Okay, maybe Sarah *did* deserve it. Her moral center was pretty warped, but that's what happens when you're raised by a serial killer. Still, I couldn't condemn her for killing her abusive husband—another gray area that haunted my conscience. I hoped the Zone would make her better, as it had people like Bill and Andre, who'd been heading the wrong way down one-way streets until they saw the light. Or the chemical flood. Whatever. People deserved second chances.

Apparently I thought bats didn't deserve any chance at all.

As I slid into the booth next to Paddy, I doubted that we would come to any agreement tonight. In our current edgy moods, we would all be hacking at the Acme problem from different perspectives, and moving forward would not be the result.

Leo was probably waiting for me to unleash the law for a nice legal search of the plant—even though he had to know that whoever was running things at Acme couldn't let us into the level where they hid the zombies. They'd fight a court order tooth and nail, and use the time to move the zombies where we couldn't find them. This wasn't about a will. It was a power struggle.

Andre would be plotting attack by AK-47. And Paddy . . . Hell only knew what was happening in Paddy's head. Frank . . . Frank was just waiting for orders.

Me, I wanted food and a good night's sleep before committing myself to the insanity of entering Acme's death trap again.

Except I knew I wouldn't be getting any sleep. I really, really didn't want to know if I'd be rewarded for sending demonic bats to hell or punished for using my powers without justice. Justice had once been a black and white word to me. No more. I had no evidence those bats were dangerous. I'd killed because I was afraid of them. That's what bigots did.

We all ordered plates of pasta. Leo squeezed in next to me and Paddy. Andre and Frank sat across from us, where they could admire my cleavage and the food in Paddy's beard. Cora slinked over to join us. She'd had to hold down the detective agency while Frank was out playing, but the office had closed hours ago.

I'd once thought Leo and Cora would make a pretty couple. He certainly noticed her curves in her skintight leopard-skin almost-dress. But other than teasing each other with flirty looks, they treated each other like furniture. Matchmaking wasn't my forte. I wasn't even certain Leo recognized Cora's snake aptitude. Like me, she probably kept her talents on the down-low in front of golden boy. The Zone hadn't warped Leo yet. Maybe.

"You do realize that Dane had to set up his fortune in a blind trust when he took the senate seat, and any part of his share of Acme will go into it?" I thought I'd lay out the law just to move the meeting along. "Apparently he's trying to prove he's presidential material by removing himself from control of any private entities. That means his trustees will take over his votes." And I had no idea who they were, but I'd bet Gloria had been top dog. Blind trusts are never really blind.

"If MacNeill is a trust executor, he gets the controlling vote," Paddy concluded gloomily.

"Since chances of your mother leaving anything to you are slim," I said, "I suggest that if you believe there really is a will and there's any chance that Mac-

Neill can find it, you start making amends with Dane. Maybe you can be included as executor of his trust in Gloria's place."

I could almost see the *not happening* thought bubble forming. I wanted to smack Paddy's head against the wall. If it had been me, I'd have put on my power suit and waltzed into Acme's office and sat down at the head honcho's desk and forced everyone to prove I didn't belong there.

Paddy wasn't me.

Although I supposed that kind of arrogance would be bad mojo for a scientist who is supposed to be objective.

"Can we get into the plant and reconnoiter?" I asked.

Andre and Cora continued their private conversation. Leo slurped up spaghetti. We were getting nowhere. As a team, we sucked.

I'd been hoping for any other way around it, but we desperately needed to get into Acme—to find the will, to free Bill, to stop the scary rumbling. But no one was talking about what I wanted to talk about. They just didn't grasp the potential for disaster if Acme slipped out of Dane's or Paddy's hands. It was all legal mumbo jumbo to them.

I preferred action to reaction, but I wasn't getting either tonight.

In frustration, I studied the other customers. Not too long ago, they'd included spies and media all out to get me. I wasn't at all certain they weren't doing the same now, although, according to Julius, Andre was higher on their hit list these days. He'd been charged with murder, after all, a rather juicy one. Nervousness about taking on a case for which I wasn't prepared made me antsy.

Ha. I spotted a familiar face. I didn't know his name, or that of his fellow reporters, but they'd all had cameras and microphones waving under my nose a few months back. It wasn't as if I'd forget their faces. I wondered if other Saturn's daughters were plagued with media nuisances while they battled demons and monsters, or if I was just special.

Andre must have noticed my expression. He slapped his hand over mine in warning. The touch tingled. I gave him my best evil-vamp smile, licking my lips and watching him hungrily. Leo had me blocked in and Cora had Andre trapped. He couldn't do anything except hold my hand and tap my rubber shoe with his leather one. Not at all satisfactory.

"Do you dance, Leo?" I purred, still watching Andre.

"Not on poles," Leo said, drinking his beer. But then his gaze caught the way Andre was holding down my hand, and he got the message. "We're not solving anything here. Maybe it's time I took you home."

Since we lived in the same building, that almost made sense. Except I'd never needed anyone to escort me anywhere, and I wasn't ready to call it quits for the night. I wiggled my fingers under Andre's. He didn't release me.

"Clancy is asking for trouble, Schwartz," Andre said, filling in the conversational gap I'd left open. "Either carry her out of here or dispatch the reporters."

He knew me too damned well. "Not my boss any-more, Legrande," I pointed out. "If I want to talk to reporters, it's my business."

"I'm your only client and I'm paying your office rent, so yeah, I get to be your boss. I don't want my lawyer irritating the press. They've been behaving so far. They'll go away when they don't see me murder-ing old ladies."

With my free hand, I pinched the hard, bronzed one holding me down. Andre didn't even flinch. Chi-nese water torture probably wouldn't loosen his grip. I didn't like being boxed in, physically or otherwise.

"I can always go back to Snodgrass, Legrande. I don't need you or your problems if you're going to boss me around. Those reporters over there could be our key to Acme. Let me loose or I'll scream. Let's see how many white knights come running."

With disgust, he shoved my hand away. A pity, ac-tually. I kind of liked the human contact. The imperi-ousness, not so much.

Leo warily let me out, looking as if he'd far rather heave me over his shoulder. Golden Viking had used that maneuver once before, when I'd been in no emo-tional shape to deal with it. He probably sensed I'd carve his heart out if he tried it now.

I tossed the mane of hair I'd yet to have cut and bit color into my lips as I swung toward the table of reporters, giving them a full view of the goods. Under normal circumstances, brown-wren me and my crooked teeth wouldn't be overtly noticeable, but black leather works for me, and these guys knew me enough to be leery.

Since I would never be the friendly sort people would welcome with open arms, I was learning to accept that response. I might prefer it otherwise, but these guys didn't count for much.

"Hello, boys," I purred, noting there were no women with them. Poor Jane was stuck at home with her two-year-old. I wondered how many men at this table had wives at home dealing with the kids while they drank beer and annoyed people like me. "Looking for some entertainment?"

"Working the poles these days, Clancy?" one of the older ones asked. "What does your boyfriend the senator think about that?"

I gave him the brilliant gap-toothed smile that Max had told me turned him on. "Why, if you believe everything the media says, Danny Boy has a pole in his apartment just for me. A more original story would be a newsman who reported *news* instead of gossip."

They slugged back their drinks and glared. I had no sympathy. If they couldn't sell newspapers with real stories instead of entertainment news, then they needed to get out of the business.

"So, what's the real news?" a balding one asked. "Give us something worth writing about."

"I'm just a little ol' lawyer, not a big bad investigative reporter. And I can't say anything that would jeopardize my client's case." I hesitated just a fraction, giving them time to absorb the fact that I actually had a client. "But the senator and Andre aren't real news.

It's the actions of Acme Chemical that should be examined. Corporations are where dirty deeds are hidden these days."

"That's your boyfriend's family gold mine," one of the younger ones said, trying to sound smart-assed. "You had a fight with Dane? That why you're over there playing footsie with a murderer?"

I sighed and glanced at the balding guy with mock sympathy. "Is this what you have to put up with every day? Does he always believe what he's told without getting the facts?"

I left them snickering at the younger guy's expense. He was probably glowering and vowing revenge, but I'd made them all think, for a change. Real news wasn't lying out in the street, waiting to be picked up. As with gold, you had to dig for it in dirty, sometimes dangerous, holes.

But those lazy bums wouldn't be digging into the dungeon soon enough for me, dang it.

I sauntered out and headed up the hill. Maybe I could catch up with the Fat Chick and chat, find out how much she knew about this business.

Within minutes, I was aware of being followed. Oversensitive to bats, I saw pink ones darting about under a purple street lamp. A yellow rat scampered across the street. The Zone liked color as well as food.

I stopped at the corner and leaned against a neon blue building to reconnoiter, as they say in the movies. If necessary, I knew how to blend into the shadows. I'm small and dark and I'd been doing it for most of my life. But I fancied these were friendly footsteps.

Leo and Cora walked toward me, acting not exactly like a happy couple but more like pissed-off bodyguards. I sighed and stepped back onto the sidewalk. "You really shouldn't follow me, you know."

"Yeah, and you really should keep your mouth shut, but we know that's not happening, either," Leo said.

I glanced at him in surprise. Leo seldom said much, and what he did say was usually politically correct. I glanced at Cora for answers, but she was eyeing him with interest, too.

Leo just took my arm and steered me up the hill, refusing to answer questions we weren't asking.

"Silent Cop Syndrome," I told Cora, talking around him. "All I did was point the stupid hounds in a better direction."

"No, all you did was antagonize Andre until his ears poured steam. And his nose smoked," she added for emphasis. "No one does that. Andre is a mite . . . peculiar. You can't just go rubbing him wrong, then walking out."

Andre was a mite peculiar, all right, but he was a big boy and not my responsibility. "I'm even more peculiar," I declared, "so people better start tippy-toeing around me, too." I meant it. Andre and I were going to go head-to-head one of these days, and people needed to back off.

"He didn't mean it about being your boss," Cora said. "He was just sounding off, like men do. You just gotta turn on your sexy, and he'll be buying carpets for your new office."

The thought of my new office made me feel better. Except it probably had secret tunnels under it, filled with Andre's computer equipment, where he filmed and copied my every move. "Is there any way of getting bug protection?" I inquired, thinking aloud.

"Like, listening-type bugs, or cockroaches?" Cora asked.

"Listening-type. And hidden cameras."

Leo finally checked back into the conversation. He'd been the one to discover Acme's devices in my last apartment. "No monitoring equipment," he noted, glancing up our empty street for surveillance vans.

I thumped his temple. "Underground, Schwartz. What does Andre have under that building? Demonic bats? More bomb shelters?"

"Union Army tunnels," Cora said unexpectedly. "Some collapsed when they were building the harbor tunnel. These houses were built after the Civil War, but they used the excavations as foundations. I don't know that they're all connected anymore, though."

"Collapsing tunnels, even better." I aimed toward the office building, then realized I didn't have a key. I bit my tongue really hard to keep from cursing Andre.

"Looking for this?"

We all turned to watch Andre coming up the hill. He'd donned dark tailored slacks and a gray silk shirt before meeting at the club, and they emphasized a walk sexier than that of any cowboy I'd ever seen on TV. In his fingers he twirled a brass key.

"One of these days, you're going to end up like Max," I warned, reminding him of the ball of flame that had ended Max's life. "You stand forewarned. I want some respect. I'm not cute, I'm not sweet, and I'm not entirely stable. So keep it cool, Legrande."

"I totally respect what you're saying, Justine," he answered mockingly, sliding the key into the lock. "Not cute, not sweet, and not stable."

I swiped the key from his hand the instant the door opened. Once inside my magnificent new office, I mellowed. *My office.* Milo leaped out to explore. Having my own office meant I could take my cat to work with me. We could guard each other's backs.

I ran my hand over the enormous wooden desk, not caring if it had been built for men with quills. It was huge and heavy and demanded respect just by its existence. That's what I wanted. Well, not the huge and heavy part.

"Tunnels, Andre?" I asked, waiting expectantly as he flipped switches. I could see the plate-glass windows would need shades for night.

"What's with you and caves? Haven't had enough bats for one day?" he asked, leading the way down a hall I hadn't had time to explore. "There is no elevator, which is why we can't rent this place. It's all stairs. Spiders. Cobwebs."

"Bad plumbing and old toilets," I agreed solemnly. "I have a friend who knows a good plumber." Jane's father had taught her all she needed to know about the business. Andre wasn't scaring me.

Cora and Leo tagged along, either out of curiosity or to keep us from killing each other. Although by now it ought to have been obvious that we both just needed to get laid, and we were doing our best to resist. There were ethics rules about going to bed with clients. Besides, it was a bad idea all around.

The floor beneath us began to rumble before we reached the stairs.

"The bomb shelter!" I cried when the sway of old floors didn't stop but worsened.

I scooped up Milo and we ran for the front door and our helpless patients.

24

As the rumbling motion of the ground continued, Leo shouted into his phone, and below the hill, people fled into Edgewater Street, screaming in alarm and expecting an explosion. The gargoyles growled uncertainly. I checked the chemical plant to the north. It wasn't completely dark. I could see flickering lights but no signs of fire. I didn't have time to study the situation. If the street was about to cave, we had to get our people out of the shelter. Rippling pavement couldn't be safe.

I could have sworn bats were swirling out from cracks forming in the streets, but by this time, I was bat-obsessed and prepared to believe anything.

Andre, Cora, and I ran toward the apartments. I

stumbled when blacktop cracked beneath my shoes, but Andre caught me just in time. Flames shot up before our noses. A gas line must have cracked.

I froze in horror. Gloria writhed and raged in the flames.

Apparently not noticing apparitions, Andre jerked my arm and navigated me around the pillar of fire. I was more than ready to follow. *I did not see that*, I chanted to myself.

Pearl and Tim appeared on their respective porches, eyes wide in terror. I shouted at them to take Milo and my car and drive south, away from the plant. I didn't know if they listened, but as we hit the porch, I tossed my keys and Milo's bag to Tim before he flickered out.

"Pearl can't drive," Andre informed me as we hit the basement stairs.

"Neither can Tim. They'll figure it out." I was hoping Milo would have the sense to go with them. Cats can't fight fire.

We saved our breath after that. In the bomb shelter, the med students were dithering, uncertain whether they were safer under the street or above. Seeing no evidence of unwanted intruders, we directed the docs to start hauling the patients up the basement stairs. Once there, we'd have to decide how to deal with them.

The rocking, swaying motion seemed to be lessening, but we couldn't take chances that 150-year-old tunnels would remain intact. Or that more gas lines wouldn't burst. I pushed Nancy Rose's gurney down the hall and helped carry her in a stretcher up to Andre's front hall, then left Cora in charge of directing the med students outside to the porch while I ran upstairs to Julius. As expected, he was in the attic with Katerina.

"We're staying here," Julius announced.

In an earthquake, general wisdom says to leave the building, but if anyone was my boss, Julius was. I'd have to respect his choice.

"Look after Andre," he ordered.

Well, maybe not entirely my boss, but also my friend and Andre's father. Complicated. "What, you want me to smack him upside the head if he starts shooting?" I asked in exasperation. "You know we have to go to the plant, don't you?"

I had avoided putting those words into the Universe for fear they'd come true, but it was obvious this was no normal earthquake. We only had one cause for our regular catastrophes, and we knew the source. And my greatest fear was that the origin wasn't in Acme's offices, but in the dragon-infested dungeon.

"Every time Andre uses violence, he loses a piece of himself," Julius warned. "I don't understand how it happens, so you'll have to take my word for it. The only way I can explain is to say he's operating on low battery power right now."

"He's operating on a *murder charge*!" I shouted in frustration. "Why don't I just tie him up and toss him to the alligators? It would be just about as easy."

I didn't linger to argue. I dashed back down to the bomb shelter, grabbed the end of a stretcher from a med student so he could prepare another patient, and helped carry another zombie upstairs.

I was operating on pure adrenaline. I really didn't have the strength to carry two-hundred-pound bums. I was useless here. I needed to be at the plant, hunting villains.

Someone must have turned off the gas line. The pillar of fire had vanished. I was terrified it would sprout anywhere I walked.

Leo had apparently called ambulances. Official medical vehicles screeched to a halt in front of the town houses. I gave up trying to help patients. Medics rushed past me, probably thinking they were dealing with earthquake victims. I hoped Acme wouldn't realize the casualties being hauled off now were their zombies from earlier.

With Gloria gone, I no longer knew the enemy. Ferguson, the pervert? Bergdorff, the guy Paddy called a mad scientist? MacNeill, the greedy shyster? I couldn't damn an entire building to hell in hopes of catching a villain.

I didn't see Andre or Cora anywhere. That was probably for the best. They'd only disagree with me anyway. Since I had no clear idea of what I was about to do, I wasn't in a position to argue. That's a tough spot to be in for a lawyer.

I jogged back to my Harley while studying the situation down by the waterfront.

Now that they realized the town wasn't being bombed, people were wandering back to the club or climbing into their cars and leaving. I saw nothing immediately hazardous, like green clouds or black floods of pitch. No more fires. The jagged cracks forming down the middle of the street didn't pour brimstone, but I still saw bats.

I could have sworn I saw Sarah in chimp form gazing into one of the cracks, swiping at bats. Maybe she'd crush any demons who tried to escape. If hell wasn't scorching her, it must only be me Gloria was after.

Given my experiences lately, I was imagining Gloria and Dane setting off fireworks in hell, but without Max as my mirror to the underworld, I couldn't verify fantasies.

Still, the flickering lights at the chemical plant were suspicious. Technically, Acme didn't have a night shift. Employees streamed out of the plant daily at five o'clock on the dot. There were guards and maybe some management or researchers who might have reason to work overtime. But it was almost midnight. This wasn't overtime.

Bill and the other patients were still inside the plant, being subjected to whatever atrocities Acme had planned for them. My DNA for justice burned through my veins like a shot of heroin, turning my normal caution to ashes.

I dug my jacket out of my saddlebag and dragged it on. The night air was cooling rapidly, and my silk shirt didn't lend itself to warmth. Besides, the leathers were from Max and made me feel safe. Stupid, I realized. But I was warm as I rode my bike down garbage-strewn alleys, avoiding anyone who might guess my direction. I zipped past the cordoned-off dead zone and up the north side to Acme. The earlier swaying had diminished to an occasional burping rumble, and the bike handled just fine.

Even a Harley can't handle a chain-link gate rolled across a drive, though. Given the bike's roar, I wasn't exactly hiding my presence, but no one appeared at the guardhouse. I wheeled into the shadows of a transformer station, took off my helmet, shook out my hair, and studied the situation.

I saw no evidence that the chain link was electrified, but I ambled around the side until I found a long weed. My rural education had its uses. I held the grass against the fence, and it didn't jump. Just to be safe, I tested the links with the back of my hand in case it pulsed slowly. I didn't want my fingers to instinctively wrap around the wire.

No juice. I could go home and mind my own business, or climb the damned fence and snoop.

Lawyers didn't break and enter. Apparently daughters of Saturn did. I really needed to work on that superhero costume, though. My gloves held up but I ripped a hole in my leather jeans going over the barbed wire on top.

Given what I knew already, I didn't need too much more evidence to convict Acme of jeopardizing lives and possibly manslaughter if any of our patients died. But for real justice, I needed the human culprit behind the gas attack and earthquakes. Gloria Vanderventer had already gone to her just reward.

I assumed the villain I needed was the one who'd sent the gray suits in the white sedans to evacuate us this morning. Was he busily covering up his dirty deeds tonight, and that's what the rumbling was about?

As I worked my way around the perimeter of the sprawling plant, searching for an opening, I reminded myself that I couldn't get mad and close the plant, legally or otherwise. Presumably, Acme made perfectly legitimate products while employing hundreds of hardworking people. I didn't know what the experimental element they were working on was—except dangerous—but for all I knew, it could be a cure for cancer.

So blowing up the plant wasn't an option, even if I knew how. Nice that I was finally learning to plan ahead. Sort of. Maybe I should do that more often—anticipate what could go wrong and plan for emergencies. I'd try that just as soon as life quit knocking me down.

One thing I could anticipate was that Andre would be aiming this way as well, but I hoped he'd have Paddy with him. Andre was sneaky and devious but he liked to appear legal—when he wasn't flying off the handle. Julius meant well, but I really didn't think Andre needed a babysitter. He was probably far better off without a loose cannon like me around, truth be told. I didn't want anyone else involved if I decided to take someone out.

Had it only been a few months ago that I'd been horrified at killing a rapist? And now my adrenaline was pumping in expectation of executing someone. At this rate, I'd be a merciless killer. I would become Sarah. That possibility gnawed one giant hole in my gut, but it didn't slow me down. Someone at Acme had crossed a line when they'd endangered the helpless—and continued to do so.

Vigilante justice rides again. Not liking it. Happening anyway. Maybe I should have brought Sarah and used her as my weapon—a different moral quagmire.

The plant had been renovated and added on to since Acme acquired it ten years ago. No coal cellars with handy chutes to slide down in this place. But I figured underground labs required air vents.

I hunted until I located the electrical control building. The door was locked, but I pried the aluminum siding open easily. As I've said, I've lived in some pretty crappy dives. Aluminum is bad for security.

I had no way of knowing if the control room actually contained ducts into the main plant, but I hadn't seen a more likely entrance.

I still had a flashlight in my bag. Given my propensity for exploring hellish places, I'd have to transfer it to my pretty briefcase should I survive the night.

Luckily, the flashlight beam revealed that this was more shed than bona fide building. No insulation or drywall hampered my access. I ripped the aluminum back to a point where I could see the machinery and wiggled through the studs and inside.

The grate for the air vent was on the wall facing the plant where it should be. I pried it off with a screwdriver I'd filched from a toolbox that really shouldn't have been stored there. I'd have a word with Paddy about security later, should I survive this.

Being small had some advantages. I tucked my

jacket into my bag and crawled down the duct without a bit of problem. I was probably picking up pink particles and breathing green gas, but I was feeling pretty confident that I was closing in on the bad guys and had Saturn on my side. Right now, I was thinking anyone causing bat-spewing earthquakes qualified as bad, if not outright evil. I could make a case for attempted murder and self-defense.

Pondering the differences between bad and evil and deciding there might be an element of redeemability in the former, I levered open another grate and dropped to the floor in the secret underground dungeon. *Bingo.*

I heard voices in the lab where I'd seen them keeping Bill and the others. So, were these syringe-wielding scientists bad or evil? *Evil* was so much easier. I could just damn them and watch them find their own way to hell. And maybe Satan or Saturn would grant my wish that my friends would regain consciousness. That notion had temptation written all over it.

Bad meant . . . they were merely guilty of a crime, right? If there had been a crime, I could conceivably call in authorities, but so far, the authorities had been turning their backs on the Zone and protecting Acme. Not the most appealing of alternatives, but I had to consider it.

I hated being judge and jury. If the scientists were just guilty, I should figure out how to teach them a lesson about experimenting on people without their subjects' permission.

I needed a repertoire of punishment to draw on.

I needed to get back to Fat Chick and check out the others to see if they had any good ideas.

Too late to think of that now. Besides, I could spend a lifetime studying and never get anything done. If Gloria kept pet demons in here, I was betting no other Saturn's daughter had encountered them or developed a better remedy.

I was right next to the head honcho's office. I tested the knob, but he'd locked his door. I guessed he was worried about that missing tablet with his pornography on it. Stupid, but worried.

Ye Olde Credit Card Trick doesn't work if you don't have any credit, but the nail file on my pocket-knife worked to open the feeble lock they'd installed on the cheap interior door.

Once inside the office, I studied the lab through the two-way glass. I didn't think a bunch of research scientists could cause the earth to tremble, but it wasn't as if I was any expert. My powers of observation were all I possessed, not magical knowledge.

I didn't see any demons in the lab—nothing with horns and a tail, anyway. No pillars of flame. Nothing obviously evil. As far as I could tell, these were simply employees following orders. I watched them for clues.

The researchers were huddled between the rows of cots, gesticulating angrily and yakking and not in the least happy. Huh, maybe they didn't like earthquakes, either. Maybe they actually thought they were helping their victims. People are arrogant like that.

I picked out Bill and Leibowitz on their cots, sleeping soundly but otherwise looking good. They were big men. I had no way of getting them out even if I knocked the scientists cold.

But despite my caution, my rage was still simmering. It needed an outlet. I wasn't finding one here. Not exactly. That Bill's jailers seemed as worried as I was prevented me from judging them and finding them guilty.

I donned a lab coat hanging on a hook. It was twenty sizes too big, but it hid my clothing and my bag, thus making me harder to identify when they checked their security cameras. I wasn't planning on confronting the scientists. Yet. I needed to explore and find out who was in charge of earthquakes and zombie thieves.

I yanked out the scarf I usually wore under my helmet and tied it around my distinctive hair. Black scarves aren't easily identifiable. I'd dispose of the evidence later and get a red one if I had to.

No one patrolled the dimly lit corridor. I kept my head down so cameras couldn't catch my face and stopped at the supply closet to add a surgical mask to my dashing white coat. I didn't normally carry weapons, but a case of surgical instruments could be useful. What the devil did any of the surgical supplies on these shelves have to do with better living through chemistry? It chilled me to consider it.

Now it was time to determine who the street wrecker was.

Sticking to the shadows along the walls, I slipped down the corridor, keeping my eyes and ears open. I knew I was underground, on the secret dungeon level beneath the public corridors. The lights I'd seen had been aboveground. I couldn't remember if there had been windows in the normal labs the next level up. Since there was no evidence of earthquake machines down here, I had to leave Bill and Leibowitz and investigate elsewhere.

I located the secret stairs and stole quietly upward in darkness. I was wearing biker boots, so I had to tread carefully. I listened at the hidden door into the main lab, but there was no way of discreetly opening a wall to hear better. I'd have to either slide the door open and confront anyone on the other side or admit defeat. We all know how that worked out, right?

As soon as the wall opened, I heard a furious voice and froze.

"Dammit, Padraig, what in hell are you doing in here? You nearly scared the shit out of me."

I didn't recognize the loud voice, but I knew the owner of the mumbled reply. Paddy hadn't been able to wait for justice, either. Or to find his mother's will.

I wished he would speak up. I couldn't tell if he was playing crazy or exercising authority. Unable to see either man, I hesitated, hoping they'd move on.

"Don't question me, you old coot!" the first speaker shouted. "You abdicated your responsibility. I've been the one managing the lab all these years in your absence, standing up to your damned mother. You can't just come in here and throw out years of work. MacNeill supports our research."

I was betting Max wouldn't like hearing that his former father thought it was fun to play with magic elements. But he probably suspected it, and that was the reason Max had been investigating Acme before his Granny Gloria had him killed. And here I was, following in his footsteps, courting hell.

Damn Paddy and his muttering. I put an eyeball to the crack, but this lab was nearly dark. A pity they didn't make black lab coats so I could blend in better. I couldn't see either of the players, but their voices carried just fine. I shimmied out of the lab coat and stuck it in my bag. Now I was in black.

"Padraig, you have gone too far!" the furious voice thundered.

Hooeee, that was one scary shout. Normal voices don't thunder, no matter what it says in novels. This voice was deep and resonant enough to rattle glassware and jangle my Saturn's daughter antennae.

Paddy the scientist didn't know what *not normal* meant.

I did. I'd seen through mirrors into hell and killed demonic bats by damning them to perdition. I seriously believed in demons these days, even if they came disguised as normal people. Or bats.

To hell with secrecy. Paddy could be in some serious shit. I slid through the crack and into the darkened lab, searching for Paddy, praying his antagonist hadn't already flung him against a wall with the strength of a thousand devils.

I wrapped a fist around the handle of one of the surgical knives I'd lifted, but I didn't think I could get close enough to use it. My martial-arts training did not lean toward knives. Throwing stars, yes, but knives were too up close and personal for someone my size.

Too late. Glassware crashed. With a thud, a lab table rattled and hit the wall to my left. A curse and a groan followed as I eased in that direction.

I prayed Paddy had broken a beaker over the other guy's head, but I didn't hold my breath. Paddy is so very obviously not a fighter. I knew in my gut that he'd been taken down.

"Thornton, Lerner!" Thundering Voice shouted. He either had minions nearby or was using a phone. "We have an intruder."

That would be me, except if I couldn't see him, I knew he couldn't see me. Which meant he must be calling Paddy an intruder. Not a good sign if he was accusing a part-owner of the plant of being an intruder in his own company.

Still, a scary voice, mayhem, and potential illegal incarceration were not enough for a death penalty. *Think like a lawyer, Tina,* I reminded myself as I eased along the wall. A task light gleamed over a desk on the far end of the large lab, and I made that my goal.

"Thornton and Lerner are currently unavailable," a cool voice on the far side of the lab replied with a familiar wry intonation. *Andre!*

I bit my tongue hard on a *damn.* The whole damned Zone could be here. I needed answers, not brawls, although I'd have liked to take my bat to Andre's head for not including me in his little reconnaissance mission.

I grabbed a nearby piece of heavy metal resembling

a toaster. Giving up on secrecy, I pushed past tables until I could see a wide, short lab coat that was Thunder Voice, presumably facing off against Andre.

I didn't know if Andre could see me in the darkness behind the broad girth that was my target. I only knew he was there from his voice, so I was hoping I still had the element of surprise on my side. I was allowed to defend others against a bully who had taken down an old man and threatened a friend. With the force of fury, I slammed the toaster thing down on an unfamiliar shiny crown.

Thunder Voice staggered, grabbed a table, turned, and fired a round from a nasty little gun in his hand. I ducked. Glass shattered over my head. I only registered that he had a piggy face before I whipped out my surgical knife and aimed for his balls.

But the turd bastard had turned his back on Andre. Always a mistake. Picking up my metal contraption, Andre rammed it even harder than I had across the jerk's balding skull. This time, Thunder Voice had the sense to go down and stay down.

I wanted to be grateful, but mostly, I was annoyed that Andre had finished the job. "Tell me he's evil and he's a goner," I thundered as best as I could in my feeble contralto. It's hard for a woman to do bass. Superheroes really ought to sound heroic. I snapped on my flashlight so I could see where Andre had got to and make sure Thunder Voice didn't come around.

Andre had dropped beside Paddy, who lay sprawled across the floor in a bed of glass. "Define evil," he said, lifting Paddy's eyelids. Paddy groaned, indicating he was still alive, and my red rage retreated to its hiding place, replaced by my stupid conscience.

Leave it to Andre to hit on exactly the argument I'd been having with myself. "Is the shit redeemable?" I asked, forgetting to thunder. After nearly breaking a man's skull and almost getting shot, I was more confused than angry. Usually, I damned people to hell when I was blind mad. In my current state, I probably couldn't fry bacon. So I was hoping Thunder Voice only sounded like a demon and wasn't actually one.

"From all reports, Ferguson's a pervert, a yes man with no spine, and probably a coward. He hit a defenseless old man. What does that make him?"

Crap. I'd seen Ferguson's computer files. Looking at pornography was disgusting and illegal if he was distributing. He was certainly guilty of breaking the law, but no one had given me an objective definition of evil. He had thundered in a not-normal voice, hit an old man, and shot at me. Except Andre and I didn't exactly belong here, so there was that crummy self-defense argument. Demons ought to have horns and tails or cackle madly or be more identifiable if I had to be both judge and jury. Maybe I should read more comic books and figure out how superheroes made these decisions.

I was ready to resign my position as a daughter of Saturn. How the devil was I supposed to envision justice in this case? I kicked the fat turd to see if he would roar some more, but he was out cold.

"It makes him a toad," I decided. Inspired by a SAVE KERMIT poster on the wall, I resisted temptation.

"He can spend the rest of his days eating insects and doing good instead of harm."

I visualized a toad. I was more familiar with horny toads than garden ones, and perverts ought to be labeled horny, except I knew horny toads were actually lizards. Pity. For lack of any better idea, I pictured something that could have been a frog or a toad. Or Kermit.

Andre nearly fell over backward when Thunder Voice shrank and bellowed in protest. Bullfrog was my guess. I gaped in astonishment. I hadn't actually expected my image to *work*.

Still bellowing, Ferguson hopped under a cabinet and out of sight.

Really, I scared myself when I did these things, and I'd sure put the fear of God into Andre's eyes. He was watching me as if I were the demon in the room.

25

I glared at Andre as if I'd turn him into a toad, too, if he gave me any lip. I was pretty shaky, but I'd be damned if I'd let him know that I'd never turned a man into a bullfrog before. I'm a smart-mouth with grandiose dreams, but until Max's death, I'd never done anything more dramatic than have a corrupt provost fired. And myself expelled. Consequences were always a bitch.

Of course, for all I knew, I was already damned for my incompetence, and turning someone into a bull-frog would get me sent directly to the devil. I needed a scorecard to keep track of my failures, but I dared him to come up with a better solution.

Shaking his head—probably in disbelief—Andre

lifted Paddy's shoulders to examine him for injuries. "Good thinking," was all he said. *Cool, Andre, really cool.*

Under normal circumstances, I would probably have found a seat until I was certain my knees would hold me up.

This time, I'd turned a two-hundred-pound bald guy into a *toad.* Or a bullfrog. As if I had a magic wand. *What in hell was I?* And there was that bad word again. Witches turned men into toads, right? Daughters of Saturn did bullfrogs?

I'd spent a lot of time months ago worrying that I was hallucinating, but now that I knew I wasn't, I really needed to get my head together and deal with my weirdness.

Before I could collapse and turn into a wuss worrying about the toad's family, the ground shook again.

Andre and I exchanged glances. In perfect accord for a change, we moved Paddy under a sturdy desk and raced into the corridor, following the thrumming sound.

We were on the right level. The roar of an engine grew louder and emanated from the second lab. Andre had his gun out, but I had a notion that shooting motors didn't lead to happy results. What did engines have to do with chemical plants? And why the devil was this one shaking the ground? Did Acme breed mad scientists? Did swamps breed mosquitoes? We were talking the *Zone* here.

Magic, Paddy had said. Maybe I'd better start believing in the improbable. Hell, *I* was improbable. I'd turned a guy into a bullfrog. Could I do the same to a machine? Were there any limits to what I could do?

One of my limits was my annoyingly overdeveloped conscience, with the occasional embellishment of logic—except when I went into red-rage mode.

The second lab was as large as the first, and equally cluttered with counters and equipment. No dangerous machinery. But on the far end was what should have been a closet door—except it was shaking.

Dodging counters, we crossed the lab and, without discussion, leaned against the wall on either side of the vibrating door. Andre turned the knob, holding his automatic ready. I had my flashlight. The door opened inward. No one shouted or started shooting.

Cautiously, I peered around the doorjamb. Andre hissed at me, but one of us had to do it. At the sight within, I straightened in awe. The shaking was so bad that I seriously considered zapping the whole room to hell. If any machine was capable of going down, it ought to be this one. I stepped inside to examine it up close.

I was no mechanic, but this contraption resembled nothing more than a giant boiler energized by an enormous generator connected to . . . I squinted and followed the various pipes and gauges up to the ceiling. A calliope? A steam organ? Steampunk, anyone?

Pipes went down into the ground as well. I studied them with distrust, expecting pipelines to hell and demonic bats. Nervously, I fought the urge to zap now and ask questions later. Only my earlier notion that people needed this plant kept me from attempting to create a bomb crater.

Although from the size of this machine and the enormity of the vibrations it was sending out, I suspected that if it blew, it would take Baltimore with it.

"That's what happens when a bunch of eggheads think they know engineering," Andre said in disgust, studying the contraption. "And that thing's likely to blow at any minute unless there's an automatic shut-off valve."

So not how I wanted to end my days—as a greasy puddle in the sky.

"Pull the plug?" I suggested valiantly. I had a sense that the shudders were sending gas or steam or some kind of heated energy up through the pipes. It was hot in here, and that ozone stink I'd noticed with the green cloud made my nose twitch. The damned thing was loud. And scary. And I really wanted to get the hell out and damn it into outer space.

My reward for resisting was realizing I was judging by appearances again. I didn't know the machine was bad. I only suspected it caused earthquakes and gas clouds. I bit my tongue on another *dammit to hell*. We were risking our lives for a damned machine that was about to rattle my teeth out of my jaw.

But the demonic bats in Gloria's cellar had shaken my cynical belief that hell was here on earth. If demons really were dancing around in eternal flame, could this contraption be pumping vapors from sulfurous zones? Was that their *magic*? Shouldn't I be a priest instead of a lawyer if I had to confront Satan's infernal engines? Or maybe I was overthinking this.

In my head, I visualized the machine turning off. It didn't.

I imagined finding the power switch. I didn't.

Saturn was a useless bitch.

Using the flashlight, we hunted but couldn't find a plug. Generators operated on kerosene or gas, so maybe that's what the thing was, although unless those pipes were vents, I couldn't see how they were discharging the fumes. I swept my light back and forth, but I couldn't find an OFF switch. This wasn't the polite little generator my mother had attached to our trailer.

"Turn it into a toad?" Andre suggested—facetiously, I hoped, as he followed the path of my light beam on the machine with his hands, searching for who knew what.

"Right. Poof. Machine, you're a toad." I snapped my fingers. "Oops. Guess that didn't work so hot." I was nervous. Andre needed to be damned glad he was cool with my Saturn talent, or I'd be turning him into a grinning Cheshire cat. I'd warned him about my instability. I was a lot shakier than I was letting on. Nervousness was bad for my soul.

For all I knew, syringe-wielding mad scientists would be down here any second.

The machine clunked on, rattling the walls, vibrating our teeth. I really didn't like the appearance of those pipes. They could go anywhere—into the plant, into another machine, into the Zone and surrounding neighborhoods. The ones going down might go straight to hell or the harbor for all I knew. Acme could be brewing their very own terrorist plot. Or an environmental disaster to beat BP on the Gulf Coast.

Apparently with the same thought in mind, Andre circled the enormous boiler. It practically filled the room, so this took some acrobatic maneuvering. If I could have seen him climbing through pipes, I'd probably have appreciated his prowess, but he was merely a vague shadow in my flashlight beam.

I was shaking, but that could have been from fear. In my limited knowledge, boilers could and did explode when they built up too much pressure. But we couldn't in all good conscience run like crazy. Not only would we have no chance of escaping, but an explosion could take out too many other lives besides our own. Bill, Leibowitz, the lab researchers, and the homeless guys, as well as Paddy, were all still downstairs.

Why wasn't anyone trying to dismantle the monster?

I inched around the room, focusing the light on Andre so he could see, sort of. On the far side, he located a panel and popped it open. I wasn't sure if I should back out of the room in case he blew it up or ease over to check out what he'd found. Since I wouldn't know a gauge from a switch, I opted for keeping an eye on the door to the corridor.

He fiddled and punched until the boiler shuddered, hissed, and expired. The generator switched off automatically.

I wiped sweat off my brow and Andre the Über-Cool did the same.

The silence was almost frightening. Only then did I realize that the emergency exit lights in the corridor had all gone out. We were now relying solely on my flashlight.

A bloodcurdling scream broke our paralysis.

I thought the shriek was more fury than pain, but that didn't stop me from running for the stairwell. The noise was definitely above us, and I didn't want to try the elevators if the lights didn't work.

I found a public stairwell, not the secret one to the lower levels. Our footsteps echoed off the metal stairs and concrete block enclosure. It smelled of old cigarettes and fried onions and ammonia. Or pee, but I wanted to give the scientists more credit than that.

We burst into Acme's main corridor and straight into the arms of half a dozen of their black-suited security goons—like the ones who had lied about Andre killing Gloria.

I bit my tongue on an instant curse until I could judge objectively. All black suits looked alike.

As startled as we were, the guards jumped at our arrival. Through the air vents, an outraged bullfrog croaked. He'd found the vents?

"The freaks have ruined us!" a white-haired, Einsteinish character in a lab coat screamed from further down the hall. "That was the last damned batch! We're ruined!"

His thick white eyebrows almost crawled up his forehead when he spotted us. "There they are! Catch them!"

As if the goons had to be told.

I kicked the shin of the brute trying to manhandle me and elbowed another. "Bergdorff?" I shouted, needing clarification before I got all red ragey. The Einstein character certainly looked like a mad scientist.

The goons were too busy grabbing at us to answer and the troll doll just kept shrieking in rage. Violent, insane rage, as Gloria and the vagrants had demonstrated.

Even though the goons accomplished nothing by jerking us around, they still had to get nasty. The one I'd elbowed yanked me off my feet by the back of my shirt and left me flailing, with the girls practically hanging out of my collar.

I was trained to act instinctively when grabbed by brutes. I swung my bag and kicked backward with all my strength. Unfortunately, the goon's arm was longer than my legs. He dodged the bag and retained his grip.

Andre sucker-punched the thug lunging for him. With a nifty twist I'd like to learn, he elbowed the bully in the solar plexus to keep him spinning, then thumped our next assailant with two fists to the jaw in a swift upward thrust that left my fighting abilities in the shade.

Not having time to be awed, I swung my puny weight sideways enough to unbalance my captor and kick his jewels. He screamed and released me. Biker boots ain't light.

I ducked another grasping fist and gut-punched the next thug who got near me, nearly breaking my knuckles. Stupid move, but by this time, I was fueled by fury and not logic. In hindsight, had I been think-ing, I would have dodged the brawl and gone for the Einstein with the answers. But I was in red-rage mad-ness and needed to take down brutes while resisting cursing them to Hades. My victim grabbed my hair. I raked his face with my fingernails and reached for the surgical knife I'd stuck in my waistband.

I couldn't, unfortunately, fight off the gun aimed at my head by the creep who came up behind me. I froze at the cold metal pressed to my temple and the meaty arm choking my esophagus. I'm barely five-five. The goon had to be covering six feet or more. I was out of my league.

Andre had no such problem. Even as I tried to slither down from the choke hold, Andre pulled his automatic out of his belt. Giving me no time to scream in panic, he point-blank shot the thug. The gun at my head clattered to the floor and I whipped free of the brute's hold. Just like an old oak struck by lightning, he toppled.

While the troll shrieked in outrage instead of shock, I stared in incredulity at the neat hole in the middle of the thug's forehead. Killing probably wasn't good for Andre's health or his future behind bars, but the man was damned good at it. They say that Special Ops training stays with you forever.

I didn't have the stomach for violent video ac-tion. I wanted to barf. I considered taking out An-dre's weapon for the sake of his immortal soul, but the brutes had now rightfully targeted me as the weak link. I was suddenly occupied, swinging left and right, offering vicious kicks at goons lumbering up on me from all sides, while swinging my knife at any others who considered coming closer.

But shock had momentarily replaced my red rage, and I'd finally woken up and realized that what I really needed to do was to break through these goons to get at the shouting white-haired troll jumping up and down at the end of the hall, unapologetically demanding our demise. I wanted answers.

Andre had his legs spread and his gun aimed, waiting for a clear shot in the tangle of arms and legs trying to halt my whirling-dervish act. The guards were nasty thugs willingly following the orders of a nutcase, but they *might* be redeemable. I couldn't damn them to hell and wish our patients back to normality, much as I'd like to try.

For the sake of Andre's immortal soul and my eternal health, I sighed with regret and conjured more toads. Or bullfrogs. I liked that solution, and it didn't require a lot of mental acuity.

I threw in a hasty picture of frogs turning into princes if kissed. I didn't know if kisses would actually transform them back to thugs, but if they had loved ones out there, maybe I'd find them and hand them a frog. Someday. If I survived. It was mildly better than letting Andre shoot them all, as he apparently meant to do.

Andre's next shot winged a fire alarm—because his intended victim had shrunk to boot-heel height and now hopped about the floor, croaking. We both stared in disbelief at the frightened, hopping frogs.

Even the guy with the bullet in his middle morphed into a flattened amphibian with his webbed feet curled in the air.

Andre turned an incredulous glare on me. The ensuing shriek of fire alarms prevented argument and shredded my already ragged nerves. And yeah, of course, the sprinkler system came on. The frogs loved it.

At the end of the hall, Einstein froze in disbelief as half a dozen amphibians hopped about where his guards should be, but Andre and I were Zonies. We were used to chaos and destruction. We took off running in his direction, trying to avoid breaking our necks on the water coating the tiled hall.

The white-haired troll sprang into action, darting into an office to the left. The slam could be heard over the shrieking alarms. IVANOV BERGDORFF had been gold-lettered onto the door.

I had the gut feeling we'd just located the true villain behind Acme's depredations.

Andre didn't even bother trying the knob. He simply blew it away, then kicked in the door.

Not wanting to lose my chance to question our target, I whacked the gun out of Andre's grip with the side of my hand.

Andre shot me a truly disgruntled look but miraculously didn't go after the gun. Maybe even he understood what he was doing to his soul when he killed. Maybe he had issues like mine. Although not quite like mine, because he'd been trained to kill, and I'd been trained to find evidence.

But I didn't figure Bergdorff would give up information just because I asked. So I jumped him before he could put that big desk between us. Landing on his back, I brought him down to the ground and rammed my knee into his spine.

"What is that infernal contraption doing to us?" I shouted, struggling to hold down the furious scientist. For an old man, he was wiry and strong.

"Making magic!" he cried. "We can cure cancer, raise the dead, own the world! It worked, can't you see? They said it wouldn't, but it did! The gas is curing their ills."

That sounded way too much like Gloria's mad tirade. I could be sitting on another power-hungry demon. Or a madman. Guilty by way of insanity? "Did you gas us on purpose?" I asked in horror.

"I needed to prove my element would work on people! It was the only way." The troll shoved, and, furious, I shoved back, kneeing him harder and grabbing his electrified hair. Andre located his gun but stayed out of my way, thank all the heavens and maybe Saturn.

"How?" I demanded, wanting to smash Bergdorff's nose into the floor but magnanimously refraining. "With pipes straight to hell? Where does that gas come from?"

"Who cares?" the troll asked, practically spitting in rage. "Don't you understand? I'm creating medical history! All those sick old people—they're cured!" He stopped his struggles in his need to explain.

"They're not better if they're comatose," I argued,

backing off slightly and wishing he were right. "And the gas causes violence."

"But don't you see? We can utilize that!" he crowed in triumph. "The ultimate weapon! We just have to refine the process." Taking advantage of my loosening grip, the devil came up swinging. He socked me straight in the diaphragm, sending me sprawling backward into Andre.

And of course Andre had aimed his damned gun while my back was turned.

Knocked off target by me hitting Andre's shins, the shot rang wild. The troll grabbed the opportunity to dive for an open desk drawer.

Figuring he was going for a gun, I rolled for cover. Andre did the opposite. He flung himself directly at Einstein.

Instead of a gun, Bergdorff brandished a familiar aerosol canister. He spritzed. Pink sparklies and a green cloud billowed in Andre's face.

Andre staggered backward, cast a startled glance at me, then crumpled, nearly two hundred pounds of male muscle at my feet. That he hadn't turned into a raging berserker like Gloria probably said something, but Andre was the final straw. He'd been trying to do *good*. And now he was comatose like the others.

Red rage instantly consumed me.

The cloud had drifted down to the carpet, where I was still gasping from the blow to my gut. I couldn't catch my breath in time. I inhaled.

He'd gassed us! The insane Nazi had gassed us!

Just as he had risked all our lives by gassing the

Zone, used our friends as guinea pigs, and turned them into zombies.

"Damn you to hell, you've killed him!" I shrieked, wiping my eyes and lunging for the madman behind the desk, who had scrambled to his feet again.

My curses never worked fast enough and usually required physical action. Stupid slow Saturn.

Bergdorff shot another cloud of gas but missed in his scramble to retreat from a raging virago. Covered in pink sparklies, I was too furious to think. I just went over his desk, aiming for his face and the can at the same time. I mashed his nose with the flat of my hand and shoved him back against the wall before nearly ripping his arm out of the socket to get at the cloud can.

"I want Andre back!" I yelled, struggling with his grip on the can. "I want my friends back. I want all the zombies back, you bastard." I dug my fingernails into his hand so hard that he finally dropped his weapon. "And I want you to suffer like them!"

With that last shout, I did more than slam my palm in his face. In my wild frenzy, I swung my fist at his jaw with all the power in me and sent him flying. He wasn't big and he wasn't agile and he obviously had a glass jaw. He slumped into a window, crushing the blinds. Before he could recover and come after me, I found the canister and shot him with his own damned gas.

He shrieked. He clutched at his eyes. And instead of leaping at me in self-defense, he turned and dived through the closed window, blinds and all.

I staggered backward, stunned. I didn't think it was really possible to throw oneself through glass and blinds at close range. He should have just bounced off. He didn't. As if a giant hand had grabbed his back and swung him through the air, he took out everything, including the aluminum frame. And then he was gone. *Whoosh*, out the window.

Maybe I hadn't killed him. Maybe he was just out there on the ground.

I glanced down at Andre's lifeless, elegant body sprawled across the floor and felt the red rage drain away, replaced by soul-deep fear that I might never talk to him again. I didn't know what was happening to us or to the Zone, but I'd never wanted anyone to die. Or spend eternity in a coma. Shaking, trying not to cry or panic, I approached the window and leaned out.

This was the main floor, one level above the basement labs where we'd left Paddy and the machine. The window wasn't much more than ten feet above ground—a survivable drop.

Einstein lay crumpled across a spiked fence surrounding an air-conditioning unit. I was pretty sure the black spike coming out his back wasn't good for his heart, if he had one. My stomach churned. Had I done that? Or the evil gas? Or . . . Saturn?

A frog hopped through the open doorway and across Andre's silk shirt, croaking. I realized the fire alarm had stopped shrieking. In the silence, I could hear the bullfrog still bellowing through the air vents. I brushed pink particles off my sleeves and started shuddering. Hard.

"Okay, Saturn, what do I do now?" I whispered, wishing I'd at least learned how to save the zombies before inviting death and destruction.

I had no idea if Bergdorff had been mad or evil. I just knew he was dead. And so was almost any hope of Andre and the others recovering.

Hands trembling, I could scarcely open my bag to retrieve my phone as I knelt beside Andre. I still had the can in my hand. I stared at it in distaste, but, not wanting to leave a weapon lying around, I stashed it in my bag after removing the phone.

Who should I call? I didn't know how Andre or Paddy had gotten in. I wasn't certain Leo would be willing to climb the fence, and we really needed ambulances and cop cars. . . .

Phone in hand, I knew my mind wasn't working right when I realized I was thinking of calling cops to help Andre. He was wanted for murder. And there was a dead body outside the window and missing security everywhere. And frogs.

I stared in fascination as the one near Andre shot out a long tongue to catch up one of the pink particles as if it were a tasty insect.

The frog didn't flinch when I glared at it, but it hopped under the desk to slurp more particles while I tested the pulse in Andre's strong wrist. He was still alive. Grasping at this one straw, I punched in Cora's number. This was Zone business. Outsiders not allowed.

26

Paddy staggered in holding a white cloth to his head. He glanced down at Andre and wearily slumped into a chair. "What happened?"

"Einstein gassed him." I put away my phone and waited for the troops to arrive. I still wasn't certain if Paddy was any saner than Einstein or Ferguson had been. Maybe magic gas had polluted their brains and the whole plant was crazy.

Paddy glanced worriedly at Andre, rubbed his head, and asked with puzzlement, "Einstein?"

"Oh, stop that," I said grouchily. "I'm tired of the crazy act. The troll with the white hair who had the cloud canister. He sprayed both of us. Andre dropped like a stone. The troll went berserk." With a little help from a raging Saturnian lunatic.

"Bergdorff?" he asked in bewilderment at my rant. His attention was more on Andre than me. "Andre got gassed? Julius will kill me." Paddy winced and pressed the cloth tighter to his head. "We've got to get him out of here before we call the cops to report Ferguson. I've already called the fire chief and told him we had a false alarm."

Ferguson? He was worried about the *bullfrog*? I glanced at the smashed blinds covering the shattered window, but Paddy hadn't even looked in that direction. Maybe I'd better not disturb his confused mental state just yet.

"Why was Ferguson trying to kill you?" I asked, trying to determine how much he actually understood.

"He turned on the magic machine again. I had to stop him." He studied Andre with puzzlement and listened to the silence. "Did Andre stop him?"

"He stopped the machine, I guess."

Paddy looked pretty pale and sweaty, so I didn't see any sense in explaining too much, especially if he hadn't seen Ferguson morph into a bullfrog.

"I want Bill and the others in a proper hospital," I continued, mournfully stroking Andre's glossy hair. I was all out of rage. I just felt hollow inside. Andre didn't stir.

Paddy slumped silently into a chair. I was afraid he'd gone out on me too.

In response to my frantic call, Cora arrived with Frank and Leo in record time. I hugged Cora in relief, and she tucked her snakes back to their own dimension. We all stared solemnly at Andre's sprawled form.

He seemed even bigger on the floor than he did standing up. I'd seen him in action. He was all solid muscle, and a whiff of gas had taken him out. My pulse pounded anxiously, but it would be uncool of me to reveal my fear for him.

While Frank checked Paddy's bruised head, our perceptive cop wrinkled his brow. "What's with the frog?" He pointed under the desk.

I accepted the distraction and glanced around. The stupid amphibian was probably poisoning himself on pink particles. Maybe he thought he was still a six-foot thug with a sweet tooth. Heck if I knew.

"Not important," I said, going into impartial lawyer mode. "We have to remove Paddy and Andre and the zombies before anyone discovers they have a mad scientist impaled on the fence."

Everyone raised their eyebrows in shock except Paddy, who was rocking back and forth like a dementee. Leo took the lead and strode across to the smashed blinds.

I shivered as he examined the broken window frame and wished this had all been a nightmare I could wake from.

"We won't find Andre's bullets in the guy down there, will we?" Studly Do-Right asked, reasonably enough.

If they wanted to check frogs, they'd find a bullet there. I didn't tell Leo that. I'd added Andre's gun to my bag before the troops arrived. "No, I gassed him," I confessed, "and he went berserk and leaped out."

No mentioning damning the bastard to hell. Leo

wouldn't have believed that anyway. If we got out of this without a life term in prison, Leo was our Zone cop like I was the Zone lawyer. A regular clan, we were. Right now, my teeth were chattering in sheer terror. I didn't much like killing people, and I didn't want to lose Andre.

"That was some leap," was all Leo said, testing the splintered frame. "Frank, you and Cora better check on Bill and the other patients. I'll find something to carry Andre on. At this rate, we probably ought to keep a supply of stretchers on hand for Tina's victims."

I hugged my elbows and glared. Cora snorted. And Frank did as he was told. Still not looking good, Paddy lumbered out of his chair to lead the way. No one tried to stop him. I hoped he had the authority to order the scientists to back off when they reached Bill.

Once they were all gone, I kneeled beside Andre and gently brushed the hair off his forehead. He was cool to the touch and didn't stir so much as an eyelid to acknowledge my presence, which left me feeling empty.

He was a handsome man when he wasn't leering or being snarky. I'd just sent Satan a soul. Saturn or Satan or Someone owed me for that. I'd already asked the Great Whatever to return my friends from comas, but rather than rely on the fickle finger of fate, I was hoping Paddy had more magic formulas. We needed Andre too much to lose him.

Except the troll had said they didn't have a solution yet.

"What the devil is that racket?" was the only other question Leo asked when he returned with a gurney just as the bullfrog roared his protests through the vents.

"Demon," I joked. "You want to see Acme's demon-transport system? It's fiendish in its simplicity." Although I supposed I'd need a definition of *demon* to know if a bullfrog qualified, but Leo wasn't buying my attempt at humor.

Leo glared and heaved Andre onto the wheeled table.

I had no way of knowing if the boiler machine did anything more than thunder and smoke. I didn't know how to blow it up without blowing up Acme. I had to hope Paddy would take care of it now that the villains were gone.

Mostly, I was worried that we weren't dealing with normal chemicals. Given the amount of damage done, the new *magic* element the stupid scientists were testing could have come straight from hell. Did greedy, arrogant men never consider long-term consequences when they had dollar signs in their eyes?

Or had Ferguson and Bergdorff really been demons and not just corrupt men?

My wicked imagination conjured gates to hell in Acme's basement, but I was reeling from exhaustion and despair and not thinking straight. How did one go about scientifically studying the underworld? If we proved it existed, could I write laws against demons?

I was thinking hard about resigning my Saturn duties. I was pretty certain it wasn't possible, but watching Andre lying lifeless on that cart, I considered it anyway.

How had the damned troll gotten that canister?

Unless there was more than one, Paddy was the only answer. Paddy must have retrieved the canister from Tim and not told us. We still didn't know if Paddy was sane. Of course, at this point, I needed a definition of *sanity*. I needed a damned library of abnormal knowledge.

I wanted to cling to Andre's hand and reassure myself that he lived as Leo wheeled him out, but I was afraid Leo would slam him into walls if I expressed my concern. Men are territorial for the stupidest reasons.

Ignoring the frogs hopping about in the puddles, we met the rest of the crew rolling Bill out of the elevator. My fear of losing friends was deeply ingrained. I touched Bill's forehead, but he didn't stir.

"We'll have to come back for the others," Frank said gruffly.

The security cameras would have had a field day, except Leo said he'd turned them off and wiped them out. Let them believe the sprinkler system had short-circuited the wiring.

Cora and Frank were intelligently wearing rubber gloves so no trace of them would be found later. Leo and I had been here before, so there was no sense in disguising our fingerprints. I hoped Andre hadn't touched anything besides his gun. Both of us had fingerprints in the database if anyone cared enough to search.

"You mean you just walked in through the gate?" I asked suspiciously as we stepped into the night and I recognized Leo's Ford SUV in the drive. "I could have walked in instead of crawling through ducts?"

Holding his bandage in place, Paddy glared at me. "I have keys. You could have asked."

And gotten gassed for my efforts? I bit my already sore tongue and eyed him with more suspicion. He seemed to be recovering in the night air. "When I know I can rely on you, I will," I retorted. "How did Bergdorff get the canister?"

He locked Acme's front door and smudged the lock with the back of his sleeve. "Bergdorff is in charge of the magic machine."

Even Frank rolled his eyes at this. "Magic machine?"

"Figure of speech. Bergdorff is mad as a hatter. I wanted to use the cloud on him and see if it would make him better." Paddy studied the darkened windows of the plant. "I left the canister in my office. Maybe I'd better go back and get it."

"Man, you lie better than I do, Padraig," I said nastily. If he'd brought the canister here, he was as much to blame for Bergdorff's death as I was. Although ultimately, as inventor of the gas, Bergdorff had killed himself in more ways than one. "Einstein's deader than a doornail, so you don't need to worry about him anymore. You'd better just hope Andre hasn't sacrificed his life for us, or I'll bring the whole place down around your ears."

It didn't sound threatening from a skinny shrimp like me, but he ought to have known by now that I was a loose cannon and dangerous when roused.

Instead of appearing properly terrified, Paddy looked sad, and not in the least guilty. "Bergdorff's dead?"

"Trust me, he won't be firing up the machine again."

"He used the canister on Andre? I'd better go back and get it," Paddy said worriedly, studying the plant. The first rays of dawn were lightening the sky over the harbor. "Did you leave it in the office?"

"Einstein took it out the window with him," I lied. I wasn't trusting that can in anyone else's hands ever again. "I don't advise you to go near the body, or I'll have two murder cases to fight."

"They know I'm there at night. The window in his office?" he asked worriedly, tensing as if he was about to take off in search of the canister. Or Bergdorff.

I grabbed his arm and shoved my phone in his hand. "Learn to use one of these, will you? Call the cops when we're safely out of here. Pretend sanity."

If glares could kill, he would have downed me then. Without another word, he departed at a lope.

Frank and Cora didn't attempt to stop him. Cursing under my breath, I climbed into the back with Bill and Andre and held their hands.

We might not think alike, but Andre was my anchor to the Zone. I didn't want to live here without him.

Which was just plain nuts, but I'd been gassed. That was my excuse and I was sticking to it.

• • •

The next afternoon, I watched the world go by outside Andre's front window while sitting on his fancy leather couch with Milo in my lap. Andre's apartment is on the first floor, so his porch blocked most of the view. But it would have been silly to ask Leo and Frank to cart him up to my barren apartment when Andre's was more comfortable and accessible. And his father had so much more experience at caring for comatose patients.

Leaving Andre unprotected wasn't on my radar, however. I didn't know when I had appointed myself Andre's guardian. If I gave it any thought, I'd realize he had an entire community to watch over him. Sarah had already been by, asking questions that I'd shrugged off. She considered Andre boyfriend material. I'd rather not set off a jealous rage in her murderous breast, but it didn't matter. I was here, and I wasn't leaving. I was probably still waiting for Saint Saturn to fix things. My world was just that confused.

My phone rang and I checked caller ID to make certain it wasn't a hamburger joint in Alaska, but Cora's number showed up. "Anything new?" I asked.

"Cops still crawling all over Acme and we've got newshounds cruising the streets. We got Bill to the hospital, but not the others. So far they're only questioning Paddy about Bergdorff."

"Bill still comatose?" I asked. I hadn't even managed to rescue all the patients, dammit. I was feeling like a complete and utter failure.

"Bill's still out. Frank's at the hospital with him and the other patients they took from Andre's. As far as we know, Paddy hasn't led the cops to the secret lab, and the research scientists are lying low. Paddy's over there now, pretending to be sane. He says we can go in and get Leibowitz and the others as soon as the mundanes are gone. He'd probably get arrested if the cops found them. Bad for business. How's Andre?"

I'd known that was why she was calling. Julius had wanted us to take Andre to the attic infirmary with Katerina, but I'd balked and insisted he be returned to his own room. I was convinced Andre would pull out of his coma, like Sarah. No one ever said I was *always* rational. But I did keep fretting over the part where Bergdorff had thought the gas only affected sick and old people. The baby docs had more or less confirmed that with the zombies.

Sarah hadn't been sick. She'd just been shifting.

Andre took regular time-outs. Maybe he shifted in his brain. Bergdorff wouldn't have known about those possibilities.

"Sleeping," I insisted. "There's a reporter outside taking pics of the warehouse," I warned, watching out the window. Fortunately, I hadn't had time to hang a shingle in front of my new office. I was thinking maybe I wouldn't. I didn't have a lot of friends in the media.

"We have people working overtime on faking them out," Cora assured me. "Apparently gas explosions happen all the time on chemically enhanced ground. The road cracks are settling back to potholes."

"Might work for reporters, but what is Paddy telling the police?"

"Leo and Paddy have them convinced Bergdorff committed suicide when the sprinkler systems malfunctioned and ruined his big, bad machine. The police think Ferguson may have sabotaged it. They haven't found him yet."

Even Cora didn't know I'd turned Ferguson and the nasty security guards into frogs. I doubted that anyone cared. I occasionally gave the frogs a worried thought, but it wasn't as if I'd figured out how to reverse my curses. I sure as hell wasn't kissing any goonfrogs.

I was feeling a little lonely and depressed, with no one to talk to about my fears and no means of alleviating them. Andre was the only one who had any real clue about me. Maybe I should call Sarah. At least she understood, even if her reactions weren't necessarily rational. She might try killing frogs to see if she was rewarded with longer legs.

"I'll let you know if anything changes," I assured Cora, knowing it was Andre she fretted over. "He has a court appointment next week. I'll have to get a postponement. We can't wheel him in like this."

I'd slept all morning on Andre's couch and prayed a miracle would have taken place by the time I woke up. Hadn't happened. Of course, it had been after midnight when I'd damned Bergdorff to Hades, so maybe I had another twenty-four hours to wait.

Outside, a physically fit man with poker-straight posture pushed a twin baby stroller past the warehouse. If that was one of the soldiers I'd condemned to nursery duty, did I have to lift the punishment or did it eventually wear off? Didn't I give them a week? Their time wasn't up yet.

I'd lose track of all the asshats I'd visualized out of my way if I did it too often. I needed to remember to give them term limits when I cursed them. For now, I was hoping that once they learned their lessons, they'd work themselves out of whatever I'd thrown them into. Or maybe they'd make radical changes in their lifestyles and the world would be a better place. Not sure the frogs had minds enough to do that, though. That had been fun at the time, but a major big boo-boo on my part now that reality had set in. Maybe I ought to gather the frogs and take care of them until I figured out how to fix things.

Tim jogged down the stairs, saw me in the front parlor, and came in jiggling my car keys. "Thanks, Tina," he said diffidently, handing them back. "Pearl wouldn't get in the car with an invisible driver, but we did okay."

Milo leapt down to say hi to Tim, and I dropped the keys in my bag. "You'll learn to control it eventually," I assured him. "Guess I need to give you driving lessons, though."

He shrugged. I'd taken him to Goodwill a few months ago to help him pick out clothes since Pearl had thrown all his out when he'd first turned invisible. He was outgrowing them already, thank goodness. He was wearing a tie-dyed pink wife-beater and lemon-green mini-shorts today. And his shaggy, nondescript hair needed a cut. I thought he could be one of the good guys that the Zone made into good men—like Bill.

"It's like having family, y'know?" he said cryptically.

I smiled as I took his meaning. "Pearl can be your grandmother, but Nancy Rose has to be your mother, not me. I'm just the annoying older sister. And you're my bratty baby brother." I'd never particularly wanted siblings, but Tim was a good kid.

He nodded solemnly. "Can you make Andre better?"

"I would if I could, but I'm no doctor. I guess we wait to see what happens." I hated that. I'd already tried visualizing our patients out of their comas, but apparently fixing things wasn't in the interest of justice. It hadn't worked. I should run over to my place and grab my tablet now that I was awake, see if Fat Chick or someone knew the answer.

"Can I have the keys back to visit Nancy Rose at the hospital?"

I pointed at the kitchen. "You can go make us some sandwiches. You need a driver's permit and lessons before I let you in my car outside of an emergency."

"You can't blame a guy for trying." He ambled off toward the back of the house.

I returned to petting Milo and watching out the window. I could go in and check on Andre, but I wasn't much of a nurse. The baby docs had all gone home now that their patients had been taken from them. Maybe I should hire one to help out Julius. Like I had any money to do that.

I was hurting bad and needed to do something.

I'd almost convinced myself that talking things out with Sarah was worth the risk when a familiar male voice jarred me out of my reverie.

"Any chance of getting food around here?"

I swung my legs back to the floor and stared at the doorway. Andre leaned against the doorjamb, wearing impeccably draped dark trousers, a blue silk shirt open at the neck, and a hungry gaze that had my insides performing acrobatics.

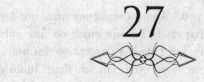

27

I'm not ashamed to say that I flung myself into Andre's arms and kissed him. It was one hell of a good
kiss, if I do say so myself. Andre might make me
crazy, but man, he had some major mojo happening.
He hauled me off the floor, flattened my breasts into
his solid chest, grabbed my ass, and applied a whole
lot of tongue until my head reeled. And other parts
south. All those hormones mixed with ecstatic joy—
combustible. I might even have been crying while I ran
my hands through his silky hair.

Julius's coming down the stairs interrupted us.
Andre muttered an expletive and reluctantly lowered
me to the floor, taking full frontal advantage while
he was at it. I wasn't averse to some titillating body

contact and a good whiff of unshaved male. I needed to make certain he was solid and real and all there. I didn't even want to punch him out for a change.

He was still my client, though, so I shoved away as my senior partner hurried in, his face alight with delight and relief.

"I'll help Tim fix lunch," I muttered, leaving the two of them alone.

"I'll go with you." Andre caught my arm, not letting me escape that easily. I'm not much on succumbing to alpha males, but I made an exception this time.

Andre's kitchen was even fancier than Julius's: larger, with more granite and stainless steel and fancy machinery that had probably never been touched. I was amazed Andre allowed Tim anywhere near it. I pried myself away from Andre's grasp to examine the refrigerator's contents.

"I am not going through this hell ever again," I warned as I removed goodies. "I need explanations. You can't just rise from the dead when no one else can and pretend everything is normal. That's the stuff of zombie movies."

The echoing silence even had Tim glancing up from the array of food I'd spread on the counter.

"Why don't Tim and I make some nice sandwiches?" Julius said politely. "The two of you can go in the other room and catch up."

That sounded ominous. Tim scowled when Andre grabbed my arm, but he had even less authority than me around here.

Andre dragged me out of the kitchen instead of

snarking, and I tensed with anxiety. Andre treating one of my questions seriously meant the answer had to be bad, indeed. Might as well clear the air while I had a chance of him listening. "How come the gas made *me* go ballistic and not comatose, but you, the macho man, went the other way? How can you wake up and the others can't?"

He dropped me back on his couch and loomed over me. "I've been inoculated," he said. "Not a word of this goes beyond this room, understand?"

His dark eyebrows pulled down in a scowl and his whiskered jaw created the kind of bad-boy image that made my heart go pitty-pat. He looked sane. But his muscles were tense enough to make me think I'd just revealed national secrets.

"You're my client. They can't even make me talk in a court of law," I informed him, growing more worried by the minute. "*Inoculated* with what? Crazy gas?"

"They didn't have the gas back then." He paced up and down his gorgeous brown and cream silk rug. "I was using anything I could get my hands on when I came back from overseas."

"Crap." I dropped my head in my hands, my over-worked imagination picturing über-cool Andre with three-day-old scruff and needle tracks up his arm.

"Paddy used a mixture of magic element in treating my mother," Andre reminded me. "I thought comatose would be better than the hell I was living. But I tried it in smaller quantities."

I rubbed my eyes. "I get it. I've smoked a joint or

two, and I didn't have the excuse of shattered nerves from being shot at and tortured. Get to the point before Tim sneaks in."

"The magic formula knocked me into a dreamworld, but not enough to keep me there, like my mother. So I shot up anytime I wanted escape." He stopped there.

I flashed him my best glower. Andre just stood in the middle of his elegant apartment, exuding fiendish magnetism and arrogance. I wanted to dump a bucket of chocolate fondue over his head and bite him. Maybe sensing my antagonism, he dropped into his fancy leather pedestal recliner—the one remarkably similar to Dane's.

"That's it?" I asked in disbelief. "So because you played with fire back then, you can get gassed now and you just take a nap and come back better than ever?"

"It's not all good," he warned. "There are side effects. I don't have hallucinations, but if I go into emotional overload, whatever is in my system reacts in reverse. I go comatose without need of gas."

Okay, I'd seen that. I'd seen him go gray around the edges. I'd seen him pass out. I knew he sometimes disappeared at inconvenient times when I needed him most. Magic gas kicking in. Got it. Didn't like it, but at least it was an explanation. And better than going berserk. Even explained his practice of über-coolness.

I worked through some of this, but it just wasn't enough. "How come Sarah came back? And the others didn't?"

"You brought Sarah back. Don't ask me how. The others . . . They didn't have my immunity." Swinging his long legs onto the ottoman, he dragged his hand through his hair and frowned. "Paddy believes the same thing as Bergdorff—that the element has a healing ability that can be distilled. In a way, it healed my psychosis. And it cured my mother's cancer. But we were experimenting with different levels of the drug, different mixtures."

"So this stuff Acme is working on really is like a drug that can cure cancer?" Wow. Damned good thing I hadn't blown up the plant. "But didn't Bergdorff say we'd ruined his last batch?" *Shit*. We'd probably doomed the world, if so.

"What good does curing cancer do if it sends the patient to another dimension?" Andre asked grumpily, leaning back. "It's like living another life beyond the veil, really freaky. I've learned to jerk myself out of it in sheer frustration, but the others . . . Maybe they *prefer* dreamland to reality. Or maybe they don't know it's not reality."

I rubbed my brow as if that would help me absorb this new revelation. "You mean, you're not just sleeping? You're hallucinating or something?"

"Or something," he agreed. "What time is it? I need a drink."

"You don't drink," I reminded him. "For good reason, apparently. Explain 'or something.'"

He didn't want to. I'd learned to recognize Andre's evasive tactics. But this was too important for me to stay uninvolved. I set Milo back down and pointed him at Andre. "Get in his face, will you?"

I could swear, my cat almost laughed. And then he roared as I'd heard him do when offended, launched from the floor at Andre's head, and tilted the whole damned chair backward with his heavy weight.

The resulting crash brought Tim and Julius running. Andre was lying flat on his back, buried under a hefty blur of ginger fur, cursing blue blazes while Milo kneaded his chest. It's possible my kitty took a bite or two, because Andre yelped and shoved the cat away.

"We're learning a new game," I told Julius, wearing my most sincere expression. "Go back to your sandwiches. Andre doesn't like losing."

Julius is a brilliant man. Verifying that his son was furious but unharmed, he led Tim out of the range of danger.

"What the devil was that for?" Andre demanded, returning to his feet and straightening the chair. "You've trained an attack cat?"

"Milo is a natural, and I sicced him on you because this is no time for you to equivocate. I've *counted* on you to watch my back, while you were hanging out in Shangri-la. I need to understand why."

"I don't know what you're warping into, but you're developing a Wonder Woman complex with your frog voodoo," he grumbled, taking a high-backed wing chair with four legs instead of a pedestal base. "What you really want is to save the world and magically bring back Bill and the others. You have to get a grip. It's just not happening. Don't you think I would help if I could?"

"Not totally sure," I admitted. "You might miss Bill

at the bar, but you don't care a whit about the others. So make this about your mother." This line of questioning had no rhyme or reason. Andre would have saved his mother if there were any way of doing it. But I just couldn't get past the possibility that if Andre and Sarah could come back, there had to be some way of saving the others. "Where do you go when you're not here?"

"I told you, it's a dreamworld. It's not real. My mother is there sometimes. I thought I saw Bill this last time, and Sarah before she woke. But take my word for it, I'm really in my bed. Witnesses tell me I haven't stirred, just like the others. My subconscious is simply mixing stuff up and making it seem real, like in dreams, except I remember some of it when I wake up."

"I remember some dreams when I wake up. This must be different if you're not telling me about it. What do you do in these dreams?" I felt as if I'd burst through my skin if I didn't get answers. I'd taken out Bergdorff for him. Andre *owed* me explanations.

He glared. "Time in dreams isn't linear like in the real world. I see and do things over there that sometimes happen later, here."

I dropped back against his plush sofa and processed this with disbelief. "When you told us we wouldn't find the will at Gloria's, it was because you'd dreamed it was somewhere else?"

"I dreamed we wouldn't find it," he corrected. "But I didn't dream *where* to find it. And things don't happen in logical order. Years ago, I dreamed of being attacked by soldiers, so I built the arsenal closet. It was pretty pointless until last week."

"Paranoid dreams." I wanted them to be more. I wanted them to be a clue that would help save our zombies. I swallowed my disappointment. "I don't suppose you've dreamed anything about us saving the comatose?"

"No, not a thing," he said wearily. "Can we let this go?"

I didn't want to. I wanted a blow-by-blow description of this world he repeatedly returned to when stressed. I wanted to go there myself, but I was apparently one of the morally questionable who went berserk when gassed. And I wasn't about to shoot up. No pleasant dreamworlds for me.

"You can't dream a winning lottery ticket?" I grumbled.

"Not deliberately, but if I did, it might be one from last year. Time has no meaning in the dreamworld." Andre watched me warily for a reaction.

If there really was a hell, why not another dimension? I just needed to expand my mind far enough to encompass the enormity. Could I believe Bergdorff's infernal contraption drew on another dimension besides hell? Probably not. Only hell would turn Gloria into a demon. But hell apparently had several layers. Circles. Whatever. Maybe the zombies were in some outer level—*like Max had been*?

Out the window, I saw Paddy hurrying in our direction. I'd have liked to take another whack at Andre but I figured we'd end up rolling around on the floor in frustration. Not a wise idea.

I opened the front door before Paddy had a chance

to knock. Julius and Tim arrived bearing trays of sandwiches and soft drinks. My tree-hugging mother had
taught me to dislike chemically enhanced lunch meats,
but since I didn't have to prepare the food, I accepted it
without complaint as we settled into Andre's front room.
Andre was still frowning blackly, so I ignored him.

"Are we all under suspicion yet?" I asked Paddy,
bringing the discussion straight to the point.

"No, they still think Ferguson did it, but they're
searching for the guards who were supposed to be on
duty, too. Their families fear the worst." Paddy tapped
his fingers against the pedestal recliner he'd taken and
glared at me from under his bushy eyebrows. "I gathered up all the frogs I could find and said they were
part of an experiment."

"They like to eat pink glitter," I bluffed with a grin.
I was relieved that he'd captured them, though.

"You have no idea how valuable those particles
are," he griped.

Pink glitter was valuable in what way? He didn't
give me time to interrogate him.

"But that's not the problem." Paddy produced a
packet of papers from inside his old blue work shirt
and handed them to me.

I wanted gloves before accepting them, but I hated
to insult the potential new owner of Acme. I took the
papers by a corner and scanned them quickly. Not
original documents but copies. The legal language of
the first paragraph was explanatory enough. Forgetting my distaste, I started flipping through the pages.
"Where are the originals?" I demanded.

"Police have them. They've called Dane."

Julius swept the papers out of my hand, skimmed them, and gave them to Andre as he finished each one.

Tim simply helped himself to another sandwich and swigged his Dr Pepper, oblivious to the momentous revelation in our hands.

"She completely bypassed you," I said in sympathy, rereading Gloria's will as Andre returned the pages to me. "I'm sorry."

"I'm not, not entirely," Paddy admitted. "It's tainted wealth. I just want continued access to the plant. I'll need to hire you to fight the will if they deny me that."

A phone rang. I recognized the national anthem. Remembering I'd given Paddy my cell, I held out my hand. Should I ever make any money—and it obviously wouldn't be from Paddy if this will was accepted—I was buying a new phone, one untainted by Zone humor.

Paddy seemed momentarily confused, patted his pockets, then rescued my El Cheapo pay-as-you-go from his pants.

I couldn't greet Max with my usual sauciness, not with everyone listening. "Good afternoon, Senator," I said in greeting, alerting him that I wasn't alone.

"Snodgrass's office just called," he said without preamble. "What the hell will I do with Hell's Mansion? The bitch didn't even trust her own son to control Acme. She gave a ten percent share to Glenys instead, which means I have no control and can't burn the place down. Can we run away to the South Pacific now that I'm a gazillionaire?"

"We were just discussing possibilities, Senator," I said politely. "I'm sure the mansion can be donated to a worthy cause or sold to developers. Your lawyers will be happy to advise you. You really need to talk to your father about the other. Closing Acme is not advisable under the circumstances." Not if pink particles might cure cancer or whatever Paddy was implying.

"Who's there, Justy?" Dane/Max demanded.

"Witnesses," I said snidely, aware that I had a riveted audience. Andre gripped his chair arms and looked as if he'd rocket into orbit any minute.

"You need to come over here and talk in private?" he asked. Brilliant man, my Max. I liked having him back, as long as I didn't have to see him in Dane's disguise.

"Not when the news breaks. Acme and I don't have a good rapport, and you don't want their goons suspicious of you. I seriously suggest that you not allow the MacNeills to have control of the plant. Do you understand?"

Michael MacNeill, Max's ethically challenged father, was also Glenys's father. Now that Glenys had a share, they'd probably control Acme, unless Grandma Ida bothered to resume her authority. Dane really needed to keep his paws out of that mess if he wanted to keep his senate seat.

Max was silent for a moment. He had been investigating Acme before he died, so he had to know his father had supported whatever went on over there.

"Snodgrass says I need to put the shares into the trust," he said cautiously. "He's one of the executors."

"There should be more than one executor. Don't let MacNeill be another."

"You want me to make *Paddy* an executor?" he asked in disbelief, extrapolating nicely.

"Other than the wonderful scene that creates in my head as he consults with Snodgrass, yeah, that guarantees a better balance," I agreed, trying not to reveal too much to my audience in case Max didn't heed my advice. "You really need Zone input."

"You're crazy," he said after a moment's silence. "You've gone around the bend. You want Nutzoid Paddy and the Zone to stand up against my . . . Mac-Neill?"

"Or make Grandmother Ida smack his hands," I agreed, not arguing with the crazy bit. I figured we were all a bit crazy.

"It has a warped sort of justice. I'll take it under consideration. I want to see you again, Justy."

"Blackmail, Senator, very bad business. You know where to find me."

I carefully closed the phone and met the gazes of my friends. "I did what I could, boys." I turned to Paddy. "Get your hair cut, put on a suit, and go see Snodgrass if you really want to keep Acme out of MacNeill's hands."

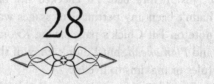

28

I collapsed in my own bed that night, knowing Andre was back to reality and do-gooder Dane/Max had inherited part of the Bane of Our Existence. That ought to put Gloria in her place—or the world had better stay away from gas lines.

I let Milo snore on the pillow next to mine to make up for not having a man beside me. I was starting to think that sane, safe Leo the Lieutenant was my best bet. He would never own mansions that opened on hell or chemical companies that gassed the helpless. He wouldn't turn gray and pass out and dream about soldiers storming the house. Or take drugs that caused those nightmares.

I tossed and turned, disturbing Milo until he stalked

off to the foot of the bed. One of the burrs under my collar was my first murder case. I was nervous about the court date next week. I'd never stood before a judge except when I'd been sentenced to jail. Not a reassuring memory. It had taken years to expunge my record and overcome the obstacles that minor conviction had created. I hated for Andre to suffer through worse.

Just before bed, I'd checked my tablet, but there hadn't been any pertinent messages waiting. I'd left a note on Fat Chick's page saying *Knowledge is power* and *Plan ahead*, but I didn't know if those counted as rules or maxims to live by.

I couldn't sleep. If I counted midnight as the beginning of the day, I'd damned Bergdorff to hell in the wee hours of the morning. It had been nearly twenty hours since then, and I hadn't seen any sign of reward or punishment. If my theory was correct about midnight being the witching hour when rewards were handed out, I wanted to be awake to argue with whoever did the handing out.

I was deathly afraid I'd be punished for damning Bergdorff, and that I'd be crippled for life or sent to the outer rings of hell instead of rewarded. Worse yet, I was stupidly hoping that if I deserved a reward, I could ask for the zombies to come back to life.

That was plenty enough to keep me awake despite my exhaustion. I heard church chimes in the distance and checked my clock. Midnight. Nothing happened. I waited. No mysterious entities appeared. I was afraid to look in a mirror. I patted my hair. It was still there. My leg was still whole. I felt normal.

Nothing. Maybe I was only entitled to so many rewards and after that, I was expected to know the routine? But how could I know if I'd judged Bergdorff correctly?

I couldn't. No judge could. I'd have to live with his execution for the rest of my life. Wincing over that realization, I turned over and collapsed in complete exhaustion.

The next morning, I got up, gulped coffee and a Nutribar, and went in to shower and brush my teeth. I hated facing the mirror and waited until it was good and foggy before I'd stand in front of it.

I opened my mouth to insert the toothbrush . . . and froze.

The crooked gap between my two front teeth was gone.

Shit. I didn't want any more physical rewards to remind me that I'd sent a man to hell. Every time I looked in the mirror, I could count the number of souls I'd sent to Satan, wittingly or not. And now I knew I'd sent another. Satan was probably smirking.

Dammit, I'd wanted to argue with the tooth fairy, ask that s/he free the zombies instead of rewarding me. I'd wished for it at the time Bergdorff went out the window. What more could I do?

The devil worked in mysterious ways. Or Saturn. Whatever.

Cursing, wondering why I didn't at least get something useful like a bigger brain for sending souls to their just reward, I got dressed in reasonably professional attire and headed across the street to my office.

My office, an earthly reward I'd earned with intelligence and hard work. I liked that much better than my pretty gleaming new smile. Stupid, useless Saturn.

I started to use my new brass key to open the door but realized it was unlocked. Frowning, I glanced through the glass but didn't see anything except my empty desk and scattered furniture. I needed to set up a file room and move the file drawers out of sight.

And get new locks, evidently. Bracing myself, I entered.

One of the black suits sat on a desk chair in a far dark corner. I contemplated hurriedly backing out, but this was *my* turf. He was the intruder.

"Who let you in?" I demanded rudely.

He rose, and, to my utter amazement, I saw he wore a red rosebud in his lapel buttonhole. A red *rosebud*. And a pink silk handkerchief in his breast pocket. In my experience, goons wore shoulder holsters, not roses and pink silk.

He was relatively young, maybe even younger than me, but male-model handsome, complete with cleft chin and thick head of styled hair. Not my type. I'm not into pretty. I think I would have recognized the rose or the handkerchief if I'd seen them before, but the square face and broad shoulders? Nah, all the goons had them. Why did I have an ugly feeling that he was one of Acme's security guards? Weren't they all frogs just yesterday?

"Mr. Vanderventer said I might wait here," the intruder said politely. "I wished to make my apologies to Mr. Legrande, but I didn't know where to find him."

Mr. Vanderventer? Paddy? Or Max?

I immediately donned my suspicious face. Very few strangers knew Andre by any name other than Legrande. Even though the lawyers at the courthouse knew his father, the murder charges had been filed under Legrande. I had no idea if Andre had officially changed his name, but I assumed he had identification. No way was I telling a stranger where to find Andre, since it would also involve his parents.

"I've advised my client to stay out of the public eye," I lied. "Who are you and for what are you apologizing?"

Before he could answer, a frog hopped from under my desk. Well, that answered the question as to which Vanderventer had keys to my door. Uneasily, I snapped on the overhead to brighten the gray morning light. Another frog was chomping down on a spider in the corner. I supposed that was a good green way of cutting down on the pest-control bills. Why had Paddy let the frogs loose in my office?

Was it my imagination, or did my visitor just lick his lips while watching the spider disappear? My stomach did a backflip.

Pink particles were valuable—as a frog-healing agent? One frog had been eating them. . . . Paddy had some explaining to do. Again.

The male model returned his attention to me, although a puzzled frown now marred his wide brow after watching his spider-nibbling brethren. "I apologize. I'm Ned McNamara. I used to work for Mrs. Gloria Vanderventer. I'm one of the witnesses against Mr. Legrande."

Whoo, boy. I studied him with interest. This was one of the goons who'd been fighting off the old lady when she'd gone over the railing? He didn't look too dangerous.

Where was my ethics book when I needed it? Should I call Julius? I staggered to the enormous office chair behind my immense desk, collapsed into it, and stared at Ned the security guard incredulously. "What are you doing in here?"

"You're kind of small for that desk," he pointed out ungraciously. "If you want to impress your clients, your décor needs better proportions." He glanced around. "You could use a decorator."

"Yeah, and fewer frogs. I repeat, *what are you doing in here?*"

"Oh, sorry. Now that I'm unemployed, I'm hoping for a more congenial occupation, but that's not your problem. I was working at Acme the other night when Mr. Bergdorff committed suicide. It was a very odd night. It made me aware that I was starting down a road I was no longer willing to follow." He toyed absently with his pink handkerchief.

"The road requiring taking orders from insane villains?" I asked sarcastically.

"I was paid to guard a wealthy woman and her assets," he corrected. "But I was not paid to lie in court. And since my fellow witnesses have all mysteriously disappeared, leaving me holding the bag, so to speak,

I intend to inform the prosecutor this morning of the truth, and take my punishment like a man, after I apologize to Mr. Legrande."

Villains could apologize and make amends?

Shouts and cries echoed from down the street, and I twitched uneasily. This was all wrong. I couldn't process it. And shouts from the direction of the Zone weren't to be taken lightly. I wanted to get up and investigate, but Andre was my very first case. I couldn't blow this.

The other witnesses had disappeared? Had Gloria's other guards also worked at the plant, where McNamara said he'd been working? Gut instinct was damned painful—I'd turned the guards at the plant into frogs. Of course they'd disappeared.

The witnesses against Andre were hopping around under my desk—where their pink-particle-swilling colleague probably had been before he poofed back to himself. Right? Did I want to believe this?

Think like a lawyer, Tina. "Very well," I told him carefully, trying to think fast, "I will call Mr. Legrande and apprise him of this latest situation. Would you like me to represent you when you speak with the prosecutor?"

His eyes widened in surprise. "You can do that?"

"If you're no longer testifying against Mr. Legrande. I believe you were both placed in a difficult situation for which self-defense was the only remedy, am I correct?"

"Yes, ma'am," he said in awe.

Ma'am. I was too young and hip to be a "ma'am." I

had the urge to smack him, except I liked that ring of authority. I'm such a slut for a little respect.

The shouting in the street grew louder, and I couldn't stand it any longer. I pushed away from the desk. "Excuse me." I hurried to look out the door. A frog followed me, but I pushed him back with my heel. I'd feed him pink particles or find a princess to kiss him after we closed Andre's case. I didn't want any lying bastard toads on the witness stand.

Lesson learned: Turn lying witnesses into amphibians. I should study up on toads, too. My jubilation at unintentionally winning Andre's case threatened to spill into hysterical laughter.

My joy knew no bounds as I stared down the street at the astounding sight of Bill and Leibowitz parading together in my direction. A few of the homeless, wearing new jeans and work shirts and appearing confused, ambled along with them. The mob of Zonies celebrating the return of the no-longer-zombies cheered and sang a rowdy verse of "We Shall Overcome." The melody was questionable and the verse inappropriate, but the emotion was spot-on. In a wave of sheer relief, I cheered from my office door, even though I despised Leibowitz.

Had my wish brought them back to life? I'd like to think killing a mad scientist had paid off and that I was being rewarded for my good judgment with something besides pretty teeth.

Ned peered over my bouncing shoulder. "Is it a parade?"

He smelled like Old Spice. Good grief. Paddy must

have taken him home to change and shower before returning him here. Rather than gag on the scent, I hurried outside, wishing I had a flag to wave while I jumped up and down and hollered happily.

The French doors on the third-floor balcony of Andre's place flew open, and Julius appeared, carrying a body. For a fleeting moment, I thought he was about to fling his wife into the street.

His wife. That flowing black hair had to be Katerina. What on earth . . . ?

She waved. She actually waved. Tears stung my eyes. I slapped my hands over my mouth to keep from shouting like a maniac. She was alive! *Andre's mother was alive!*

She was back from dreamland. As were Bill and Leibowitz.

Realizing I was still jumping up and down and screaming, I stopped to preserve what was left of my dignity, but tears of joy streamed down my face. The Zone—or Saturn—had done something right.

"They all woke up last night," a familiar amused baritone informed me.

I swung around to see Andre leaning against the burned brick wall of his warehouse, admiring the early-morning parade. He beamed proudly, if with a slight air of bewilderment.

Did I thank Saturn for this blessed turn of events? Was the zombie recovery because my invisible DNA factor had answered my prayers? I might start believing in capricious gods yet, although then I'd have to start thinking of Sarah as a sister.

"Who's Pretty Boy?" Andre nodded at Ned, who was watching the parade through the window.

"The last thread of the prosecutor's case against you," I replied insouciantly, happier with this topic than with that of gods. "I don't think the state will want to press charges against you once they learn all the other witnesses are hiding in a bog."

"A bog?"

"That's your mother up there." I changed the subject, enjoying my secrets. "Why aren't you up there with her?"

"We hugged earlier. Right now, I wanted to thank you for whatever in hell you did to bring her back."

He took my hand and held it as if he meant it. He believed in me.

His trust was overwhelming. I didn't dare glance down to where his strong brown fingers clasped mine. I didn't get enough human touches, and a wave of emotion threatened to smash through the floodgates. I let my hormones steer me down a safer path.

I liked Andre's touch entirely too well. Not as much as kissing, but he was still my client. Not for much longer, though, I bet. Did Andre go comatose after sex?

"I don't think what I did had anything to do with hell," I said thoughtfully. I might blame Satan for giving me sexy hair and straight teeth, but I couldn't believe imps from hell would return the comatose. So maybe there really was an all-powerful Saturn. "Do you think Bill and your mother saw things like you did? Maybe they can warn us of events to come?"

"We can ask when it quiets down," he agreed, studying me. "Do you think they'll answer our questions any better than you do mine?"

"Probably not, because it doesn't make sense. Yet." I smiled at another sight coming up the street. "Tim has Nancy Rose back. I guess I won't be making him my secretary."

Remembering Ned, I turned around. He was catching a fly against the window. I might have to rethink adding frogs to my punishment repertoire. *Although . . .* I regarded him thoughtfully.

He seemed more the type who'd be interested in pink than his lockjawed buddies.

I leaned in the door and called to him. "Ned, you can apologize to Mr. Legrande now, but I'd appreciate it more if you'd teach a friend of mine how to dress appropriately."

He came out to join us, and I nodded down the street at Tim, attired today in hot pink flip-flops, purple capris, and a black skull-and-bones T-shirt I think he'd filched from my closet.

Ned held out his hand to Andre. "Sorry, old man. I was wrong to lie." He cast a glance at Tim. "Will a dozen lessons be sufficient to cover my legal fees?" he asked. "I'm still unemployed."

Apparently picking up on the newcomer's oddity, Andre snickered. "Hire him, Clancy. We have a new Zonie."

Why not? In jubilation, I released Andre so I could

rush down the street and throw myself into Bill the Bartender's arms. "Glad to have you back, soldier," I whispered in his ear.

Before the big man could react, I jumped down, caught Lieutenant Leo's arm, and, to the tune of "We Shall Overcome," danced a jig in the sunlight.

Tomorrow, I'd worry about pink particles and bullfrogs and the gas can in my purse. Today, I celebrated life.

ACKNOWLEDGMENTS

As some of you may already suspect, I am not a gushy person. But even Tina cannot make a book happen by magic. A lot of people put a lot of hard work and brain waves into creating a book, and I'd like to thank them all. Most especially, I would like to thank my agent and her assistant, Robin Rue and Beth Miller; my editor, Adam Wilson; and Pocket's marvelously talented art department. Without them, this book would never have happened. And the real icing on my cake is the Cauldron, who didn't laugh me out of the room when I said I wanted to write a book about a heroine who could unwittingly damn people to hell. You all are my rocks!

And my ever-patient husband gets hugs and kisses for understanding that sometimes I just need pizza.

More bestselling
URBAN FANTASY
from Pocket Books!

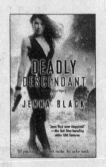